THE ART OF FALLING IN LOVE

CARRIE CLARKE

This is a work of fiction. Any resemblance to real places or people, living or dead, is entirely coincidental.

eBook Format: 978-0-6456982-0-6

Print Format: 978-0-6456982-1-3

Cover Design: Akapit Ryan Alexander Gilchrist

This book is written using Australian English. So you might find unfamiliar spelling or phrases. There is also a liberal scattering of Scottish words, which are explained in a glossary at the end. If anything in particular perplexes or interests you, please contact me at hello@carrieclarkeauthor.com.au. I'd love to hear from you.

 A catalogue record for this book is available from the National Library of Australia

CONTENTS

For my Dad. Who gave me a love of words, if not seafood.

CHAPTER ONE

NICK

The lift doors are seconds away from snapping shut when slender, blue-stained fingers slide between them and they rebound open. A tangle of absurd curls bounces into the space after them.

"Thank you *so* much," the owner of the fingers and curls throws breathlessly at me with a blinding smile. A smile that somehow manages to tell me she knows I'd made no effort to hold the lift; she thinks I'm rude, and it's her intention to embarrass me. Quite a lot to pack into four words and one smile, really.

Sadly for her, I don't do embarrassed. And today, of all days, when I'm struggling with the guilt of my conflicted emotions, I can't seem to drum up any response other than irritation. "You're very welcome," I reply, matching her sarcasm, note for note.

Not content with slowing me down once, she lunges for the open-door button. Charging through the foyer appears to be every office worker in the Sydney CBD, all heading for the lift. A moment ago, I was alone. A much-needed moment of solitude in a day I hardly know how to navigate. Now, thanks to her, I'm surrounded by a seething mass of humanity and their swirling energies. She gifts them a smile infused with genuine warmth as she shifts backwards to make room and loses her balance, stomping firmly on my foot with her ridiculous spike heels. I catch her by the shoulders and stand her upright, barely managing to contain my grunt of pain. I know it wasn't deliberate, but I'm not in the headspace to be forgiving right now. I simply want to wallow for a while. Alone.

"Oh, I'm terribly sorry. Did I hurt you?" She glances over her shoulder at me. She continues to shuffle backwards in the face of the oncoming wave of humanity.

"Don't give it another thought." I scowl at the scratch across the top of my previously unblemished Stefano Bemer shoes. This already bad day seems determined to get worse.

At last the lift is as full as it can possibly get, and the irritating cause of the crush is pushed close up against me. I'm tall and so is she. And she's wearing towering heels. Which means her perfectly rounded arse is pressed tight against me right where it shouldn't be, and her tangled nest of curls is tickling my face.

As we speed upwards, I'm forced to hold my breath. Those curls tickling my nose smell like wildflowers. Like my grandmother's garden. The last thing I need today is sentimentality and nostalgia.

She pressed no other button, so I assume she's coming to Carter, Pierce and Millwood. Not surprising. We get lots of beautiful young trophy wives in our offices, looking for a lucrative divorce settlement. What is surprising is she doesn't appear to fit the usual profile. No sign of Botox, hair extensions or fake tan. Not the usual trophy wife at all.

I glance down. No tasteless yet expensive ring on her left hand. Not even a dent where a ring may have been. Long elegant fingers are decorated with nothing more than those weird blue stains, short unpainted nails and an enormous purple stone on her middle finger.

The lift has gone from a fast express to an all-stops journey. People are getting off on every floor, yet there still seems to be no room, or air, in the lift. The wildflower scent and the press of her rounded arse have raised the temperature and are in danger of raising something else. I stay as still as possible, but my irritatingly attractive tormentor is shifting back and forth, making room for our fellow travellers as they come and go. I close my eyes, which only intensifies my other senses, defeating the purpose. I think about my first-grade teacher Miss Best and her hairy face wart. That always works. Except this time, it doesn't.

Finally, to my almost overwhelming relief, the last passenger leaves the lift and the wildflower curls and lush arse move away.

"I truly am very sorry about your shoe. I hope they aren't your favourites?" Her expression is apologetic, a small, rueful smile showing off the dimples in her glowing cheeks. *Jesus wept*. She looks like Glinda the Good Witch, all sunshine, sparkles and smiles.

"Not anymore, thanks to those lethal heels." I can't keep the annoyance out of my voice. "Perhaps you should consider trainers if you have trouble keeping your balance?" I know I'm being rude, even for me. But I simply don't have the emotional energy to temper my response today. Rather than upset her, though, my rudeness goads her into a glare.

The lift doors swish open, and I sweep my arm out in mock gallantry. I'm treated to another of her subtext smiles, a waft of wildflowers and an unobstructed view of her very nice derriere as she waltzes past me. I swear I hear her whisper, "Such a gentleman," under her breath as she passes.

I head straight to the sanctuary of my office, where I can put the strangely distracting woman right out of my mind. Sitting front and centre on my desk is a Post-it Note reminding me—in caps—of the meeting I don't want to attend. *Christ on a bike.* I have no idea why we must do this. And of all the days of the year to pick, it had to be today.

My assistant sweeps in with my coffee in her capable hands. "Don't forget the mee—"

"Yes. I know. The meeting." I hold up the Post-it Note. "How could I forget?" At that moment, my phone starts to vibrate in my pocket. "You set an alarm? For God's sake, Mandy. I know how to get to a meeting on time."

She puts the coffee on the desk in front of me. "Of course you do. You are also quite capable of accidentally on purpose forgetting meetings you don't wish to attend." And she's out the door with one of her evil grins and a toss of her head. I hate her sometimes. I need a new assistant. Except she's excellent at her job. And I love her to bits.

I have a few minutes before the meeting, and I'm feeling restless, so I fill in the time by stopping by Will's office. Our grandfathers started this business together in 1960. Will joined the firm right out of uni, while I went to Oxford on a Rhodes Scholarship before joining the firm. Exactly as my father wanted.

"Remind me again why we're doing this?"

"Doing what?" He glances up from his computer with a frown.

"Why we're going to—as he so eloquently put it—'re-energise and modernise' the office? We have the best tech money can buy. What else do we need?" I drop into one of the worn-out visitors' chairs in front of Will's desk and wince as it creaks under my weight. His office isn't as big as mine, since I'm a senior partner. But at least he doesn't have to work surrounded by antiques, which are beautiful, but not in the least comfortable or convenient.

"Oh, well," Will answers. "Let me just save this contract I'm reviewing for our biggest client—on this high-tech computer—and take time out from my busy day to explain to you why we need to look like a successful law firm operating in the twenty-first century instead of a second-rate insurance company from the 1970s." He saves the document on his screen with a flourish and turns to face me across the desk.

"We *are* successful—our billings speak for themselves. Why do we need to spend good money botoxing the office to prove it?"

Will roars with laughter, head thrown back against his leather chair.

"I know it's not your intention, Nick, but you're hilarious. Take it up with Harry. Although I'm warning you, he's made up his mind. You won't win. Now be a pal and bugger off so I can finish this before the meeting, will you?"

I stalk back to my office and search for something to distract me. It wouldn't do to be punctual for this one. Let them sweat. It will drive Harry crazy. It's not my habit to indulge in passive-aggressive behaviour, but I'm struggling with this whole endeavour. Our firm trades on its long history, and I know my father was dead against any changes that made us seem like one of the slick new firms. I get where he was coming from. Our reputation is tied up in old-fashioned service. But changing with the times wouldn't have killed him. Unlike the booze and cigars. Nevertheless, this firm was his life, so to be doing this today seems like a betrayal of his vision.

I settle in and attempt to concentrate on a contract, with little success. The incident in the lift keeps returning to distract me. Which does nothing for my already sour mood.

I walk into the conference room ten minutes late and do a quick double-take. Standing at the head of the table next to the wall-mounted screen is the woman from the lift. So, not a trophy wife at all. Well, perhaps she is, missing ring notwithstanding. But that's not why she's here today.

Without acknowledging my tardiness, I drop into my preferred seat at the table—we are all such creatures of habit—and cross my arms. "I have twenty minutes. Let's get on with it."

"Thank you all for taking the time to meet with me. As I understand it, your objective is to update and modernise the offices of Carter, Pierce and Millwood, while at the same time honouring the history of your long-established firm—" she starts in a voice like top-shelf scotch. Ugh. I could use a drink right about now, despite the fact it's not even midday.

"We already know that," I speak over the top of her, earning me a glare from Harry.

"Yes, of course you do." She gives me another one of those blinding subtext smiles. "I simply wanted to make sure you know I understand what it is you are looking for."

And then she proceeds to ignore me. For sixteen minutes, she doesn't once look my way. Not even a glance. I have no idea what she has said, and nor do I care. All I can hear is the teacher's voice from Charlie Brown as I watch her lips move. Her quite luscious lips, I can't help but notice. Which, of course, irritates me even further. The last thing I need right now is an inconvenient attraction. Especially with a potential work colleague. Not to mention I have a girlfriend. Of sorts.

The snap of her laptop lid brings me back to consciousness.

"Thank you so much for your time. Does anyone have any questions?"

"Oh, I don't think so ..." Harry looks around, eyebrows raised, at the other partners, some of whom look like they're drooling. Others appear mesmerised. "That was exceedingly thorough. As you are aware, we have a couple of other designers to speak to, but we are anxious to get started, so we should be able to let you know by the end of the week."

That's it. I'm up, out of my seat and out the door without a word. I need some space to breathe. In the end, I may have to concede on this, but I don't have to like it.

Alone in my office, I drop my forehead to the worn leather and wood of the antique partner's desk. Dad's desk. It has been a year to the day since I watched the paramedics battle to save my father in the foyer of this office. Battle and fail. The desk—the entire office—still smells like Dad. Like his after-shave and those ghastly cigars he smoked when everyone else had gone home for the night. This desk, the chair, the bookcases, even the masses of leather-bound legal books—modern copies of which are also kept in the legal library—belonged to his father before him.

The room is a constant reminder of my father and how I never quite lived up to his expectations. My sister says I wear it like a hair-shirt, and maybe she's right. It scratches at my soul to be here day in and day out, reminding me of those expectations and the path he set out for me at birth. A path I promised to follow. Promised on his deathbed. Well, the floor, at least. But lately, it feels as if I've taken a wrong turn somewhere.

I sit bolt upright at the soft knock on the door and try to pull my face into a neutral expression. "Come in."

I'm surprised when it's Harry. Soft is distinctly un-Harry-like. He settles his massive frame on the sofa, which means I have to get up from the desk and sit on the sofa opposite him. He searches my face and gives a gusty sigh.

"How are you coping today?"

"I'm fine, Harry," I reply, although we both know I'm lying. "Apart from wasting almost an hour of my time in a meeting about primping up the office."

"Hmm. Well, there was no need to be quite so rude to Lulu MacLeod. I understand you're not on board with this redecorating, but it has to be done. Even your father agreed."

I feel an uncharacteristic twinge of regret. Perhaps I was unnecessarily rude to Ms MacLeod. But after the episode in the lift, I couldn't seem to help myself. To say my emotions are running close to the surface today would be an oversimplification. Unfortunately, Lulu MacLeod copped the brunt of that. "You might be stretching the definition of *agreed* a little bit, don't you think?"

Harry frowns. "Yes, I guess so. But it's happening, nonetheless. And Lulu MacLeod gave us a brilliant sales pitch. Although I am sorry it had to be today. It's a tough day for all of us."

Harry's eyes are sorrowful and, not for the first time, I wonder how he and my father ever became friends. Chalk and cheese. Yet there's no denying they were close.

I sigh and rub both hands over my face in irritation. "I know it needs doing, but I don't have to like it." It's clear Harry doesn't understand how conflicted I am by the whole enterprise, and I don't have the energy to explain it to him. I'm not even sure

I can explain it to myself. "Just so we're clear, there will be no changes in my office. At all."

"No touching anything of your dad's," Harry agrees. "A coat of paint and carpet, that's all. To match the rest of the office. Oh, and maybe new sofas..." Harry's grin is sheepish.

"Jesus. This had better not interfere with workflow." I stand, arms crossed, signalling to Harry the conversation is over.

"Try to keep an open mind, hmm?"

That manages to bring a smile to my face. Open-minded is something Pierce men are not.

CHAPTER TWO

LULU

Wow. If I had thought he was obnoxious in the lift, he really outdid himself in that meeting. He didn't bother to introduce himself, but Harry referred to him as Nicholas. Whoever he is, he came across as an entitled arse in serious need of an attitude adjustment.

On the plus side, I aced the presentation. I'd nailed my outfit. Well, almost. There isn't much I can do with my crazy hair. But the high-waisted, wide-legged linen pants paired with the white shirt were the perfect mix of corporate and creative. I looked smart and put together, and I had a killer pitch. So, I was confident. Despite my tardy lift nemesis.

"How did you go? You look fantastic." My best friend Rosanna looks me up and down when I meet her for coffee later in the afternoon.

"Good. I think." I take a gulp of the chai she ordered for me while she waited.

"You don't sound sure."

"Well, the presentation went well. It seemed like pretty much everyone was on board. Harry Carter, the managing partner, was super positive …"

"But?"

"There was this one partner; I think his name is Nicholas. He didn't even bother to introduce himself. I travelled up with him in the lift. I had no idea who he was, and we got off to a bit of a bad start." I settle into the comfy velvet wingback chair and cross my legs.

"What happened?"

"He was so rude, Ro. I was running for the lift, and he didn't even attempt to hold it for me. Then I lost my balance and accidentally trod on his very expensive shoe. I felt terrible. It left a great big scratch. I apologised, but it didn't seem to help. I would've offered to replace them, but his attitude really got my hackles up. Then he was late to the meeting, scowled through the whole thing and left without saying a word. I'm pretty sure I didn't impress him."

"Well, he's only one of how many partners?"

"Eight."

"Maybe he's a cranky old fart." Rosanna picks at the banana bread we're sharing.

"Cranky? For sure. Old fart? Definitely not. You should see this guy. It's just as well he was an arse; otherwise, I might have embarrassed myself by drooling."

"Ooooh. Do tell. On a scale of one to Alexander Dreymon, how hot was he?"

"Oh, a full Alexander Dreymon." I close my eyes and think. "He has the lips, you know? And the eyes. Not to mention he must be at least six foot two. And the suit ... He looks like he stepped right off the page of *GQ* magazine." I laugh and roll my eyes, remembering the feel of him pressed against my back in the lift and the quick shiver which ran down my spine as he walked into the meeting, despite his scowl. Or maybe because of it. He has a stellar smoulder.

"Wow. I think I could put up with quite a lot of arse-holery for that." Ro smacks her lips together, grinning.

"And he smells delicious too. Like expensive leather and sex." I let out a sigh. "Why are the gorgeous ones always arseholes?"

Ro laughs, shrugging. "Because they can be, I guess."

"Anyway, I'm just there—I hope—to do a job. No fraternising. Besides, he made it very clear he didn't like me."

"Didn't like you? How could anyone not like you?" Ro might, of course, be a tad biased.

"I have no idea. I scratched his shoe, so I guess he was understandably pissy about that, but I felt like there was something else. Regardless, I need this job, not romantic complications. It's a super high-profile law firm, so it could lead to all sorts of other work, and until my paintings start to sell, I need to keep myself afloat." I press the last crumbs of the banana bread with the pad of my finger and slide them onto my tongue. "I have to focus on work and finishing the painting I'm working on. I've almost convinced Sebastian Black to consider my work for a solo exhibit. I'm nearly there. I'd like maybe a couple more paintings to show him."

"Didn't I tell you The Black Gallery was the right place for you?" Ro holds up her hand for a high-five, which gets a smile from the elderly couple at the next table.

"I'm not over the line yet. He won't commit until he sees some more of my work." I shrug. "But it's looking hopeful. Anyway, enough about me. How are you doing?"

Rosanna rolls her eyes and pouts. "Nothing new to tell. Work is going pretty well. The costumes we're making for this season are to die for, but I'm still not getting a chance to do much designing beyond adding the frou-frou." She frowns. "And boys are stupid. You know, sometimes I don't think Marco is interested in me at all. Do you think maybe he's gay?"

I burst out laughing. "Maybe. If he isn't falling all over himself to get a gorgeous girl like you into bed, I can't think of any other explanation."

Rosanna and Marco have been dating for years now, and their sex life has been a point of dissatisfaction from the beginning. Marco says he wants to 'wait until they're married'. But so far, he hasn't proposed. Their families are close and old-school Italian. Marco also works for Rosanna's dad. The drama it would cause if they broke up is more than Ro feels she can bear.

"Maybe some retail therapy will make me feel better?" Ro sighs, her big brown eyes pleading.

Yes, I think a new pair of wedge sandals might be exactly what I need to take my mind off my nerves, and off Nicholas the Tardy and his big broad shoulders. And those lips.

For the next few days, I'm busy putting the final touches on my last design project and trying to squeeze in some time to work on my latest painting.

By the end of the week, I've finished the painting and am working on rough ideas for the next. I've had some success getting my paintings into smaller galleries based on my dad's reputation, but this one—if I can convince Sebastian to hold it—will be my first solo show. With any luck it will help me make a name for myself. I want people to want my work for itself, not because of who my dad is. I love my decorating business, but if I could make a living out of painting, I'd do it in a heartbeat.

I've pretty much convinced myself the CPM project will go to someone else when Harry's assistant, Gillian, calls late on Friday afternoon.

"Lulu, Harry was wondering if you could come into the office on Monday. Say, around noon?"

"Of course. Twelve is fine."

"Afterwards, he'd like to take you to lunch if you have the time?"

"I'd be delighted. I look forward to it."

Right, so I have the weekend to get my imagination under control. Because despite his rudeness, and my attempts to put him out of my mind, I've had more than one sex dream about Nicholas the Tardy and woken up with feels I haven't had in so long I can't remember.

It's been a while since I've been attracted to anyone. Longer still since I've even been on a date. I'm not interested in a relationship, and men always seem to want more than I'm prepared to give. I don't like hurting people, so I avoid dates. Simple. Except when you meet someone like Nicholas, who, even with his obnoxious personality, has so much sex appeal my insides feel like warm caramel at the thought of him. Dammit.

At two minutes before twelve on Monday morning, I'm sitting in the foyer at CPM. My right leg starts to bounce as it does when I'm bored. Or nervous. Or bored and nervous. I'm not usually the nervous type, and I don't know why I should be today. I've got the job. But I can't seem to stop the jiggling. I refuse to consider the possibility it might be because of Nicholas the Rude.

Harry bowls down the corridor, all smiles and handshakes. "Lulu, so good to see you again. Let's get down to brass tacks, shall we?"

It doesn't take long for us to go over the details of the job and agree on budgets.

"Before we head out to lunch, let me take you on a tour of the offices."

We start down the corridor and pass through each department, leaving the partners' offices until last. It would be a kindness to say the offices are tired, despite the expensive computers on every desk and the spectacular views that make Sydney Harbour look close enough to dive into. The dull grey carpet is worn and stretched, and the desks look as if they were made in the 1960s. And not in a good mid-century modern kind of way. In a this-used-to-be-a-public-service-office kind of way. But it does give me an idea. A way to modernise the office while maintaining a strong reference to their 1960s beginnings.

Harry's son, Will, a junior partner, leaps out of his seat when he sees me. "So glad you're going to be working with us, Lulu." His wide grin and handshake are warm and welcoming, but I feel an icy chill down my spine. In my peripheral vision I notice my nemesis stalking into the office next door, pointedly ignoring us.

"Oh, Nicholas, just in time." Harry spots him too and drags me to his door. "I don't believe you two were introduced the other day. Lulu MacLeod, this is Nicholas Pierce, one of our Senior Partners."

"Nice to meet you, Nicholas." I hold out my hand, meeting his steely grey stare. How it manages to be both hot and cold at the same time is a mystery to me.

"Ms. MacLeod," is all he says, in a black gravel voice. His hand is large and strong, with surprising callouses on his palm, as he shakes mine. It's not often I feel small, but that's the effect Nicholas has on me. Not only is he tall, but he's broad too, his wide shoulders creating the perfect inverted triangle with his narrow hips. The chill running down my spine spreads at the touch of his hand, and I feel goose-bumps scatter across my skin. It's fire and ice and goes straight to my lady parts. For a beat too long, neither of us breaks the hold. Or eye contact. And then he shakes himself and drops my hand as if burned, alerting me to the fact that whatever it was, he felt it too. The strange push/pull of dislike coupled with attraction.

"I'm taking Lulu to lunch to celebrate our agreement. Why don't you and William join us? Lulu doesn't want to have lunch alone with an old bloke like me, I'm sure."

"I'm afraid I'm very busy today, Harry." Nicholas attempts to put his desk between himself and the rest of us.

"Nonsense. Mandy said you have nothing scheduled. We'll just go downstairs. I won't take no for an answer." I try to hide my smirk at how Harry has outmanoeuvred Nicholas, who scowls but doesn't argue.

Will is already shrugging into his suit coat beside us. "Come on, Nick. You have to eat. Let's go."

And so, I find myself once again in a lift with Nicholas Pierce, his delicious aftershave and impressive shoulders. I glance down and see he has another expensive pair of shoes on today to go with his perfectly tailored suit. It's probably not wise to bait a new client, but I can't help myself.

"What lovely shoes, Mr Pierce. Are they new?"

"Yes, they are. My *favourite* pair was ruined last week." He looks pointedly at my shoes, brand-new wedges, which are almost as high as my stilettos.

Will laughs. "You have favourite shoes? All the years I've known you, you still manage to surprise me."

"What a shame. Were they expensive?" I try hard to look sympathetic, but I'm pretty sure it comes out more mocking than anything else. I know full well how much his shoes were worth. I'm no stranger to expensive designer clothing, but he doesn't need to know that.

"Quite, yes." He scowls at me again but doesn't fill Harry and Will in on how the shoes were ruined.

"Well, those are very smart too. You should take better care of them." That gets a strangled oath from Nicholas the Cranky and looks of bewilderment from Harry and Will.

The restaurant on the ground floor of their building is high-end, conversations hushed, silverware heavy and glassware sparkling. It's not the sort of restaurant I usually eat at, and I'm glad I spent so much time choosing my outfit. I might not fit in perfectly, but neither do I stand out like a broken toe.

Harry and Will keep the conversation flowing through lunch, which is just as well because Nicholas the Cranky says nothing at all beyond ordering his meal. He scarcely looks up from his plate unless he's asked a direct question. Until I order a chai latte. Which earns a snort.

"Do you have something against chai, Mr Pierce?"

"Not at all, Ms. MacLeod. I just didn't realise we were in nursery school." He sits back in his chair. I'm speechless. Harry looks mortified.

"Don't take any notice of Nick," Will jokes, trying to smooth over the awkward moment. "He missed the class on manners at prep school."

My leg starts to bounce again. Dammit. No, wait. It's not my leg jiggling the table. Someone else is jiggling. Oh, my God—it's Nick. We have the same tell. If you'd told me five minutes ago I have anything in common with Nicholas the Rude, I would've laughed out loud. I'd never have picked him for the nervous tic type. He seems so in control of himself and his emotions. I'd go so far as to say he's buttoned up tight.

"Well, I'm quite wired enough without drinking coffee. Perhaps you should try it?"

"Ha. Maybe you should, Nick. Might make you a little less ... you," Will comments with a laugh.

"I'm perfectly happy being me; thank you, Will."

"Really? How lucky for you to be so happy with yourself." I give him a sugary smile as his gaze locks with mine, and another of those shivers runs down my spine. This guy has a glare that could freeze lava. Harry's and Will's eyes bounce between us.

"Perhaps some of us have more room for improvement than others. Now, if you'll excuse me ..." He leaves the thought unfinished as he rises from the table and stalks away, his stride as smooth and dangerous as a panther, without even waiting for the short black he ordered.

He's almost at the door, when a very pregnant woman tries to stand up from her table, but can't seem to get the chair out. She's struggling, and the chair starts to unbalance. To my astonishment, Nicholas stops midstride, rights the chair, pulls it out from the table and helps her to her feet. I can't hear their conversation, but I can see the kindness on his face. Who'd have thought?

CHAPTER
THREE

NICK

I n the end, I not only have to put up with the offices being redecorated, but with Lulu MacLeod being the one hired to do it. Yes, her presentation was professional. And perhaps she had some good ideas. I wouldn't know. I wasn't listening. I was too busy looking at her lips. I mean, mentally crafting a client strategy. But I shudder at the thought of her prancing around the office with her preposterous hair and her irritating dimples and her delectable arse.

Not that any of the other designers impressed me. But at least I could ignore their waxed moustaches and too-short pants. Unlike Lulu. I don't know what it is about her that gets under my skin, but I can't seem to get her out.

However, I'm outvoted, so here we are. Stuck with Lulu MacLeod poking her delicate little nose into every corner of the office without even a week or two to get used to the idea. First thing, bright and early Tuesday morning, she'll be here. At least she won't be in my office.

Adding insult to injury, Harry manipulated me into a 'celebratory' lunch to seal the deal. There was small talk, which is not my forte. I concentrated on my meal and tried to ignore the chatting and laughing, which wasn't difficult. The occasional waft of wildflowers floating across the table, on the other hand, was not so easy to ignore. By the end of the meal, my left leg had started to jiggle. A sure sign of my discomfort. When she ordered a chai latte, I couldn't stand it anymore, and I got out of there without even waiting for my coffee. Which, based on my jiggling leg, I definitely didn't need.

At least the mystery of the blue fingers has been solved. As well as being a decorator, Lulu MacLeod is an artist. Shocker. I should've known based on the weird clothes and hippie jewellery. Not to mention the hint of a tattoo I swear I saw peeking out from under her sleeve and wrapping around her delicate wrist.

My day has not improved by the time I arrive for my obligatory dinner with my mother. I have a nagging headache and a hair-trigger temper. Not the best frame of mind in which to deal with my mother, otherwise known as Meddling Mary.

"Nicholas? Is that you?" Mum calls as I close the door behind me with a little too much force.

"Who else would it be?" I mutter to myself. "God forbid anyone arrives at this overblown mausoleum without a formal invitation." I take a deep breath. I need to keep those thoughts on the inside of my head. "Yes, it's me," I call louder. My footsteps echo on the cold marble as I head into the cavernous family room—a misnomer if ever there was one—where Mum sits with her pre-dinner sherry and an art auction catalogue.

Kissing her lifted cheek, I slump into the chair opposite, tearing at my tie and undoing my collar.

"Is Claire home for dinner?"

Mum purses her lips in disapproval, her grey eyes as cold as the North Sea. "Claire? No. Why on earth would she want to stay home and eat with her family when she can gallivant all over town with God knows who?"

"Good for her." I wish I was doing the same. Although, I have never been a gallivanter, more's the pity. I'd more likely be at home, working.

"You look like you had a bad day. Anything you can talk about?" Having been the wife of a lawyer for thirty-five years, Mum knows there are often things that can't be discussed at home.

"Yes, I had a shocker of a day. Harry has hired a designer to redecorate the office. She's, without a doubt, quite mad. It's a ridiculous and pointless waste of money."

"Well, at last. It's certainly long overdue. Harry and your father had been debating it before he died, and then, of course, it had to be put on hold." I should have known she'd take this position. Appearances are everything to my mother.

"I'm well aware of the history, Mum. The whole thing is already becoming a massive headache, and it hasn't even started yet."

"What pleasant company you are tonight." Mum's eyebrow rises along with the rest of her as she goes to the drinks trolley.

"I saw that eyebrow."

"I have no idea what you're talking about. Drink?"

Mum drives me crazy, but one thing you can say in her favour is she's utterly unflappable. No matter who is losing their heads around her, she maintains her dignity. Her only tell is her right eyebrow, which rises to her hairline when she's displeased. A tell, I am sorry to say, I inherited.

"I hear you haven't seen Eleanor recently ..." She lets the sentence hang, waiting for an explanation as she pours scotch into a heavy crystal tumbler for me.

"Not lately." Eleanor is a woman I've been seeing for a year or so. Since not long before my father died. If I had to find a word to describe my feelings about our relationship, it would probably be indifferent. But she and Mum are close, so the less I say the better. I'm getting a great deal of pressure to make it official. Pressure I'm resisting.

"She'll find someone else if you're not careful." I know that's supposed to be a threat, but it doesn't have the effect Mary is hoping for.

"Eleanor is a very suitable partner for you. Not to mention her father will do wonderful things for your career. Don't procrastinate too long." Ugh. The eyebrow again. Twice in two minutes. Not a good sign.

"None of your business, Mum." Even I can hear the edge in my voice, but Mum ignores it and continues her campaign. I take a large gulp of the scotch, hoping it will dull the irritation I'm feeling.

"You're thirty-three, Nicholas. You need to start making your move into politics. Which means you need to show you're stable and settled. Being a senior partner on the basis your father died won't give you the credibility you need. Richard has already said he'll make sure you get preselection in a safe seat."

"Well, thank you so much for the vote of confidence. Supportive as ever." She's right, of course, about both politics and Eleanor being a 'suitable' partner. If that is, indeed, what I want.

My father had a plan, hatched over many bottles of expensive scotch with Harry. I would eventually go into politics. Will would take over at the firm as senior partner. And thus, they would take over the world. Or at least our little corner of it.

As Dad lay dying on the office floor, his last words were a demand I follow through on their plan. And of course, I agreed. What else could I do?

But lately, I've begun to have doubts. This was Dad's plan, not mine. And he's no longer here to see it through. This leaves me in the unfamiliar position of being a little adrift, a situation Eleanor would not appreciate, since it's her father who's been lined up to shoehorn me into a seat in parliament. It's very clear Eleanor wants to be a politician's wife.

"Don't say you weren't warned," Mum cautions as I help myself to a second glass of scotch. Then, being the master strategist she is, she drops it.

·♥·♥·♥·♥·♥·

"What the fuck?" I bellow as I open my office door late the next afternoon after a frustrating morning in mediation.

"Oh, Nick. You're back. Sorry. I was hoping she'd be finished before ..." Mandy trails off lamely as she looks past me.

Standing on my father's desk—my father's antique, leather-topped desk—is the irritating piece of work herself. Lulu MacLeod. I'm speechless. A rare occurrence for a lawyer and almost unheard of for me. At work, at least.

"Oh, good afternoon, Nicholas. I'm sorry, I'll be out of your way in a twinkling." The tape measure she is wielding whizzes into its casing with a snap, and she kneels—*kneels*—on my desk to scribble on a bright blue pad sitting on top of a pile of my case files. Twinkling?

She's barefoot. So I suppose is should be grateful for small mercies. Her toes are painted fire-engine red, matching the fluffy top she's wearing with a pair of faded jeans. Standing again, she stretches, and Mandy and I are treated to a display of toned and creamy midriff.

The snort I hear from behind me is quickly but poorly disguised as a cough.

I finally find my voice. "I believe I made it *excruciatingly* clear this office was not to be touched in these shenanigans?" I give Mandy a look known to fell Supreme Court judges, but which seems to have no effect on her. She's small but fearless. I can feel my eyebrow disappearing into my hairline. "Mandy, under no circumstances is this woman to be allowed into my office. Whether I am here or not." Turning again to the lunatic on my desk, I point to the door behind me. "You ... OUT. Now."

"I'm almost done. And then you won't have to see me ever again. I just needed to get the measurements for these bookcases." Lulu jots something else on her pad and stretches again to measure the ancient bookcase behind my desk. This time we're treated to the sight of a belly ring glittering on her smooth flesh. My mouth starts to water, and there's a clenching low in my belly.

I turn again to Mandy, who is studying her shoes, her ruthlessly cut, dark bob hiding the smirk she's valiantly trying to suppress. "Give us a moment, please."

With a nervous nod and a quick look of sympathy at The Interloper, she heads off to her desk as I nudge the door closed with my toe. Turning back to the office, I see The Interloper is now sitting on the desk, casual and relaxed, legs swinging, hands planted beside her knees.

"Ms MacLeod," I begin, trying hard to use what my mother would call my indoor voice. "You may be under the impression you have carte blanche to wander anywhere you wish in these offices. Let me correct you. This particular office is now, always and forever, off limits. There is to be no redecorating or *reimagining* in this office."

"Hmm. Yes, I can *imagine* there is precious little *imagining* ever done in *this* office." She beams, eyes bright with amusement. "Be that as it may, I have been asked to do a job. And I intend to do it. Including replacing the early *Rumpole of the Bailey* vibe you've got going on here."

She holds up a hand to stop my interruption as I start to speak. "Yes, I know the desk and bookcases are off limits. But there is still a lot we can do. I've got everything I need now. Have a lovely afternoon." And with that, she jumps from the desk, picks up her pad and tape measure and is out the door of my office before I can even formulate a response.

I'm still frozen in place, hands on hips, when she scampers—there's no other word for it—back in. "Oops. Forgot my shoes." She picks up the ludicrous wooden clogs she left behind and is gone again, leaving nothing behind but smouldering irritation and her wildflower scent, reminding me again of my grandmother's garden in spring. The smell of innocence.

"She's quite mad," I grumble to Will that evening as we wait for the lift to take us to the basement carpark.

"Mad? She's a delight. She even had old Edith eating out of her palm this morning." Will sighs, referring to the oldest employee we have. She should have retired ten years ago. Or twenty. But nobody is foolhardy enough to suggest it. Not even me. So, she stays. Ruling the library with an iron fist.

"She was standing on my father's desk this afternoon."

"Ouch. Did she damage it?"

"No, she took her shoes off. But I work at that desk. Her bare feet were all over it," I spit. "She wears a belly ring. And a toe ring," I add, as though it were relevant to anything.

"Yes, well, she's very arty. Goes with the territory I guess. I'm sure it hasn't escaped your notice that she's gorgeous." Will's expression could only be described as lascivious. Which, for some reason, raises the hair on the back of my neck.

"If you like rainbows and unicorns, I suppose."

"If you have eyes and a pulse you mean." Will nudges me in the ribs and steps into the lift.

Rolling my eyes, I stab the button for the basement and attempt to change the subject.

"How is Josh settling back into life in Sydney?" Will's closest friend Josh, an old school friend of ours, has recently returned to Sydney after ten years working in London and New York.

"He's great. I expect you'll see him yourself soon. He's going to crew for me in the Twilight Races this season."

"I look forward to beating you both, then." Will and I have been competing against one another since our fathers taught us how to sail at the age of ten. Nothing beats being out on the harbour on a warm summer evening. Unless it's winning a race on a warm summer evening. Especially against Will.

"You wish." Will laughs, then claps his hands together as an idea strikes. "You know, Josh has bought a place in Manly. My sister is helping him with blueprints for some renovations. Maybe I should introduce him to Lulu? I could set them up, and she could help him with decorating. She's kind of his type, and he hasn't been seeing anyone since he got back. Two birds, one stone." He grins like he's had the best idea in the history of ideas. For reasons that escape me, it seems like one of the worst ideas ever.

I've never been much of a sleeper—four or five hours is enough. But tonight, sleep seems impossible. It's four am, and I'm still tossing and turning. Reliving the conversation I had with Lulu MacLeod in my office. Except it wasn't a conversation. It was a skirmish. An altercation. A confrontation. And she had the final word. In fact, she had all the words. Apart from my brief explosion when I arrived, she ran the whole ... exchange. This can't be allowed to continue. I'm a lawyer, for Christ's sake. I make a living out of coming out on top in an argument. If I can't manage to control an encounter with an interior designer, I should be rethinking my career choices. I roll over yet again and attempt to pound my pillow into submission. In the morning—well, later in the morning—I will make sure my position is clear.

I eventually fall asleep around four-thirty, then sleep through my alarm, so I'm later than my usual seven-thirty start at the office the next day, already out of sorts. First order of business—coffee. Mandy is not in yet, so I head towards the staff kitchen, where I hear laughter and voices, all tripping over each other. I round the corner, and there she is, Lulu MacLeod. The Interloper herself, surrounded by three junior associates. All drooling. All looking like scouts have set up tents in their cheap suit trousers.

Today she's wearing a ridiculous all-in-one pantsuit, and my cock twitches alarmingly in my trousers. I'm no better than the junior associates, which ratchets my temper up further still.

"Do none of you have anything to occupy you?" My voice is quiet, but my tone is hard. At their guilty stares, I glare back. "Because if you have nothing to do, I have some precedent research I need to be done. Or you could proof read some contracts for me. And I'm sure Edith could use a hand shelving books in the library. She has such trouble reaching the top shelves these days ..."

I think the land speed record is broken as they scuttle out of the kitchen with not much more than a nervous, apologetic glance at Lulu.

"Good morning, Nicholas," chirps The Interloper, the tiny diamond stud in her nose winking at me. It's way too early for that sort of perkiness. In truth, it's always too early for any sort of perkiness.

Now is my chance to redress the power balance I somehow lost control of yesterday.

"Not particularly." I look her sternly in the eye. Who knew that colour blue existed in nature? Giving myself a mental shake, I continue. "I would appreciate it if you would refrain from distracting the staff while you are here, Ms MacLeod. They have a great deal of work to do, and we are not paying them to stand around flirting and giggling like teenagers."

"Of course not. I wouldn't dream of distracting them. We were discussing the kitchen facilities and whether an additional coffee station closer to their work area would improve their productivity. You know, since they work such long hours and need to stay alert." She grins at me, her long elegant fingers wrapped around a coffee cup. Fingers which are today stained blue and green. There she goes again, getting the upper hand.

"Right. Well. That might, in fact, be a good idea," I concede, to which she beams.

"I do have them from time to time," she throws over her shoulder as she saunters off. "Have a lovely day."

I watch as she sashays away, the pantsuit clinging alarmingly to the curve of her incredible arse. At least we won't be treated to another viewing of the belly ring. Thank God.

But yet again, she got the best of our encounter.

CHAPTER FOUR

LULU

I waltz out of the kitchen with a determined swing to my hips, glad I wore my favourite boy-short knickers, which make my arse look amazing. Because I know he's watching. There's nothing quite like getting the upper hand in a debate. And Nicholas the Tardy is now Nicholas the Disapproving. Something tells me he will have a long list of titles by the time I finish here, and none of them will be flattering. Except maybe Nicholas the Smouldering. I do like a good smoulder, and his is Olympic gold medal standard.

Getting to know the people who work here is part of the job. I can't design a workspace for them that will help their productivity if I don't understand what it is they do and how they do it. But if Nicholas the Disapproving cuts it short every time I have a conversation with someone, this job is going to take forever.

I decide to head to the other side of the office where the library is. Hopefully, he won't notice me there. Office gossip is gold, and I find a rich seam of it with the librarian, who everyone seems to be terrified of, but who is as sweet as anything. Edith tells me Nicholas is a senior partner because he took his father's seat when he died last year. Which, when I think about it, explains a lot. I know more than I would like about losing a parent before you're ready. Maybe I should cut him some slack and be extra nice to him next time we cross paths.

Ahh, best-laid plans. I have every intention of cutting Nicholas the Disapproving some slack. I truly do. He just makes it so hard to not bite back.

We got off on the wrong foot—almost literally—and we don't seem able to get onto the right one. I'm not sure what it is about me he doesn't like. For the most part, people find me pretty likeable. And I'm not sure how to deal with the hostility that rolls off him in waves.

In a matter of hours, we are toe-to-toe again, this time over bathrooms, of all things. This firm is so old-fashioned they still have an executive washroom—put in no doubt at great expense—and only used by partners and clients.

I'm sitting on the sink sketching the layout when the door opens.

"Oh, for crying out loud. Is there nowhere safe in this office anymore?" Nicholas the Disapproving fumes.

"Oh, hello there. Fabulous, you're here. I have some questions." I smile over at him. He's taken off his suit jacket and loosened his tie, so he looks a little more approachable than usual. His dark hair is standing on end as though he's been pulling at it, and his sharp jaw has the beginnings of a five o'clock shadow around the kind of lips women spend thousands on fillers to achieve. Scrumptious. How deceiving looks can be.

"I'll bet you do." Why does that sound suggestive? Surely that was only in my imagination. Maybe it's a trick of the enclosed, intimate space.

"It appears there are no female partners at CPM. Why is that?" I ask as Nick prowls across the room. Prowls? Since when did I get so dramatic? But prowls is the only word for the way he moves. I slide off the sink and stand tall as he comes almost nose-to-nose with me. So close I can feel his heat and smell his cologne. The pit of my stomach clenches. Okay, maybe somewhere lower down than my stomach. I can feel my nipples turning to pebbles. I think my mouth even starts to water. Ugh.

"Female partners? What on earth are you on about? How is our business structure any of your concern?" he growls, adding to my discomfort by sending one of those icy and inappropriate shivers down my spine to between my legs. This spine-shiver thing is starting to get old.

I feel the need to lick my lips to make sure I'm not drooling. "Well, I'm thinking this should be a gender-neutral space, but I didn't see any women at the meeting. Which got me wondering ..."

"No. At present, we have no female partners," he barks.

"Well, that's not very inclusive of you. Have you ever had a female partner?"

Nick's lips thin, and his eyes narrow. I didn't mean it to sound salacious, yet somehow it did. I can feel his tension, but it's not all irritation. His pupils have swamped the silvery grey of his eyes. The air between us seems tight and hot, my skin super sensitised. I can feel every stitch and seam in my clothes. If I didn't know better, I'd think he was just as affected as I am. His breathing is loud in the echoey space. For a crazy hot second, I think he might kiss me. But he crosses his arms and takes a step back.

"I would suggest, Ms MacLeod, that in future you keep your pert little nose out of things which are none of your concern and stick to things you know. Like the colour of the drapes and throw pillows. Now, if you will excuse me, I'd like to use the facilities in private." His tone makes it clear the discussion is over.

I'm momentarily taken aback, not only by the rudeness of his words but by his hard-as-granite tone. Not to mention my physical response. It only takes me a second to regroup and put on my preferred armour—sarcasm. "Oh, yes. I'm terribly sorry.

Let me get out of your way and allow you to use your archaically sexist, executive washroom in private."

Honestly. No female partners in this day and age. Bloody male privilege. Haven't they heard of gender equality? How out of touch are these people? Sadly, the door has a soft close on it, so I can't even slam it on my way out. Dammit.

I have no idea why Nicholas causes such a strong reaction in me. Well, no. That's not quite true. He annoys me. He annoys me because he's rude, unfriendly, uncooperative and, it would seem, sexist. Whilst, at the same time, being pretty much the sexiest human being I have ever laid eyes on. Well, met in person, at least, because Liam Hemsworth is pretty damn unbeatable in that department. Those lips. Hello.

By the end of the day, I find Nicholas is also Nicholas the Miser.

I know, I know. It's not good to eavesdrop. But in my defence, I didn't set out to hear their conversation. It just happened. It's not my fault they left the door ajar, and once they started talking, I could hardly let them know I was there, could I?

Harry's assistant had gone home for the day, but she left some old office plans on her desk for me, which I want to take home and look at this evening.

As I'm picking them up, Nick's black gravel voice rumbles out of Harry's office door.

"I'm afraid I can't agree. Five per cent is ludicrous, Harry."

"It's more than the CPI, but roughly the same as other firms are offering as an increase. I've done some digging." Oh my god. They're talking about staff pay increases. I'm frozen in place, trapped between the door to freedom and Gillian's desk, too scared to move in case they hear me. "Most are offering between three and five per cent for admin, and the same for junior associates."

"Well, I'm not going to agree to it." Wow. Nick is also stingy. I've seen first-hand how hard the staff work in this company.

Harry's voice comes closer, and I hold my breath, hoping to God he doesn't look out and see me because there's nowhere to hide.

"You'll have to give some ground, Nick ..." and the door clicks shut, silencing the rest of the conversation. I grab the plans and skedaddle before one of them comes out. That is a conversation I shouldn't have heard. Yet more evidence Nicholas the Smouldering is not someone I should even be dreaming about, let alone thinking about. If only someone would send my subconscious—and my hormones—the message.

Over the next couple of days, it seems I can't be anywhere without Nicholas the Sexist Miser appearing and starting a squabble. And honestly, about the littlest things. Whether a new copy room is needed. Whether the reception area should be bigger or smaller. Whether hot-desking is a workable plan. Okay, that last one is not so little. But by the time we got to that, I found myself taking the opposite view, even though I secretly agreed with him. For no other reason than to annoy him. Well, that, and because I was annoyed his view was the same as mine. Getting under his skin is just so much fun.

It seems like everyone in the firm is a little bit in awe of Nicholas, with the exception of Edith, who has known him since he was in primary school, and Mandy, his assistant. Someone must have ratted out his behaviour towards me because a week into my work in the CPM offices, Mandy corners me in the boardroom while I'm sketching and measuring and she's setting up for a big meeting.

"I hear you and Nick have had a few differences of opinion whilst you've been here," she comments as she lays folders full of paperwork, pads and pens in front of several chairs. I guess Mandy is somewhere in her forties, with the neatest hair I've ever seen and a wardrobe of don't-mess-with-me suits all the other admin staff envy.

"You could say that. Honestly, I don't know what I've done to rub him the wrong way, but he seems determined not to get along with me." I cross my fingers behind my back because this is not even a little bit true. I know why we don't get along. I bait him mercilessly.

Mandy laughs and rolls her eyes. "Yes, he can be quite contrary when he wants to be. But his bark is far worse than his bite."

This seems like a good time to do some digging. "I'll take your word for it. I was shocked there are no female partners here, and he got quite angry when I asked him about it." I can't mention the pay discussion I heard, not least because it affects Mandy. But I wish I could. Strangely, she answers my question for herself.

"Yes, he would. He's passionate about diversity and inclusivity. He's been working on a policy for a while, but getting the older partners to agree has been an uphill battle. It's enormously frustrating for him. He and the other partners are always butting heads."

"That's odd. Why didn't he say so?" If he had, our whole argument could have been avoided. It occurs to me that maybe he enjoys not liking me.

Mandy shrugs. "I don't know. He's a complicated character. Very ... oh, how would you put it—reserved?"

"He seems perfectly able to express himself to me," I reply with more than a little frustration, which seems to be the overriding emotion when it comes to Nick. Well, that and the unfortunate attraction I can't seem to ignore.

Mandy laughs. "You do seem to bring the worst out in him. But he genuinely is a very good man. And he's having a rough time right now. Only yesterday he had a blow-up with the partners over admin wages."

"Oh, really?"

"Yes. He was fuming all afternoon. The partners want to offer a five per cent increase and Nick is pushing for ten. I thought he was going to blow a gasket when he came out of the meeting." She sets a tray of sandwiches and fruit in the centre of the table, adding napkins and glasses in front of each seat.

"He wants to offer a ten per cent raise?" My stomach does a dive into the deep end of the guilt pool at my leap to judgement.

"Yes. It might surprise you to learn, he's a very generous man. Don't be fooled by the gruff exterior. It's all a front."

"Well, he sure does a good job of hiding it." I sigh. Looks like I keep getting it wrong when it comes to Nick the Unpredictable. I remember the kindness he showed the woman in the restaurant. What a conundrum Nick is.

"I wouldn't take his attitude personally, Lulu. I don't think it's you. He simply doesn't want things to change around here. This is the only place he ever got any attention or approval from his father, so it's difficult for him to see change."

It's so not any of my business to ask, but I can't help myself. "So, they weren't close?"

"Hmm. That's a difficult one. Nick idolised Norman. But he was a tough father, not the warm and fuzzy type, if you know what I mean. It didn't matter what Nick did, what he achieved; it was never enough."

"*Jesus wept.*" A bark sounds from the doorway, and Mandy almost jumps out of her smart navy pumps, shooting me a nervous glance. "Are you always where I particularly don't want you to be?" Nick grinds out, eyes narrowed, nostrils flared.

"Not always," I reply sweetly. "And I will be out of here in plenty of time for your meeting. As a matter of fact, I'm finished now and will be on my way."

"Good. We don't have time for your shenanigans this morning."

"Shenanigans? Hmm. And here I imagined I was doing my job." I turn to Mandy, who is trying to suppress a laugh. "It was so nice to chat while we were working. Have a lovely day." And with that, I saunter past Nicholas the Confusing, trying and failing not to take a big deep breath of his delicious cologne.

I was so sure I had Nick pegged, but it seems like maybe I was way off base with my opinion. Which is not good at all. I could almost keep a lid on my inconvenient attraction while I believed he was irredeemable, but it's getting harder by the day. And letting these feelings loose feels fraught with danger.

CHAPTER FIVE

NICK

I scowl as The Interloper once again flounces away from me, her sunshiny blonde curls bouncing. I turn and glare at Mandy, who at least has the good grace to look a little sheepish. Unfortunately, our every encounter seems to end this way. The annoying piece of work pops up unexpectedly all over the office, smiling, laughing and somehow charming everyone whose path she crosses, leaving me feeling frustrated and out of sorts.

It seems she's researching office workflow and canvasing the staff on what would make their life easier and more productive. It's irritating in the extreme to find her constantly under foot. Even my notoriously daunting assistant appears to be under her spell. I'm positive I have returned from meetings to smell her strangely pleasant scent lingering on the air in my office, despite my clear instruction she not be allowed in at any time.

As suddenly as The Interloper began torturing us, she disappears. A week goes by without a sighting of her. Thank God. If I had to listen to her throaty laugh while trying to concentrate one more time, I think I might have redecorated the office with someone's blood.

And so much for her being a professional. She just up and disappeared. I knew the moment I met her she was flaky. I think it was the crystal jewellery. I'd bet she even reads tarot cards.

"Haven't seen your decorator around this week, Harry. Did she give up on us? Bit too difficult for her?" I say with a smirk as we pass each other in reception one afternoon.

"Oh, no. Not at all." He gives his trademark hearty laugh. "She has everything she needs for now and is working on putting together the proposal and detailed costings. She expects to have it ready for us to look at by the end of next week. I'll let you know when we have a time locked in."

"Yeah, pretty sure I'm in a deposition that day, but good luck with it."

Harry's already pink face flushes further, and his bushy silver brows furrow.

"I don't think so, Nick. I want full attendance from the partners at this meeting. We all have to agree on what we're approving. It's going to be pretty pricey, and I don't want anyone saying they don't like it after the event. I'll give you plenty of warning so you can make sure you're available." And with a thump on the back, he leaves me conflicted in his wake.

Now that I know she won't be in the office anytime soon, I can take a deep breath and relax. The past week, like all weeks, has been busy and I have lived in expectation of finding The Interloper lurking around every corner. Not having that to contend with, at least until she returns, is a relief.

I have no idea why the rest of the week drags and I'm too busy to give it much consideration. But drag it does until Friday finally rolls around.

"Nicholas," she purrs as she slips a hand onto my shoulder, bending to brush her lips over my cheek before I can stand. Eleanor is beautiful in a composed and polished way. She looks perfect, as always. Perfectly put together. Perfectly groomed. Perfectly on time and perfectly calm. "I was so glad you called. It's been an age."

She slides gracefully into the chair opposite me at her preferred table in her favourite restaurant. Where all the right people dine.

Even though we've been seeing one another for around a year, we both have busy careers, and often weeks will pass without us even managing to catch up. It hasn't escaped my notice that this doesn't bother me in the slightest, and my sister Claire has plenty to say on what this reveals about our relationship.

I'm not sure what prompted me to arrange to see Eleanor tonight. Certainly not the overwhelming desire for her company. But I'm aware the lacklustre nature of our connection is at least half my fault. Maybe all it needs is for me to try a little bit harder to ignite the spark.

"It's been crazy at work lately. How are you?" I notice how smooth and tidy her hair is, falling neatly to her shoulders, framing her delicate jaw. Odd, but I have never realised how delicate she is.

"Don't even mention it. I understand how busy you are. Things have been hectic for me too."

I hold up the bottle of wine, indicating her glass, and she nods, folding her hands in her lap and crossing her legs. It's all so neat and perfect.

As she takes a sip of her wine, I notice her perfectly manicured nails. No strange green and blue stains, nothing but pale pink polish and one small, tasteful ring. Strange how I've never noticed before how short her fingers are.

Neat. That's Eleanor. Neat and proper. Very, very proper. The right family, the right school, the right job. A very neat and proper fit for me. For an aspiring politician. On paper, perfect. And yet …

Our sex life—occasional as it is—is all very neat and proper too. Luke warm at best. I know she is expecting some sort of commitment from me. In large part due to the interference of my mother, who is undoubtedly the one who put the idea in her head. There's a reason we call her Meddling Mary. Yes, Eleanor would make a very proper wife. And yet …

For reasons which escape me Eleanor picks up the menu. We always come here. And she always orders the same thing. Entrée size. With dressing on the side.

Dinner arrives and Eleanor picks through hers, finishing not much more than half of it. Very different from The Interloper, who ordered a pasta dish when we had lunch and ate with gusto. Although why I should think of her right now, I have no idea. I can't help but feel I'd rather be home eating pizza and reviewing briefs.

Eleanor's glass of wine remains half full by the end of the meal, and she shakes her head with an almost-smile when I suggest dessert. For the life of me, I can't recall what we've talked about, but it was no doubt pleasant. Eleanor is an intelligent and well-informed woman, but it all just feels so pointless. Rather like the whole relationship.

We're finishing our coffee when I realise it's now or never. Music is one of my few passions outside of work, and Will has been telling me about this amazing young English guy producing incredible work out of his bedroom. As it happens, he's playing at a bar in the city tonight.

I slide my credit card into the bill folder and hand it off to the waiter.

"I hear there's this great new jazz musician who's playing at The Back Lane tonight. I thought we might go and check him out. What do you think?"

"The Back Lane? Isn't that a dive bar down in The Rocks?" Eleanor screws up her face like she's stepped in something disgusting, which is on the cards if we go to The Back Lane. It's pretty seedy, I gather, although I've never been. But some of the best musicians in the city play there. And it's time I tried something new.

Eleanor glances around as if fearful of being overheard. "I believe they were raided for drugs recently." It comes out almost as a hiss.

"That was months ago, and it was blown out of proportion. A couple of guys were smoking a joint in the back lane. And this guy sounds amazing. Plays every instrument on his tracks. Including the double bass." It's all I can do not to roll my eyes at Eleanor's reaction.

"I don't think it's appropriate for you to be seen going to that kind of bar. What if the press got hold of it?"

I sigh. I could have foreseen this. I did foresee this. It was pointless hoping for ... more.

"It's not illegal to go to a bar. It was just a thought. Let's forget it. I'm going to the bathroom. Won't be a minute." As I stand, I throw back the last of my wine in one slug.

I lean on the long marble sink, taking a few deep breaths. My collar feels too tight and I splash water on my face. Eleanor refusing to go to the bar is such a small thing. But it feels much bigger. Like a metaphor for our relationship. For my whole life. And I know I can't do this anymore.

When I return to the table, Eleanor puts her hand on my arm. "Would you like to come back to my place, Nicholas? It's been such a long time since we spent any time together." What she means is it's been a long time since we had sex, and her suggestion feels like a consolation prize for not going to the bar.

I know she expects me to say yes. Eleanor is a beautiful woman, without a doubt. But as I look down at her, there is not a single thing inspiring me to spend more time with her, and certainly not in her bed. It occurs to me that although we've been seeing each other for quite a while, I don't know her in any real sense.

I push back my chair, getting distance from her, both physically and metaphorically.

"I don't think so, Eleanor. I've had a crazy week and have a lot of work to get done tomorrow before the races." This, despite the fact that moments ago I was suggesting we kick on to a bar. By reflex I start to suggest a raincheck, but something stops me. It could be the expression on her face—somewhere between relief and annoyance—or her refusal to step outside her comfort zone, but the feeling of now or never I started the evening with overcomes me and I know it's never.

She jumps into the silence. "I understand. Next time perhaps."

"I think probably not, don't you?" I say, without giving myself the opportunity to swallow my words. She looks slightly startled but makes no move to speak. "We both know this isn't going anywhere, so let's call it a day now." I don't relish the idea of hurting anyone, but I find I can't continue this charade. Deep down, I know she won't be truly hurt. Annoyed at the wrinkle in her plans perhaps, but not hurt.

"Is this because I don't want to go to a ghastly club?" Annoyance slips through her usually serene exterior. I have only occasionally caught sight of a nasty side to Eleanor, but I'm well aware it's there under the polite mask.

"No. Of course not. We both know this has been coming for a while."

Clearly rattled, Eleanor is uncharacteristically inarticulate. "Oh. I had thought, I mean, your mother said ..." And there we have it, confirmation Meddling Mary has indeed put ideas into Eleanor's head. I have no doubt Mary has promised her the position of politician's wife. It would be a good fit for Eleanor. But I don't believe I would be a good fit for her. Or her for me.

"Let's put anything my mother has said to the side, shall we? This is a decision for us, and I believe we might be best to leave it as friends." I watch as she marshals her face into her usual mask, and true to form, she doesn't cause a scene.

"I see. Well. I'll give you some time to think this over." Her cool tone matches the mask, although I don't miss the stubborn line of her lips. "But you should be aware I won't wait forever, Nicholas. And you will need me if you want a safe seat when you decide to run for parliament."

She's right. Her father was going to make sure I got parachuted into an unlosable seat. I feel a twinge of guilt over my promise to my father. But stronger than the guilt is an unfurling feeling of relief.

Before I have time to register what she's doing, she's out of her chair, scooping up her purse, turning sharply on her heel and marching out of the restaurant, with nothing more than a look that tells me in no uncertain terms I have not heard the last of this.

I have no idea what prompted me to break up with Eleanor tonight. I came here with the intention of trying to kindle something from the cold ashes of our relationship. Yet all of a sudden it was all I could do not to shout in frustration. It didn't escape my notice my left leg jiggled for most of the meal.

Feeling unsettled, I debate whether to go to the bar on my own, but eventually head home, annoyed with myself, and spend a few hours working before falling into bed.

I wake with a start to a darkened room, the glow from my bedside clock telling me it's nearly three am. The throb from my cock tells me I've had another one of those dreams. Full of wild hair, bright eyes and long fingers.

These dreams about Lulu are getting more intense. I'm not blind. I can't deny she's gorgeous. But she's also an annoying pain in the arse and I can't stand her. I've never met a woman who disturbs and distracts me the way Lulu MacLeod does. So why do I wake up in the middle of the night with a hard-on that won't go away unless I take matters into my own hands, so to speak? I certainly never had dreams like this about Eleanor. What the hell is wrong with me?

As for Eleanor, it's evident she's been drinking my mother's Kool Aid—or sherry—as the case may be. I'm relieved I finally did what needed to be done and broke it off with her. She might make the perfect political wife, but I'm beginning to understand I need more than a 'suitable' partner. However, right now, my whole life feels like it's taking a sharp left turn and these unsettled feelings are not something I'm used to.

It hasn't escaped my notice that my feelings of dissatisfaction with my life have increased over recent weeks. Since Lulu MacLeod landed unceremoniously in the middle of my previously unruffled existence. Nor that my unwelcome attraction to her has not waned on further acquaintance. Quite the contrary.

After a morning spent drafting responses for a client, I head to the sailing club for the first of the weekend races. Will and Josh are already there, setting up the rigging on Will's boat.

"Josh. Great to see you. It's been a while." We do one of those half-handshake-half-back-slapping hugs so popular with men. Although we all went to school together, Josh and Will were in a different crowd from me. Or rather, you could say, they were in a crowd. I was the loner who spent every waking moment studying. I was the prefect who more than once turned a blind eye to the things they got up to so I didn't upset Harry, and, therefore, my father. They looked at me as a boring nerd, and I looked at them with envy. Envy that no matter what trouble Will got into, Harry still loved him. Even envy that no matter what Josh did—good or bad—his father didn't seem to care. There was such freedom in that. In my family, you lived by the rules or else. I never cared to find out what 'else' might be.

"Who's crewing for you today?" Will asks, slicking sunblock across his face.

"Ben. Have you seen him around?" Ben is one of Will's two younger brothers. They are very much alike, although Ben is, according to my sister at least, the far better looking of the two. Based on his track record with women, I suspect this is true, but they are both tall and gangly with pale red hair, dark blue eyes and party-boy temperaments. As the youngest son, Ben takes his partying, and not much else, very seriously.

Will laughs. "Last seen dunking his head in the harbour. A little hung over, I think. Looks like you won't be beating us today."

"Don't bet on that. Actually—you should bet. Loser buys dinner?"

"I'm here. I'm here." Ben staggers up, his hair darkened by a dunking, eyes puffy and bloodshot. "I'll be fine. Don't you worry, Nick. I'll be set as soon as I grab a bacon and egg roll ..." He disappears, leaving me to set up the rigging alone. I have no idea why I keep asking Ben to be my crew. Yes, he's an excellent sailor; however, more often than not, he's the worse for wear. But it's all about ballast, for which he's perfect, regardless of his hangovers.

"Right, let's get these boats in the water. Go hard or go home, Nick." Will offers a mock salute as he returns to rigging his boat.

I feel much better after the race. It's amazing what a little salt water, wind and sunshine can do for my frame of mind. Not to mention a win. We didn't win by much, but a win is a win.

After cleaning the boats and packing up, we find a table on the verandah and order a round of beers.

"Okay—dinner's on me. Happy to eat here at the club?" Will picks up the menu, although we all know it by heart.

"Not for me, lads. I have a date." Ben gulps the remains of his post-race beer and stands.

"A date? Don't you mean a hook-up with one of your fuck buddies?" Will laughs.

"Tomahto, Tomayto, old man," Ben quips, leaving the three of us with a wave.

"Speaking of women ..." Will starts. "There's someone I'd like to introduce you to, Josh. She's an interior designer and artist. Fun, beautiful, talented. Exactly your type."

For some reason my hackles rise. "Cut it out, Will. It's thoroughly inappropriate to be pimping out a work colleague. Do you even know if she's single? Or straight?" I know full well she's straight. I didn't imagine those vibes in the executive washroom.

He looks affronted. "I'm not pimping her out. I'm simply offering to introduce them. Josh hasn't been seeing anyone since he got back, and maybe Lulu might break his dry spell. And yes, I checked. She's single."

Judging from the discomfort on Josh's face, and the bruise which looks remarkably like a love bite showing slightly above the neck of his t-shirt, I suspect Will might not have all the available information on Josh's love life.

"Believe me, mate, a date is the last thing I need," Josh groans. "Good race today ..." It's clear he's desperate to change the subject.

Ever oblivious to undercurrents, Will continues, "And speaking of getting laid, I think Greer might have had a gentleman caller." Josh starts to look a little green at the mention of Will's sister, and shifts in his chair. I try and suppress the grin I feel pushing at my lips.

"Yeah, I called around to her place this morning to see her. Anyway, there she was in her bathrobe, with two sets of breakfast dishes still on the counter and a definite just-been-had look about her."

"Jesus," mutters Josh.

In all my years practicing law, I have never seen anyone look guiltier. Interesting. Seems like Will hooking Josh up with Lulu won't be happening. What I do anticipate happening is Will getting quite a shock in the not-too-distant future. I tune out the rest of their conversation, instead trying to identify the feeling knowing Josh won't be interested in Lulu has caused. It feels almost like relief, which can't be right. Unless it's relief someone I consider a friend won't be getting tangled up with such an annoying piece of work as Lulu MacLeod. That must be it.

CHAPTER SIX

LULU

The mirrors in this lift are a godsend. I'm winging my way to the CPM offices on the fifteenth floor, this time weighed down with copies of my proposal document, ready to present my ideas to the partners. I put the folders on the floor and try to wrangle my hair into some semblance of tidy—business like is never going to happen—to no avail. This time I opted for a dress. Which had nothing to do with the prospect of seeing Nick the Tardy. Or perhaps today he will be Nick the Cranky. Or even Nick the Disapproving. You never quite know what you're going to get with Nick Pierce.

But back to the dress. It's a very sensible and corporate navy, which is not my usual style. Yes, it shows off my legs, which I work hard for—well, sort of; making time for exercise is a bit of a hit-and-miss affair for me—and my breasts which, luckily for me, I came by naturally, thanks to my gorgeous mother.

Gorgeous. Which brings me, again, to Nick the Tardy. Whether he is crisp and fresh in the early morning or slightly rumpled and shadowed in the late afternoon, he's the sort of man who turns heads wherever he goes. I wish I had a free hand to slap my own wrist. Bad Lulu. Mustn't think like that. However attractive he might be—and however many sex dreams I may or may not have had about him—it is abundantly clear he thinks of me as an irritation at best and a menace at worst.

All the partners are in the conference room except for Nick the (as it turns out) Absent.

"Nick, unfortunately, sends his apologies, Lulu. He was disappointed not to be here, but he had a client emergency." Harry looks uncomfortable with the lie. He may even be blushing, but it's hard to tell, what with his already ruddy complexion. I manage to hold in my snort of disbelief, but for some reason, my chest hollows out. Honestly, it's a good thing Nick's not here. He would only criticise. At least this gives me the opportunity to sell my ideas to the other partners without having to deal with his bluster. I'm glad he's not here. So why do I feel so ... deflated?

"What a shame, but I'm sure you'll be able to catch him up." I pin on a smile. "Shall we get started?"

The presentation goes brilliantly. All the partners are on board—even the oldest and stuffiest of them. I've managed to create a look that's contemporary while at the same time being classic and giving a nod to the history of the firm. Kind of mid-century modern with a twist and a healthy dose of understated luxury. And as the cherry on top, I was able to incorporate a whole host of sustainability and recycling features so their office not only looks good but will help reduce their footprint, and, ultimately, save them money. Not to brag, but I think even Nick the Disapproving would like it. Maybe. Well, as much as he likes anything.

"That was brilliant." Harry jumps from his seat, no small feat for a man of his size, clapping his hands, his face definitely more pink than usual and beaming with delight. "What do we think?" His gaze sweeps the partners. For a largely jovial man, he sure can bust out the evil eye when he wants to, but it doesn't appear to be necessary. It looks like everyone is impressed.

"I love it." Will is grinning from ear to ear.

For a few minutes, I get swept up in the general hubbub of congratulations until Harry calls everyone to order.

"Well, thank you so much again, Lulu. We'll all take a look at this over the weekend. William will collate all the comments, and we'll be back to you early next week with some feedback. How does that sound?"

The meeting breaks up, and Harry walks me to the lift.

While we wait, he takes a surreptitious look around as though he's checking we won't be overheard. "While I have you, I wanted to tell you how disappointed I am that Nick wasn't here today." Despite his jovial mood in the meeting, I can see Harry is royally pissed. "This is an important project for us, and I want to get it moving. Is there any chance you could get the proposal sent over to his apartment over the weekend so he can take a look at it?" Puppy-dog eyes are an endearing look on him.

"I don't know, Harry. I'd rather talk him through it ..." And the thought of spending alone time with Nick Pierce is simultaneously appealing and horrifying.

"It's a big ask, I know, but perhaps you could call in to his place and run him through it real quick? Maybe this evening?" The pleading look he gives me is more than I can take.

"Fine. I have plans this evening, but I guess I could call in on my way out."

"Marvellous. See my assistant, and she'll give you Nick's address. I do appreciate this, Lulu, and splendid work." He takes off down the hall before I have time to change my mind.

If I had half a brain, I'd drop the presentation in an Uber and send it on its way. Being alone with Nick the Delicious seems like asking for trouble.

Armed with the address for Nick the Absent, I head home to get ready for my night out. Normally, I don't go to too much trouble—I'm not one for hair, makeup and fancy clothes. But since I will be calling on Nick the Disapproving, I feel like I need to up my game and put on some armour, so to speak. And who knows, maybe he'll do me a favour and not be home?

As I open my front door, my phone erupts with a familiar Face Time ringtone, and I scramble to fish it out of my bag.

"Da. You're up early." I got my mad hair from my dad, except mine is blonde like Mum's and his is a dark gingery red. Right now, it's sticking up at all angles from under a worn woolly hat, stubble now more silver than ginger covering his cheeks.

"Hello, my wee princess. I wanted to see how your big meeting went. How are ye? Ye look bonnie."

"Oh, Da. It's so good to hear from you. The meeting was a big success—they all loved it. I'm so excited to get started." I drop my bag and the heavy portfolio I've been carrying on the coffee table and fall onto the plump cushions of my enormous sofa.

"Of course they loved it. You're brilliant, hen. They'd be soft in the *heid* not to love your work." Whenever Dad spends more than a week or two in Scotland, his accent, usually nothing more than a gentle burr, comes roaring back, along with a liberal peppering of Scottish words.

This time he's been in Scotland for almost two years, ever since my grandfather died. He's now responsible for the house and estate he inherited, along with an eye-watering level of debt. He takes his responsibility for the estate very seriously, and although the National Trust has offered to take it off his hands many times, he refuses. Our family have been the lairds for hundreds of years, and he doesn't want to be the one to walk away, which is odd considering he spent so many years in Australia. But then he was the younger son. When his older brother died unexpectedly, his attitude shifted. Now that I know he won't be coming back to Australia any time soon—and that he will never live here again—I miss him like crazy.

"How is everything? The news said you've been having some wild weather."

"Och, yes, we are indeed. I do miss the Sydney summer, hen."

I lie down and stretch out, kicking off my shoes to join the collection already gathered on the floor around the sofa, and settle in, ready for a good long session.

Dad shares all the news of the cows and sheep, the local personalities and his plans to get the estate back into the black with a whisky distillery, and I fill him in on the CPM project and the work I'm doing for my exhibit.

I'm an emotional painter. The more emotional I am, whether negative or positive, the better I paint. Over the past few weeks, despite having so much work to do for CPM, I have been painting like a woman possessed. They're pretty good, too, if I do say so myself.

"Let me see your latest work, *mo chridhe*," he asks.

I head over to my work area, turning the phone so the camera picks up my latest paintings. Even though our styles are completely different, Dad has a brilliant eye for colour and composition, and we while away an hour without even realising it.

"Oh, crap. Dad, I have to go. I'm going to a party with Ro, and I have to drop off the presentation to one of the partners on my way out. I'm going to be terribly late." Heading into the bedroom, I open the cupboard, still wondering what to wear.

"I'll let you go then, hen. You take care of yourself. Think about coming for Christmas, would you? I can't get away, but it would be wonderful to see you if you can stand the cold."

"I'll try, Da. It depends on work. I miss you." We both tear up. Contrary to his wild and woolly appearance, Dad is a complete softy and struggles with us being so far apart.

"I miss you too, my darling. Talk soon."

As soon as I hang up, I'm in the shower, shaving my legs, washing my hair and soaping every inch of me. Not for Nick the Disapproving, of course. In case I meet someone interesting at this party. You never know. I'm not a relationship kind of girl. You're less likely to get hurt that way. But a good one—or two—night stand never hurt anyone, and it's been a while. Perhaps if I meet someone interesting, I'll stop having those thoughts about Nick Pierce. If ever there was a less appropriate man for me to be fantasising about, I couldn't imagine him.

As I'm drying myself, I have an epiphany. I know precisely the dress to wear. Not for Nick the Smouldering, obviously. For the unknown guy at the party.

Once I'm dressed, I snap a quick selfie and send it to Ro, who is my go-to for all things fashion. All things life, to be honest. She answers with heart eyes emojis and half a dozen thumbs up, so I know I'm good to go. I let her know I'll be late and I'll meet her at the party. Putting Nick's address into Uber, I gather my portfolio and head downstairs.

CHAPTER SEVEN

NICK

I've had a shit of a day. I should have taken the first hint when my alarm failed to go off and I overslept. Then some idiot rear-ended my car when I stopped for a red light and had the gall to suggest it was 'only yellow, you could totally have made it, man'. A note on my desk reminded me Mandy wouldn't be in—bloody hell, who takes a day off for an anniversary lunch?—along with a reminder that the presentation by The Interloper was at three pm. Big fat no to that. Not today. Fortunately, I had a client in need of a come-to-Jesus talk and quickly scrambled a meeting for two thirty. Not a great time for a meeting on a Friday, but it would get me out of sitting through the presentation. I was definitely not in the frame of mind to deal with The Interloper today. Sometime in the past couple of weeks, this woman has gone from being a thorn in my side to a pain in my arse, to an ache in my cock.

Finally, I'm home. Changing out of my suit and into some comfortable jeans and a t-shirt, I check my phone for calls and emails one more time before silencing it. Generally, I make myself available 24/7, but tonight I need a break. I queue up my favourite jazz playlist and I'm pouring my second scotch when the door buzzer sounds.

Looking at the intercom screen, I almost drop my glass. For fuck's sake. What is she doing here? Standing in front of my building is The Interloper herself, a bulky folder under her arm.

"How did you get my address?" I bark into the intercom.

"Good evening, Nicholas. Yes, I *would* like to come up. Thank you so much." She beams at the camera, in what I am sure she thinks is a beguiling way. Yes, alright. It is beguiling. But it doesn't mean I have to be beguiled. Because I'm not. I'm the opposite of beguiled. Whatever that might be.

"Why?"

"Well, unfortunately, you missed my presentation today, which I'm sure was utterly devastating. Harry wanted you to have the proposal so you could review it over the weekend. He's keen to get started." She lifts her shoulders. Her smooth, creamy shoulders. Which I can see because she's wearing some sort of off the shoulder dress. My jeans begin to feel tight, and she's not even in the room.

"Harry gave you my address?" Note to self; have words with both Harry and Gillian on Monday.

"Well, his assistant, if you want to be technical, but yes. Can I come up?"

"You can leave it in the foyer and I'll pick it up in the morning." The last thing I need is The Interloper in my apartment. I know from experience how long her perfume lingers. I'd have to get the place fumigated. Otherwise, my cock would likely drop off from too much handling. Hand being the operative word.

"Hmm. Sure." She smiles again as I push the release for the door. Mission accomplished. I'll pick the folder up in the morning and be able to avoid her for another few days. No sooner have I sunk onto the couch than there is a cheerful tapping on the door. Oh no, she did not.

Apparently, she did. I throw open the door. "How the hell did you get up here? This is a secure floor."

"Your lovely neighbour followed me into the building, so I rode up with him. Wasn't that a bit of luck?" She glances over her shoulder at the idiot who lives across from me as he disappears inside his apartment with a goofy—and more than a little creepy—leer at The Interloper. I'll have to speak to building security about him. Again.

"Fine. You have two minutes." I turn my back on her, and she barely manages to catch the door before it closes.

"I'll need ten, actually. I hope I'm not interrupting anything?" She grins, sailing past me into the living room, appearing not the least bit concerned she might be interrupting anything. "And yes, I'd love a drink. Thanks." She leans closer to take a delicate sniff of my glass. "Scotch would be fine."

I try not to look at her as I pour her scotch. Her mad, unruly hair is out and dancing around those bare shoulders. Fuck. Those collarbones. Don't look. Don't look. Her dress is the colour of crushed raspberries and brings out the flush in her cheeks and the bright blue of her eyes. I won't look at how it clings to every curve. Or stops halfway down those smooth thighs. Don't look. Don't look.

Ever since that day in the executive washroom, I have been struggling with my unwelcome and inappropriate physical response to The Interloper. Oh, who am I kidding? It's been building since she rubbed her magnificent arse against me in the lift. I'm self-aware enough to realise this is what has, to a large extent, fuelled my animosity towards her. Having her here, alone, in my space, feels dangerous. And arousing. Did I mention dangerous?

My cock is already throbbing in my jeans, and I send up a silent prayer of thanks for the t-shirt covering that sin.

"Right." I hand her a scotch as she drops her small purse on the couch. "Give me the folder, give me the spiel and give me some peace by getting gone." I hold my hand out for the folder, which she ignores.

"Oh, it's no trouble bringing this over on a Friday night. I'm going to a party, and this is practically on my way. Don't give it another thought. Nice place you have here. Very minimalist. Very ... you." She glances around, taking in the sleek, mono-chrome décor.

By now, I know how she gets the upper hand in all our en-counters. She ignores anything I say and has the conversation she wants to have, albeit one sided. It's incredibly disconcerting and often has the effect of making me feel embarrassed by my own rudeness, which is an unknown phenomenon for me be-cause I generally don't do embarrassed. Which, of course, pisses me off even more. My feelings are becoming a vicious game of chase your tail.

"Why don't we sit here at this table, and I'll talk you through it?" Lulu pulls out a chair and settles at my dining table, lining the folder up with the chair next to her and patting the seat with a shameless grin.

"Ten minutes," I grit out as I try to subtly shift the chair a little further away from her.

"Right. Well, you might be wondering why I didn't do this as a PowerPoint presentation. That's because it's simply not pos-sible to get the colours true enough and the texture of the fabrics clear. So, I like to have a touchy-feely document." She glides her hand over the front page, touching and feeling. Shifting her chair closer, she opens the folder.

For the next ten minutes, she talks, articulating her vision for the office, turning pages in the document, which are tagged with colour patches, fabric swatches, carpet squares and even timber samples. I hardly hear a word she says, mesmerised as I am by her long fingers stroking over velvets, linens and leather, and by her infuriating, intoxicating perfume wafting towards me as she waves her arms, explaining whatever the hell she's telling me. It's not that I don't want to listen. But my hormones seem to hijack my thoughts whenever she's within sniffing distance.

"Well?" she finally says, looking at me expectantly. This is where I need to tell her it all looks great so I can get her out of my apartment. If she's not gone in the next couple of minutes, there's no telling what I might do. A tendril of sunshine hair drifts across my face as she turns to face me, and I concentrate hard on Miss Best and her hairy face wart so I can get up out of my chair without embarrassment.

"Yep. All looks good. Leave it with me. I'll have my comments to Harry by Monday." I head towards the door to let her out.

"Are you serious? That's it?" She jumps out of her chair, hands on hips, brows drawn together and those luscious lips pursed. "This presentation is a work of art—if I do say so myself—and all you can say is 'I'll get back to you'?"

I turn and glare at her, hands on my hips, mirroring her stance.

"Yes, that's it. You did the job we paid you to do. Bravo. As I said, I will review it, make notes and have my comments to Harry on Monday. Thank you *so much* for taking the time to bring it over and walk me through it in my *personal* time." My voice drips with sarcasm. But at least it's not dripping lust, which most of the rest of me is doing.

"Argh." She stamps her foot. Yes, actually stamps her foot. Like a toddler having a tantrum. Which only draws my attention to her feet, below a set of spectacular calves and ankles. "You know what? You're an arsehole. Unbelievable. Impossible. I've never met anyone as rude and difficult as you. I'm trying to do a job here, and all you do is block me at every turn. Is it me you don't like or are you always like this?"

She's right. I don't like her. But I want her in a way I haven't felt in a long time. That's not true. I want her in a way I haven't ever felt. Which scares me. And makes me like her even less. Suddenly she's so close we're almost touching, hands on hips, eyes glittering, cheeks flushed.

"I honestly don't get it. I worked my butt off to give you a design I know resonates with the history of the firm. What more do you want from me?"

And that's when I lose control. The hands that were only moments ago planted firmly on my hips are tangling in her wild hair, pulling her face towards me. It takes everything I have to pull back, to meet her gaze, to control my hands and my mouth.

I can't breathe, much less think. Then Lulu grabs my shirt, and I'm lost. It's not gentle. My lips crush against hers, tongue demanding entry. Her lips open, and she uses my shirt to yank me closer, slamming the length of her body against mine. It's incendiary. All teeth and tongues and grasping hands.

Tearing my mouth away from hers, I feel like I've left a layer of flesh behind, exposing me in a way I've never experienced before.

"That's what I want. Happy now?"

"Not yet," Lulu gasps, chest heaving, and I can hear the lust in her voice, leaving me in no doubt about what she wants. The blue of her irises has been swallowed up by her pupils, and she makes no move to pull away.

"You drive me fucking insane. If I don't fuck you, I'm going to lose my mind." And my lips are on hers again, one hand still tangled in her hair as the other slides down her back to her perfect ass, pressing her tight against me again so she can feel how hard I am. I should stop. I know I should stop. But not even Miss Best and her wart could turn this around now.

She's an assault on the senses. The wildflower scent that once seemed so innocent has morphed into something hot and provocative and fuels my madness. I taste whisky and blood as our mouths tear at each other. I'm desperate to see her, touch her, taste her. All of her.

CHAPTER EIGHT

LULU

I taste blood and whisky and man, and I've never been so unhinged in my life. Nick's wicked lips leave mine, but his grip on me doesn't loosen. His mouth moves down my neck and across my collarbone. He kisses with his teeth as much as his lips and tongue. Like he's devouring me. And it's spectacular. Who'd have thought a man like Nick has so much passion locked up inside him?

Somehow, I find myself pressed up against the back of the sofa. Nick's knee is between my thighs. I can't help but arch my back, pressing harder against his erection, grinding. His fingers slide under the top of my dress, skimming my shoulders before pushing my dress down. I'm not wearing a bra, and my breasts spill out. They're not big, but not small either, and my nipples are as hard as his cock. He doesn't hesitate. His mouth is on my breast. He sucks hard at the soft flesh before covering my nipple, biting gently, then sucking, flicking the tip with his tongue. I'm so turned on my whole body is shaking. My skin is hot and tight and I feel my arousal soaking through my knickers.

With a yank, I pull his t-shirt over his head and drop it, sucking and biting the smooth, warm flesh of his shoulder, my nails digging into the hard muscles of his back. He topples me onto the sofa's cushions, his knees landing on either side of my hips as he follows.

My dress is now around my waist, baring my breasts and my sheer lacy knickers, which Nick grabs with both hands, ripping them from my hips.

"Fuck," he mutters. "You're driving me crazy. I want you wet. I want you wet and begging."

I'm already there. He shifts until he's between my thighs.

I can't form words to answer. But I open my legs wider, and he can see just how wet I already am.

"I need to fuck you. Tell me to stop. Tell me now." His words are mumbled as his lips never leave my skin, but I hear every word as though I can read his mind.

"No. Don't. Don't you dare stop." I'm breathing so hard I can barely get the words out.

That's all he needs to hear. Rising on his knees, he slides his zipper down. Pushing the denim and his boxers down his thighs, Nick takes his erection in his hand. It's long and thick and beautiful, a drop of pre-cum already beading and tracing across the head. He strokes himself as he fixes his hungry eyes on my face.

"Last chance," he rumbles.

Rather than answer, I reach out and take him in my hand. The word condom whispers in the back of my mind, but I can't hold on to the thought. Can't think of anything but the need to feel him inside me. My eyes never leaving his, I rub the head of his cock between my legs, grazing my clit. Pressing his hips forward he slides the tip into me, holding it there with tiny pulses for what feels like forever before lunging forward, filling me in one hard thrust.

I can't help but cry out, but there are no words. Only noises, gasps and groans. His thrusts are rough, like his hands and mouth, and I love it. My hands are in his hair as he sucks hard on my neck. Then he's rearing up, dragging my hips up his thighs and pulling my legs up and over his chest. He doesn't even break rhythm. His fingers dig deep into the flesh of my hips and I know they'll leave bruises. This is angry fucking at its best. And I love it. I love it all.

I can feel the pressure building, and I'm gasping for breath. Then Nick's thumb slides over my clit and suddenly I'm exploding, my body stiffening then quaking with release.

"Yes, that's it," he gasps as his back arches and I feel his cock pulse as he follows me over the edge, roaring his release.

Nick drops forward, bracing on his forearms, eyes closed, his forehead resting on mine, his sweat dripping onto my face. We're both breathing too hard to speak. He's still inside me, still hard. Time slows, along with our breathing, and then those silvery eyes are open, seeming to see right inside me to the secret self we all keep hidden. I should be worried, but for this fleeting moment, I feel like I can see inside him too, both of us unguarded, before the shutters come down in his eyes.

"Well, that wasn't quite what I was expecting," I croak.

Nick stands, hitches his jeans up and heads to the kitchen. I hear the fridge opening and ice clinking. Sitting up, I drag my dress over my boobs and down my thighs, pushing my hair out of my face. I must look a mess, but right now, I can't find the energy to care.

"I don't know what came over me. I apologise." Nick hands me a glass of water, his face expressionless below his just-fucked hair. He can't meet my eyes, which is unlike him, and I know I won't like what's coming. But I refuse to make it easy for him by jumping in with a response. The silence stretches between us. "This was a mistake. It should never have happened." His voice is as expressionless as his face. He's dropped straight into lawyer mode with barely a blink.

I take a moment to process his words, my brain still sluggish with orgasm hormones. "You're sorry? A mistake? Seriously? You really are a piece of work." Infuriated by his words, I gulp some water, put the glass on the coffee table and stand up, searching for my bag. As furious as I am with him, I'm equally annoyed at myself. What was I expecting?

"If you could have your comments on my proposal to Harry on Monday, I would appreciate it. And don't worry, nobody will ever hear about this from me." I can feel my cheeks blazing and angry tears are starting to gather in my eyes. I need to get out of here. Fast. Before they start to fall and he thinks he's hurt my feelings. Damn angry crying.

I turn at the door. Nick is still standing beside the scene of the crime, head bowed, glass of water dangling from his very clever fingers.

"You know, you didn't need to be such a prick. It was just angry sex. I get it. You don't like me. I don't like you. I wasn't imagining a happy-ever-after or anything. I'm not any happier about it than you."

He looks up, finally meeting my eyes, and even from a distance, I can feel the regret rolling off him. "It was unprofessional. We have to work together. Unfortunately." Leaving me to wonder what he is sorrier about—having had sex with me or having to work with me. Both if I had to guess.

"Yes. That is unfortunate. But you know what? I can keep it professional if you can." And with that, I slam the door behind me.

By the time the Uber arrives, I'm no longer in danger of an angry cry. I text Ro to let her know I won't be making it to the party after all—I'm in no fit state to be seen by anyone after what just happened—and head straight home. She calls me in a matter of seconds, and I can hear the party going on in the background.

"Is everything okay? I thought you were on your way?"

"Yeah, I'm okay. But I've done something monumentally stupid." Those angry tears are threatening again.

"What? What did you do? Weren't you going to Nicholas the Tardy's to ...? Oh my god. You had sex with him, didn't you?" It's like she has a sixth sense. Maybe she's psychic.

"Ugh. Yes. Angry, angry hot sex." I feel the curious look of the Uber driver through the rear-view mirror, but honestly, I'm beyond caring.

"You dirty bird. Was it amazing? Hang on, let me go somewhere quieter ..." The sounds of the party recede and then stop as I hear a door bang. "So? Details?"

"This is not funny, Ro. I have to work with this guy. And now he's seen me naked. Well, almost. And I've seen his orgasm face. And afterwards ..." I fill Rosanna in on our post-sex conversation.

"What a bastard. Well, at least now you've scratched the itch. You should be able to put it behind you and move on. Which should be much easier since he was a prick. Yes?"

"Yes. I guess."

"You still haven't answered my question. Was it amazing?"

"Oh, Ro. You have no idea."

"Huh. You're right there, I don't." I wince. I didn't mean to hit that nerve with Ro. "But give me something to work with here, Lu. On a scale of one to ten?"

"Eleventy thousand."

"Ohhh. I think I just had a sympathy orgasm."

"I'm already in an Uber on my way home, and I'm still feeling aftershocks." I sigh, which gets a snort from the Uber driver.

"Are you okay? Do you want me to come over?"

"No, you stay and enjoy the party. I'm almost home. And I'm okay. Promise. All I want to do is take a hot shower and forget it ever happened." I feel sticky and smell like sex. Like Nick.

"Okay—if you're sure. Let's catch up for breakfast tomorrow, and you can fill me in on all the details. Call me if you need me. Love you."

"Love you too."

Even after a long hot shower, I can still smell Nick on my skin. Still feel his fingers digging into my flesh, his teeth nipping. Faint bruises are already beginning to bloom, and seeing them makes my whole body throb with unwelcome need.

Restless, I prop a fresh canvas on my easel and squeeze out angry colours—purple and red and dark, dark blue—on a palette. Painting is my therapy. Whatever it is I'm feeling comes right out of my brush and onto the canvas. Sometimes it's beautiful, and sometimes it's ugly. But it always centres me in a way nothing else does.

Before I know it, it's four in the morning and I'm standing in front of a finished painting. I clean up my brushes, strip off my overalls and fall onto the bed exhausted but with my mood somewhat restored.

As exhausted as I am, sleep just won't come. I can't stop thinking about what was hands-down the best sex of my life. But the thing getting under my skin the most is that look. When he opened his eyes and looked right into my soul before slamming the shutters down. It might have been angry fucking, but somewhere deep inside me, something stirs. Something I can't quite put my finger on. The bottom line, though, is tonight was a train wreck. Nick is at least as responsible as I am. More, if truth be told. So, I refuse to feel guilty. This will in no way impact my ability to do my job. And in no universe will it ever happen again. I have no intention of falling for anyone. Especially Nicholas the Complete Bastard Pierce.

CHAPTER NINE

NICK

Saturday morning I wake up with a hangover, the likes of which I haven't had for I don't know how long. After Lulu left I polished off the rest of the bottle of scotch before spending the night tossing and turning. It's not often my conscience bothers me. I'm pretty in tune with my moral compass and, for the most part, follow its lead. Last night was the exception. The catastrophic, cataclysmic, calamitous exception. I feel like shit. The problem is, I'm not sure what I feel most shitty about. The sex or the conversation afterwards. Then there's the way I responded to her presentation. Take your pick. You're spoilt for choice, Nick.

Trying to ease the throbbing in my head, I pop some paracetamol and take a long shower. At least the throbbing in my cock, a constant companion to thoughts of Lulu of late, has subsided. Coffee in hand, I lay down on the sofa, only to find her torn knickers where I dropped them and the smell of wildflowers on the cushions. I head for the bathroom bin, and my blood runs cold when I realise it doesn't contain a used condom. I never have sex without a condom. Ever. Which goes to show how out of control I was. This just keeps getting worse. I'm about to drop the knickers in the bin when, for reasons I don't care to explain—even to myself—I put them in my bedside drawer.

I try to get some work done, but my attention keeps wandering to the damn folder sitting silently on the dining table. Judging me. Yes, I was an arsehole last night. It's obvious Lulu is talented and has put in an enormous amount of work. But as she pointed out, all I could say was 'I'll get back to you'. Ah, shit. When did she go from being The Interloper to being Lulu? Sometime between me attacking her lips and her slamming the door on her way out, I suppose.

Finally, I give up trying to work and open up the binder. An hour later, I have to say I'm no less pissed. I don't hate it. And I hate that I don't hate it. And I don't hate her either. What I am is impressed. Twenty-four hours ago, I wouldn't have believed it possible, but now it seems like everything about Lulu—The Interloper, I correct myself—is, well, less annoying.

Not only has she come up with some beautiful design ideas, but she has understood workflow and suggested some interesting innovations that could even make us more productive. And all this without creating an over-the-top, hyper-modern environment. She has managed to pay homage to the age and personality of the firm. But what I really love is her use of recycled and repurposed materials, fixtures and fittings, and the inclusion of features to make recycling easier and more efficient. She has, in fact, gone above and beyond anything I could have imagined. Which only serves to make me feel more arseholey and irritated. Fuck.

I bash out a quick email to Harry with my thoughts. Probably not the time to do it. My irritation shows. When I read it over, it seems to be the definition of damning with faint praise. But I've already hit send. All this is most unlike me. I'm considered and measured and even-handed. Knee-jerk reactions are not my normal approach. Something about her seems to render me unable to moderate my behaviour. I can only hope Lulu—I mean The Interloper—doesn't get wind of it.

My mind turns to last night. I completely lost control. I can't remember the last time I was so unbalanced by a woman. Oh, no, wait. I can. Never. That's when. I am clueless as to why this woman, in particular, gets so far under my skin. At the office, she drives me crazy in a bad way, but last night, she drove me crazy in such a good way. It was worth every moment of irritation to feel that overwhelming desire and to have it returned just as passionately. I choose not to think about the moment before I realised the enormity of what I had done. The moment when we felt connected on a whole other level. It makes no sense. And it scares the crap out of me. So, I'm not going there.

But none of this changes anything. Obviously, it can't happen again. Unfortunately. Because—apart from sexually—we are not at all suited. Her talent and professionalism notwithstanding, she is in no way the sort of woman I should have a relationship with. She's monumentally inappropriate as a partner for me. Regardless of whether I decide to stand for parliament. Or stick with the law. Or whatever it is I decide to do.

I shudder at the direction my thoughts are taking but push those nagging doubts to the back of my mind. In all honesty, I'm not interested in a relationship. But if I was, I know I would need someone sensible, measured and well connected. Someone from the same background as me. Not to mention we would tear each other to shreds. Nor do we have anything in common. Apart from the aforementioned incredible chemistry.

Surely there is someone out there who falls somewhere in between? Perhaps I just haven't met the right people.

Of course, none of this excuses the way I spoke to her afterwards. It was unforgivable. I'll be lucky if she doesn't report me to Harry for sexual harassment. Or worse.

Head pounding, I give up on getting any work done and text Claire. Her life might be a mess, but she's great at seeing things clearly when it comes to other people. And there's nobody else I can talk to about this stuff.

·♥·♥·♥·♥·♥·

"Fuck, I'm glad you cut The Ice Princess loose." Claire flops into the chair opposite me at the yacht club. We agreed to meet here for lunch since I have a race this afternoon.

"You shouldn't call Eleanor that," I chastise, with no genuine conviction. "I take it Meddling Mary is pissed off? I've been dodging her calls."

"You could say that." She grins and takes a gulp of the wine I ordered for her. "You look a little under the weather. Are you okay?"

"Yeah, just hung-over."

"You? Hung-over? Wow. What happened? Lose a big case?"

"No. Nothing like that. But I did screw up. Royally."

"Wait a minute. Let me put it in my diary real quick." She makes a show of pulling her diary up on her phone. "Nick screwed up. When exactly? I need to get the date right ..."

"You know, I didn't call you to be mocked. I called for advice. But if you'd rather ..."

"No. No. Of course. I'm sorry. You want advice? Shoot."

"There's this woman ..."

Claire grins. "Ahh. So, there's a reason The Ice Princess has been iced."

I give her a glare, and she mimes zipping her lips.

"She's the designer working on the remodel of the offices. She is possibly the most irritating woman I have ever had the misfortune of meeting. And I fucked her."

"As in, literally fucked her?" Claire almost falls out of her chair she leans so far forward, desperate not to miss a word.

"Yes."

"Well, that doesn't sound so bad. Unless it was terrible. Or she's a stage five clinger. Then it's bad."

"That's not the bad part. Afterwards, I was a total arsehole to her. Told her it should never have happened."

"Did you make her cry?" Claire scrunches up her nose and purses her lips.

"No, I didn't make her cry. She was furious. Told me I didn't need to be such a prick; she understood it was just angry sex and she wasn't expecting anything. And then she left."

"Yikes. Not your finest moment, brother." Claire takes a moment to think. "Okay. Well, it's not so bad. Sounds like you're on the same page. And she's not hurt, which is good. Which begs the question, what exactly are you worried about?"

"Well, I have to work with her. And she's so incredibly annoying. And I looked at her proposal, which was actually pretty good. Better than good. But I can't tell Harry because I've been against it all along. And I was so rude to her afterwards. And seeing her again will be ..." I run out of steam and shrug my shoulders. Why do human interactions have to be so complicated?

I can see Claire doing her best to control a smile with little success. "Okay. Here's what I'm hearing. You find her irritating, but you're attracted to her. You want to hate her work, but you can't. You don't want to fuck her again, but you really, really want to fuck her again."

I take a moment to digest all that. "Yes." Much to my irritation, that sums it up completely.

"The sex was good?"

"Not that I want to discuss details of my sex life with my sister, but yes. Better than good. But under no circumstances can it happen again." The turn this conversation is taking has me shifting in my seat. I can't think about how good the sex was now, with my sister sitting next to me.

"So you said. Why not?"

"Well, for one, she probably hates me right now. With good reason. And we have nothing in common. It wouldn't work."

"What wouldn't work? A relationship? Who said anything about a relationship? Why can't you be fuck buddies? People do it all the time."

"Yeah—people like Ben. Who don't take life seriously." I can't quite hold back the snort of derision. Despite the fact I can't help but like Ben, his life choices are questionable at best.

"It wouldn't kill you to take life a little less seriously. Sex is supposed to be fun. A memo I imagine The Ice Princess missed." Claire snorts at her joke.

"You're not helping, Claire. I can't afford to get involved in a scandal. If I'm going into politics, I want to be squeaky clean. I refuse to end up a political cliché with dirty secrets coming out." Even as I say the words, I know the door on this option is closing quickly. Kicked by my own foot. And I feel not a shred of regret.

"Hmm. Well, you know I'm not behind the whole politics plan anyway. That was Dad's dream for you, not yours. But back to the point at hand. So, maybe apologise for the way you handled things after. And don't be an arse about the redecorating. If she did a good job, be gracious and tell her so. And if you happen to trip and land with your pee pee in her vajayjay again, no harm done. Let's order." It seems so simple when she says it.

I order a burger and fries to soak up the hangover and, as I start to tuck in, Claire returns to our original conversation.

"So why is this woman so irritating?"

"Ugh. Well, she's perky. Always laughing and smiling. You know how I feel about perky."

"Yes, terrible crime against humanity to be happy ..."

"And she's an artist. She wears outlandish clothes and always has paint stains on her hands."

Claire mimics Munch's *The Scream* "Oh no. The horror."

"And she's all alternative. Drinks chai. Wears crystal jewellery. Takes her shoes off in the office. She has a stud in her nose, for Christ's sake. And a belly ring."

"Wow. She sounds terrible. I wonder how you managed to fuck her at all."

"Well, okay. She is very beautiful when you get past everything else."

Claire gazes over my shoulder. "Hmm. Sounds to me like maybe whatever you're feeling for her might be making you uncomfortable. Oh look, here come Will and Ben." She grins knowingly, and I shudder to think what's about to come out of her mouth.

"Will, take a seat. How are you?" She manages to ignore Ben completely. I think they had an almost-thing once, and they've been wary of each other since. "Nick's been telling me you're having your office redecorated. How exciting."

Will is, as ever, clueless about where Claire is headed with this. "Good to see you, Claire." Will kisses her cheek and settles into the chair next to her. "Yeah. We got the proposal yesterday. Lulu, the designer, did a great job."

"Lulu, huh? Is she nice?" Claire grins at me over the rim of her glass, waggling her eyebrows, prompting me to give her a tap on the ankle with my foot under the cover of the table.

"Yeah. She's very talented. And funny. And gorgeous. Although I'm sure Nick has filled you in."

"Oh yeah, Nick has filled me in, alright. Sounds like you've got a little crush going on there?"

"Pretty much every guy in the office has a crush. Except Nick, of course. They don't seem to get along. She's very different from Eleanor, I guess."

Understatement of the year.

Claire is having trouble keeping a straight face. "Yes, sounds like she is. I'm looking forward to seeing the finished product. And meeting ... Lulu, was it?"

Did I say Claire sees things clearly? I take it back. She's crazy. I have no idea why I turned to her for advice, because I'm never going to hear the end of this now.

Thankfully, the conversation moves on, Josh joins us, and by the time we get up to prepare the boats for the race I feel at least a little less hung over.

"I can't wait to meet Lulu. She sounds great," Claire whispers in my ear as she kisses me goodbye. "Maybe I'll call in to the office sometime soon." And with a cheeky grin, she heads off to cause mischief somewhere else.

CHAPTER TEN

LULU

Ro and I make a good pair when we meet on Saturday morning at our favourite café, where the décor is dingy and could be described as early Dame Edna, but the pastries are to die for and the hollandaise sauce next level.

She's hung-over and I'm ... well, I don't honestly know what I am. Is an orgasm hang-over a thing? I eventually got maybe two hours' sleep, and I feel wrung out like a limp rag this morning. Not to mention sore in all the very best ways. And low-level concerned about the lack of a condom. Although Nick doesn't seem like the type to be carrying anything nasty around. I hope.

"Honestly, Lu, I think you just need to brazen it out when you see him. He'll be as uncomfortable as you—more even, since he was the one who acted like a jerk." Ro still has her sunglasses on, despite the fact she chose a table in the darkest corner of the café.

"It's not nice to hear someone regrets fucking you."

"Well, to be fair, it doesn't sound like he regrets fucking you per se. It's more like he regrets that having fucked you, things will be awkward. Which is not the same thing at all." She signals for a second coffee without even having finished her first.

"I guess so. And it's not like I have any interest in a relationship with him."

"Oooh, shocker. In a departure from tradition, Lulu hooks up with an emotionally unavailable man. Wait. No. Situation normal."

"You do understand the role of the best friend here, don't you?" I glare at her across my eggs benny, my go-to emotional crisis breakfast. "It's to be supportive."

"Being supportive and being an enabler is not the same thing. Look, I get why you don't want to put yourself out there. Your dad's heart was broken, and you don't want it to happen to you."

"You're forgetting I did put myself out there once. In college. Remember?" I huff with a glare.

"Damon? The guy you dated for, what, eight weeks?" She all but spits her coffee in disbelief at my reframing of history.

"Who then cheated on me. And lied to me about it." I push sauce around the plate with a piece of sourdough, dragging up the last of the buttery goodness.

"Don't try telling me he left you broken-hearted. I was there. I saw the relief on your face. But one day, Lu, you're going to have to let go and give some guy a chance to get in. And I don't mean your knickers. For your own sake, if nobody else's."

I struggle to think of a suitable reply. "Not this day." I eventually answer.

"Did you just quote Aragorn at me? Sadly, it's too early, and I'm too hungover to give that the retort it deserves."

Ro's coffee is delivered and, as usual, she ignores the flirty glance of the cute barista. It never ceases to amaze me how oblivious she is to the effect she has on men.

"Honestly, I don't want to talk about it anymore today. It's making my head hurt." I can feel the pout on my face.

"Okay—but one last thing. I was promised details."

"No. You weren't. And anyway, I gave you details."

"Eleventy thousand out of ten is not details." Ro tips down her sunglasses and gives me a laser-glare.

"Ugh. Okay, it was great. The earth moved. He has the most beautiful penis I've ever seen, and he knows what to do with it. Satisfied?"

"Sounds like you were. Which begs the question, why can't it happen again? He's hot, smart and emotionally unavailable. Exactly your type. And the sex is great. Why not do it again?"

"Did you miss the part where he said he regretted it?"

"No. I heard you. I'm just not buying it."

"Well, I'm taking him at his word and staying the hell away. Drama is the last thing I need right now. Although, I did get a pretty good piece of work out of it." I show her the picture I took of last night's painting. Ro and I met at art school where, despite our different majors, we bonded over high school trauma. Being a costume designer, she has a great eye and I value her opinion.

"Whoa. That's some emotion on a canvas right there." She takes the phone and studies the shot. "I love the colours. They scream pissed off and passion. I hope you're going to show it to Sebastian?"

"Of course. I'm not sure how it will fit with my other work, but it's worth showing him, I think." I push the little voice of doubt in my head aside. Ro and I have talked my imposter syndrome to death. I know if I mention any doubt, she will pounce on me, and I'm not up to dealing with a lecture, no matter how well intentioned, today.

"If sex with Nick the Arsehole can get this sort of work out of you, I think you should definitely do it again." She laughs as she hands the phone back.

"Hmm. If only it were that simple."

I take Rosanna's advice, and after breakfast and the obligatory retail therapy—it's quite incredible how much a new handbag can perk you up—I call Sebastian Black. Who not-so-subtly invites himself over to look at the paintings I have ready. I prop what I think are my best half-dozen around the walls for him to look at, but he zeros in on the painting I did last night.

"Darling, this is magnificent. The passion simply *leaps* off the canvas. I love it." His nose is practically pressed against the paint, sharp hazel eyes narrowed.

"Be careful. It might still be a little wet." I hand him the glass of bubbles he asked for. He takes a turn around the room, the heels of his uber-trendy patent leather shoes clicking on my wooden floors, inspecting each painting in turn.

"More. I need more, more, more of this. Darling, you're ready. I will have a look at the schedule on Monday and let you know when we can slot you in for a solo exhibition. I've got a feeling in my waters that this will be the start of a wonderful relationship. And my waters are never wrong."

Sebastian pinches my cheek like an elderly uncle, despite the fact he can't be much more than a handful of years older than me, not to mention several centimetres shorter. He's a tiny bird of a man with big a style and a big personality, which he uses to camouflage a ruthless business mind. Throwing himself dramatically onto the sofa, he tips back his glass and takes a long drink.

Great. Now I have Nick the Arsehole to thank for the best orgasm of my life and my first solo exhibit.

Will calls me into the CPM offices on Thursday morning to be debriefed, which is much faster than I expected. It's either bad news and they didn't like it, or they loved it. I'm pretty confident most of the comments will be positive, but I have no idea what Nick may have said. By the time the lift doors open on reception, I can feel my stomach turning over at the thought of seeing him again. In a blessed stroke of luck, he is nowhere to be seen, and I make it to Will's office without incident.

"I have to say, Lulu, we were all blown away by your designs."

"All?" I ask, arching an eyebrow. I know Will knows who I am referring to with my question.

"Yes, of course." Will's cheeks go pink. He's a terrible liar. Which must be a drawback for a lawyer, I think. I let it go. I already know who *wasn't* blown away. There's no need to embarrass Will by asking.

On my way out, I'm not so lucky. Nick comes to the door of his office as though he was lying in wait for me.

"Ms MacLeod. How nice to see you again." He looks like a shark about to attack when he smiles at me. If I didn't already know he was a lawyer, I could take a good guess based on his expression alone. "I was wondering if I might have a word. Regarding my office."

With Will standing beside me, there is no way I can politely decline. "Of course, Mr Pierce. What would you like to discuss?"

Without a word, he steps to the side and sweeps his arm through his open office door so I have no choice but to enter, getting a lungful of his delicious cologne as I pass, which sets off all sorts of unwelcome reactions in my lady parts.

"Okay, well, I'll leave Nick to see you out, Lulu. I look forward to seeing those minor adjustments and getting started." Will pumps my hand, his eyes flicking from my face to Nick's, seeming to sense something is afoot, before he returns to his office.

"Please, have a seat." Nick indicates a chair and perches on the edge of his desk, crossing his legs at the ankles and folding his arms, body language stiff and uncomfortable. I remain standing. Whatever it is he wants to say, I'll listen and get out as quickly as possible. Being too close to Nick Pierce is not healthy for me.

"I'm fine standing. What is it you wanted to say?" My pulse is racing, and I don't know whether it's seeing his gorgeous face again, nerves at what he wants to say, or maybe anger because he made some negative comments about my designs. Oh, let's face it. It's all of the above. What I do know is that if I sit down, my leg will start to jiggle, and I really don't need him to witness that. I feel myself crossing my arms in a classic protection move mirroring Nick's, and I have to force them down to my sides. Showing fear is not an option when faced with a shark. The air in his office is thick with tension.

"I wanted to apologise." His tone is formal, making it clear he is trying to establish some distance between us. Which should feel good but somehow has the reverse effect.

"Apologise? For what exactly? For your appalling behaviour on Friday? Or for not even giving my designs a fair and unbiased viewing?"

If he had the grace to look even a little bit ashamed, I might have been able to calm down. But his face remains a mask, although he can't seem to quite meet my eye, and there's a distinct pinkness on his perfect cheekbones.

"Both."

"Right. Well, you can keep your heartfelt apologies, Nick. I have no need for them. Or of your good opinion."

"I assure you my apologies are genuine, Ms MacLeod, and I am well aware you haven't the slightest concern for my good opinion. You do, however, have them both. Your designs for the offices were impressive and professional, and it was churlish of me not to say so. I wasn't ..." He peters off, and as his silver eyes finally lock with mine, a jolt of arousal shoots straight to my core. Dammit.

"You weren't ...?" My whole body is hot, cheeks flaming, nipples tight. My voice quivers ever so slightly.

"I wasn't thinking clearly. I was taken aback by the ... intensity of what had happened. And concerned you might misinterpret my intentions."

My spine stiffens.

"Yes, because you've made it quite clear you're completely smitten with me." Ah, sarcasm, my old friend. "Let me reassure you. I'm not that naïve, Nick. Nor that blind."

"No. Your message was delivered, loud and clear." He looks down as if contemplating the tips of his shoes.

"Right. Well, if that's all, I'll be on my way." I turn to leave, but he stops me with a gentle hand on my arm. I feel it all the way to the bone.

"There was one more thing, actually. It appears we didn't use any form of,"— he clears his throat, visibly uncomfortable with what he's about to say— "protection."

That stops me cold. He's right. Shit. I'd forgotten that priceless little detail. I never do that. Even though I have an implant, I always insist on a condom.

"Worried I might try and trap you, Nick?" Which is a bitchy thing to say in the circumstances, but as always, I can't seem to help myself with him.

He looks a little offended. "If you were to find yourself pregnant, I assure you I would take my responsibility very seriously. You need have no concerns on that score. I also want to reassure you there is no risk of me passing on any infections." His tone is so formal I can almost imagine him as a Victorian gentleman caller. It's pretty obvious this whole conversation is torture for him.

"I'm clean too. And you don't need to worry about being my baby daddy. I have an implant. So, it looks like we're all good." And even though we're talking about pregnancy and STIs, my body continues to heat, remembering the feel of his hands and mouth and cock, imprinted on my skin like an invisible tattoo.

"I'm glad. I just wanted to clear the air and make sure we both understood where we stand." Despite his cool words, I feel the heat rolling off him in waves. He finally looks up and his gaze burns as it travels my face from my eyes to my lips. I don't remember moving, but somehow, I'm right in front of him. He straightens from the desk, uncrossing his arms and suddenly we're nearly touching.

"*We* don't stand anywhere, Nick. I'm here to do a job. Nothing more." My voice is a husky whisper.

"Good. You're a very attractive woman, Ms MacLeod, but there can be no further ... personal contact between us. It would be improper and ill-advised." His words feel like lines from a

Regency romance novel. I picture him as Mr Darcy, and despite the circumstances, almost smile.

Regardless, his meaning is crystal clear. He has no interest in pursuing me. Yet the heat in his expression says the opposite.

Our bodies are two magnets. Drawn together without intent. His hands lift and hover near my cheeks as though he wants to touch me. We're so close now my breasts are lightly brushing his chest as our breathing synchronises. His head dips. Our breaths connect our open lips. Neither of us seems able to look away. I can see he's as lost in this moment as I am. I want to kiss him like I want to keep breathing. My eyelids start to close ...

A sharp rap on the door breaks the spell and we jump apart. Nick is in his chair behind his desk before I can blink.

"Yes?" he calls, his voice harsh.

The door opens and Harry pokes his head in as I sink into the chair Nick offered me earlier, my legs shaking, my knickers damp and my whole body burning.

"Will told me Lulu was in here, thought I'd pop in to say hello." Harry settles himself in the chair beside me. "Is Nick giving you a hard time, Lulu?"

I recall the hardness I felt brushing my belly only moments ago, and my breath catches.

"No. Not at all. We were discussing the colour scheme for his office." My voice comes out a little strangled, even to my ears, and I glance at Nick. His mask is back in place, and his attention is trained on a point over Harry's shoulder.

"Oh, good, good. Glad to hear you're getting on board, Nick." Harry takes his reading glasses off and peers at me. "Are you quite well? You look a little flushed."

I glance at Nick's impassive expression, but his eyes remain locked on that spot above Harry's shoulder. "Yes, I'm fine. Maybe a little overdressed for this weather, I think."

Harry's brows draw together in confusion, which is not surprising since the offices are sitting at a very comfortable cool. Keeping a lid on this thing between Nick and me—whatever the hell it is—is going to be harder than I thought.

CHAPTER ELEVEN

NICK

By the time Harry stops blabbing and offers to escort Lulu to the lift, I'm able to stand without embarrassing myself. And Lulu. This attraction is becoming damned inconvenient. Not to mention inexplicable.

Christ on a bike. I didn't even touch her and I was rock hard. I've never experienced such a visceral response to a woman. I can't seem to shake the feelings she stirs up. Yet we couldn't be less suited.

The sort of woman I need is someone like Eleanor, although it appears that is not the sort of woman I want. If by want you mean cannot keep my hands off. But how on earth would a woman like Lulu be a suitable partner for a politician or senior partner?

The little voice inside my head, which sounds suspiciously like my sister, whispers again that those things were my parents' dream for me, not mine. I've been ignoring that voice all my life, but it keeps getting louder, especially since Dad died. And yet I made him a promise. Breaking my word isn't something I can do carelessly. I need to make a decision. Either start listening to the voice or silence it for good. Trouble is, I have spent so many years assuming this was my path that I have no real idea what I would do, given a choice.

One thing I do know is I can't deny the magnetic pull I feel when Lulu is in the room, nor the way she plays on my mind when she's not. I succumbed to that pull on Friday night, not to mention what almost happened in my office today, but I can't let it happen again. Somehow, I need to find a way to resist her until this damn project is finished and I won't have to see her again.

I have a couple of weeks of blessed relief from seeing Lulu, during which I manage to convince myself all will be well. A train of thought which comes to a screeching halt one Monday morning when I arrive to find tradies putting up protective sheeting in the lift.

"A little notice would've been nice," I bark at Mandy as I stomp into my office.

"There was an email on Thursday. Did you not read it?" She gives me one of her patient looks, but I can see the grin hiding behind it. She's enjoying this. "It had a full schedule for the work. I could forward it again if you like? But this shouldn't affect you at all. Until the third week of work. Then we'll get you set up in one of the conference rooms for a week or so—" Mandy is very efficient. She would have made sure I got the email. I can only assume I ignored it. No prizes for guessing why.

"No, we damn well won't," I snap. "You tell Harry if they want to interfere with this office, they'll need to do it over a weekend. I will not have my work schedule disrupted." And with that, I slam my door on the racket I already hear starting up in the outer office. Yes, I overreacted. The prospect of Lulu being in the office on a regular basis has me rattled. I would have liked some time to mentally prepare myself. Turns out two weeks was not enough.

I stay holed up in my office all morning with the door firmly closed. Not because I don't want to run into Lulu—although I don't—but because I'm busy. Not having to see her is simply a happy by-product. And yet, I have trouble concentrating, wondering what is going on outside. Our offices are all fully soundproofed, so I can't hear anything with the door closed except for the occasional thump or crash.

By mid-afternoon I'm going a little stir crazy. I refuse to acknowledge that perhaps it's the thought of seeing Lulu drawing me out of my office. Mandy is not at her desk, and I desperately need a coffee.

As I head to the kitchen, I spot Lulu leaning over plans on the conference room table, deep in conversation with a tradie. The table has been pushed to one wall and furniture fills the rest of the space, piled high and covered in drop sheets. Her Medusa hair is pulled into a haphazard knot on the top of her head, although most of it seems to be making a successful bid for escape. As if she can sense me watching her through the glass wall, her head comes up. Our gazes lock, and just like Medusa she turns me to stone. Well, part of me anyway. If anyone was around to see the glass wall melting between us, I would have a lot of explaining to do. It takes me longer than it should to break eye contact and head back to my office. Without my coffee.

At least I will only have to risk seeing her until Thursday this week. On Friday, the partners are taking the senior admin staff, and Edith—because she would pitch a fit if she wasn't invited—out on the company yacht. Not only is a day on the water one of my favourite things, but it will be a welcome relief from the danger of running into Lulu MacLeod at every turn.

My grandfather and his partner were both keen sailors, and the first extravagant purchase they made once the firm found some success was an eighty-foot yacht, as they were measured in those days. It costs a fortune in berthing and upkeep, but selling her has never even been on the radar for any of us. We use her to entertain clients, for the occasional staff function and sometimes a partner will use it for a weekend or holiday. Days out on *Partner* are, without question, my favourite days of the year.

A few years ago, we replaced the old sail system with self-furling sails to make it easier to manage when non-sailors are aboard, since none of the other partners are particularly keen and Harry is no longer fit enough to be much help. With the new sails, Will and I can manage her for the day without any problems, regardless of the weather conditions.

I get to the yacht club early on Friday to ensure everything is set with the boat and enjoy some quiet time. It's a picture-perfect spring day. Warm sun, a slight breeze, and a cloudless sky. The boat's teak deck gleams warmly under my feet as I step aboard barefoot, relishing the gentle movement of the water. I lay out all the cushions and towels we store in the cabin when the boat is not in use and make sure the heads have been stocked with paper, soap and hand towels. I've scarcely finished checking the lifejackets and ropes when I hear a call from the dock. It's the caterer with several large eskies full of snacks, lunch and drinks. We hoist them into place, and I have a few minutes to relax in the sun before the first of the staff should start arriving.

No sooner have I cracked my first mineral water—I'm designated skipper today—than I hear a shout from the dock. Harry is striding towards me in the most garish Hawaiian shirt I have ever seen, with his wife Stella by his side. And … No. It can't be. But it is. Keeping up with Harry's huge stride is The Interloper herself, hair twisting wildly in the breeze, enormous sunglasses dwarfing her face, and exquisite long legs, tanned and bare, under cut-off denim shorts. *Jesus take the wheel*. Today has gone from delight to disaster.

"Nick. Ahoy there." Harry turns all *Pirates of the Caribbean* whenever he gets near any large body of water.

"Harry. Stella. Ms MacLeod. What a surprise." My tone makes it clear it's not a pleasant one.

"Well, we couldn't leave Lulu slaving at the office while we're out having a relaxing day on the water, could we?" Harry gives Lulu a one-armed hug.

"Oh, I don't see why not."

Stella looks up at me sharply, surprised by my dry tone, but doesn't comment. "Nick, honey. How good to see you. It's been too long." Stella has known me all my life and treats me like a much-loved nephew, which I find somewhat confronting. I love it, but at the same time, it's confusing since the emotional dynamic in my house growing up fell somewhere between a military boarding school and a gulag.

"Permission to come aboard, Captain," Harry shouts, clambering onto the deck with very little grace and turning to help Stella. Which leaves me to help Lulu.

I stretch my hand across the small space between the dock and the deck. She slips out of her thongs and drops them into the bag on her shoulder before putting her hand in mine. The hairs on the back of my neck rise, and for a moment, neither of us moves, eyes glued to our clasped hands, before she props a bare foot with pink painted toes on the edge of the deck and hoists herself up with little to no help from me.

"Thank you." She lets go of my hand as if she's been burnt as soon as she's safely on deck.

"You're welcome." Which, of course, she isn't. Not even a little bit. Especially not dressed like that. It's an embarrassment waiting to happen. Which is entirely my fault since I can't seem to control my reaction.

"Let me show you around ..." Harry starts, putting his hand on the small of Lulu's back and guiding her away from me along the deck.

For a moment, I'm transfixed by his hand, or rather, what is directly below. Finishing just under the curve of her arse, Lulu's shorts are a hair's-breadth from being indecent. The bottom of her floaty top doesn't quite meet the top of her shorts, showing off a disturbing combination of skin and swimming costume. I take a swig of my water to ease my suddenly dry mouth and roll my eyes at the inappropriateness of her clothing. Yes, okay, we are on a boat. But this is a company function. I'm pretty certain everyone else will be more covered up than The Interloper.

It's irrelevant that not one of the other guests has a figure so worthy of the outfit. I can only hope the swimsuit doesn't get a showing.

Before I can drag my stare away from the sight of her legs, Lulu glances over her shoulder. I can't see her eyes behind the sunglasses, but the little smirk she gives me lets me know she caught me staring, red-handed.

I'm saved from further contemplation of Lulu's legs by the arrival of a couple of the partners and their assistants, and sure enough, everyone is in sundresses and lightweight pants. For the next twenty minutes, there is a constant stream of people needing help onto the deck. At last, everyone is settled on the benches or the deck at the boat's bow. Will and I cast off and motor out into the main channel through Pittwater. Once we're in position, we put ourselves under sail.

There are no better sounds than the cry of a seagull, the flap of a sail, and the slap of water against the bow of a moving boat. All of life's troubles seem insignificant when faced with the beauty and enormity of the wind and sea. Apart from the courtroom, this is my favourite place to be. Now, I have to share it with Lulu MacLeod. And her spectacular legs.

CHAPTER TWELVE

LULU

The boat is like something out of an old Hollywood movie. I keep expecting Katharine Hepburn or Grace Kelly to appear on the smooth teak deck. All the modern conveniences, like satnav and sonar, are cleverly disguised in the classically designed boat. And the weather is as stunning as the boat. If only Nick the Confusing wasn't on board. Not only on board, but apparently in charge. At least the mystery of why a lawyer has such deliciously calloused hands has been solved.

Nick seems at one with the boat, moving across the deck with perfect balance. Nick in a bespoke suit is a sight to behold. But today, he's in dark blue longline board-shorts with a white t-shirt clinging shamelessly to his broad shoulders and setting off his tan to perfection. We're all barefoot to protect the deck, and who knew there was such a thing as foot porn? Nick's feet are long, strong and tanned, flexing as his neatly manicured toes grip the deck. I have to lick my lips to make sure I'm not drooling. I dare not look higher because a quick glance at his calves earlier suggested calf porn is also a thing. Lucky for me, he spends the morning steering the boat, so I'm able to avoid him.

Harry offers me a glass of sparkling wine but I decide to stick to water. I'm not much of a drinker. Ro says I'm a lightweight, and the last thing I need is to lower my inhibitions with Nick here in boardshorts and that clingy t-shirt.

Nick drops anchor in a secluded little bay protected by high sandstone cliffs. The calls of magpies and currawongs bounce and echo around the bay; the smell of the gums crowding the ridgeline mingles with the scent of salt and warmed teak decking. The water is smooth and glassy and so inviting. But it seems like I'm the only one aboard who wore a swimming costume, so I'm hesitant to jump in.

"I can see you eyeing off the water, Lulu." Stella nods her head towards the sparkling blue. "If you have your swimmers on, go for it. Although I warn you, it'll be cold."

"Are you sure that's okay? Nobody else is swimming …"

I don't want to embarrass anyone. I might have underdressed a little for this crowd. But we're on a boat for crying out loud. I knew the partners were stuffy in the office but had expected them to let their hair down, at least a little, on a sailing boat.

"Of course. I'd go in if it didn't mean my hair would look like steel wool afterwards. It's perfectly safe. I swim here all the time when Harry and I come here. Now's the time. We'll be serving lunch soon."

I take her at her word and, a little self-consciously, slide my lace and linen top over my head and drop my shorts to the deck.

As I push off from the prow in a half-acceptable dive, I hear a splash from the stern of the boat. The water is cold on my sun-warmed skin. I dive deep, and as I break the surface with a gasp, I find myself almost face to face with Nick Pierce.

He looks no happier to see me than I am to see him. Giving me a silent glare, he drops his face into the water and, with powerful strokes, swims away as though being chased by the great white he sometimes reminds me of.

I refuse to let him ruin this glorious day for me, so I turn on my back, do a couple of lazy backstrokes, then let the gentle rise and fall of the water take me. I watch the shifting patterns on the inside of my closed lids, painted magenta and crimson and claret by the midday sun. Time ebbs and flows with the water until I hear the steady slap of swimming strokes coming closer.

"If you're intending to swim back to the club, you're headed in the wrong direction. Or perhaps it's New Zealand you're heading for?"

I flip upright and spin towards Nick's voice. I hadn't realised how strong the current was, or perhaps I've been floating longer than I thought, because the boat is a very long way off.

"Hmm. New Zealand does sound nice. But I think it might be a tad ambitious."

"I'll help you back to the boat." He swims closer, seemingly intent on getting me into an armpit tow.

"Thank you. But I'm quite a capable swimmer." And because I can't help myself, I add, "Race you."

Before he has time to process my words, I'm off, swimming quickly towards the far-off boat. After a moment, I can hear his steady strokes as he starts after me, but by then, I'm already metres away.

Of course, Nick is a much more powerful swimmer than I am, but I'm fast and had a good head start. We reach the boat at the same time, both grabbing for the bottom rail of the stairs someone has dropped over the side for us. I can't help but grin at his look of grudging admiration.

"You're fast," he gasps, a little out of breath.

"My dad used to call me dolphin girl. He says I was a fish in a previous life." Maybe it's a trick of the light or the water, but I almost imagine his eyes are twinkling. "I wish we'd made a wager."

"And what would you have bet?"

Neither of us makes a move to climb the ladder. We hold the bottom rung and tread water. A boat full of people is at the top of the short ladder, but here in the water it feels private. Intimate. We're both breathing fast from our swim. Our hands slide towards each other on the ladder, fingers touching. Our legs begin to tangle and, despite the cold water, I can feel my body heating as we float closer together.

"Hmm. That's a tough one. Perhaps carte blanche on your office?"

Nick throws his head back, showing off his perfect white teeth, and his laugh sounds more like a bark. "Never gonna happen, Ms MacLeod." But his expression is warmer than I've ever seen, and his frown not quite as deep. The swell of the water washes us still closer, and my breasts brush his muscled chest, nipples tight from the cold water. Or maybe it's the contact with his chest. I couldn't tear my eyes from his if my life depended on it.

"Lulu," he starts, and I think it might be the first time he's called me by my first name. "I wanted to say ..."

Suddenly, Will's head pops over the side of the boat. "Lunch is ready. Need a hand there, Lulu?" Shaking the hair out of my face, I smile up at Will.

"No. Thank you. I'm good."

As I hoist myself out of the water onto the ladder, I can feel Nick's stare burn a trail from my shoulders down my back to my arse, causing the simmering heat of a moment ago to burst into a scorching throb deep in my belly. I can't let myself wonder what he had been going to say. I have to keep a lid on these feelings.

When he follows me up the ladder and stands dripping on the deck, I realise that even though we've had sex, I've never really looked at him naked. His shoulders are broad and tanned, his chest lightly covered in dark hair, tapering to a narrow trail that disappears beneath the low waist of his wet board shorts, which are clinging to his package and his thighs, leaving nothing to the imagination. Holy hell, it's impressive. He's impressive. It's lucky I can convince myself my nipples are hard because of the cold water. Otherwise, I might be in a bit of a pickle.

·❤·❤·❤·❤·❤·

Lunch is as delicious as I expected, although the company is patchy at best. Most of the partners are older and pretty buttoned up, and many of their executive assistants are, too. But Stella, Harry and Will are all fantastic company, and I adore Mandy, who has a dry wit and takes no prisoners.

I watch Nick surreptitiously as he loads up a plate and takes it over to where Edith is settled in a comfy chair.

"Thank you, sweet boy," she says, smiling and patting his hand as he puts the plate and a fresh glass of wine in front of her. Even under his tan, I can see a blush creep up his cheeks.

"Is this okay? Is there anything else you would like?" he asks. The sun has moved, and he adjusts Edith's seat so she's in the shade again. As he looks down at her, I can see the warmth and affection on his face, despite his sunglasses. An affection reflected in Edith's smile.

"No, that's lovely, Nick. You go and have your lunch now. I'm fine here with my wine and nibbles."

"Okay, but let me know if you need anything else." Taking me completely by surprise, he lifts her thin, age-spotted hand from his arm and kisses it before placing it gently on the table next to her glass.

Only then does Nick return to the buffet and load up a plate for himself, coming to sit beside Stella, Harry, Will and me. I can't help but remember the woman in the restaurant. There's a sweet and caring side to Nick that's as appealing as it is surprising.

"Did you know Will and Nick are keen sailors, Lulu?" Harry asks as we finish off the meal with a decadent fruit and cheese platter.

"No, I didn't. At least not until I saw how they handled the boat today."

"We sailed her in the Sydney to Coffs Harbour race the year after we finished uni. Came in third and had a brilliant time," Will adds. "Nick takes her out for the weekend all the time, don't you, Nick?"

"Yes, as often as I can," is the short reply, although his tone is relaxed and almost friendly.

"Do you like to sail, Lulu?" Will tops up my drink.

"This is my first time, actually. But I love the water. When I was a kid, I was in Nippers and we were always at the beach. I love the feeling of salt dried on your skin and sand between your toes."

"Nick was in Nippers too, weren't you, Nick?" Harry jabs Nick in the ribs with his elbow, obviously trying to get him to contribute a little more to the conversation.

"Yes. I was. For a while." Nick is leaning back on his elbows, legs stretched out in front of him, shirtless but at least dry now. The poster boy for stress reduction right there. With his bitter chocolate hair rumpled by the breeze and a pair of Ray-Bans hiding those piercing eyes, he seems much younger—and more approachable—than he does in the office. This is bad. Not only have I found out he's not the jerk I first thought, but we have a surprising number of things in common. Crap. I don't want to like him, but I can't seem to help it. It occurs to me that maybe it's not Nick I don't like, but the way he makes me feel.

"You should ask Will and Nick to bring you out on the boat one weekend. I think you'd love it. You haven't lived until you've slept the night on a boat. It's even better than a train for rocking you to sleep. And the early morning mist on the water is beautiful. Very inspirational for an artist, I'd think." Stella nudges Will for a top-up of her drink.

I can feel Nick's scrutiny on me from behind his sunglasses, but he makes no comment.

After lunch, I change out of my damp swimmers into the spare underwear I brought with me, and we sail for a while, taking advantage of the freshening afternoon breeze. I welcome the break this gives me from having to talk to Nick, although his presence as he moves around the boat adjusting sails and tightening ropes is still a magnet for my eyes.

The sun is low in the sky by the time we berth at the yacht club. The partners and their staff waste no time in making themselves scarce, leaving Nick and Will to clean up the boat on their own. I offer to help, but Stella insists on leaving 'the boys' to it and we take a seat with Harry in the yacht club bar to wait for them. A day in the sun has me feeling a little light-headed, and I would be happy to head straight home, but refusing Harry and Stella proves impossible. By the time Nick and Will join us, there's a bottle upside down in the ice bucket and Harry is ordering a platter of nibbles to 'soak up the bubbles' he and Stella have knocked back.

Another bottle down, and I know it's past time I took myself home. Harry and Stella—who were my lift—appear settled in for the duration, having run into some old friends.

"That's fine. I'll call an Uber," I tell them.

"Nonsense. You'll have to wait hours all the way out here, and it will cost you a fortune. Nick is heading back to the city now. He can give you a lift. Can't you, Nick?" Nick looks like he might object, but Harry gives him a look, almost daring him to refuse.

"Of course," Nick replies. But his tone suggests 'I would rather eat slugs'.

By now, Harry has an arm around each of us and is guiding us towards the door. "Excellent. Excellent. Have a safe trip."

And that's how I end up alone with Nick on the soft leather seat of his Tesla. Ugh. Of course, he had to drive an environmentally efficient car. Why couldn't he drive a great big gas-guzzling truck? Nick Pierce is turning out to be someone I could actually like.

CHAPTER THIRTEEN

NICK

I spend the first twenty minutes of the drive back to the city giving myself a stern talking to. Who knew Lulu's wild-flower scent, when mixed with salt water, would smell like sex in a bottle? Great sex in a bottle. And now, thanks to Harry, I'm stuck in a car with her for upwards of an hour courtesy of Friday evening traffic gridlock. Reliving something I should be forgetting.

Not to mention the 'moment' we had in the water. I don't think I'm imagining it. Like I didn't imagine the moment in my office either. Or even the one in the executive washroom. I need to find a way to get control of myself. Fast.

When I saw her waltzing down the dock this morning, I almost swallowed my tongue. As if it wasn't bad enough to have to see her in shorts, she took them off and went for a swim. I'd have picked her for a bikini girl, but she wore a sleek, low-cut black one-piece with little bits cut out unexpectedly all over. It made her tits look amazing. And her arse. And did I mention her legs?

Legs which are now crossed temptingly on my passenger seat, slightly pink from the day in the sun. This train of thought is not like me. I'm not one to objectify women, but bloody hell. She makes it so hard not to notice. I'd be ashamed of myself if there were any room left in my overheated brain for thoughts or feelings other than this unwanted lust.

Once I'd recovered from the shock of seeing her with Harry and Stella, I managed to convince myself I could avoid her for the day. How I was going to do that on an eighty-foot yacht, I had no idea. And, of course, it didn't work out that way. I couldn't take my damn eyes off her. Thank God for reflective sunglasses because, like a cartoon character, I felt like my eyeballs were out on stalks, following her everywhere. By the time we dropped anchor, it was either jump in the water to cool off or embarrass myself—and Lulu—in front of a boat full of my colleagues.

And then she had to go and jump in too. I must have been in a lust-induced coma the night we had sex, because although I think I can remember every detail, her body in a swimming costume was a revelation. She's all sleek muscles and smooth skin and slender curves. And so strong and graceful in the water. Who knew that would be such an incredible turn-on? It seems like everything she does is designed to reduce me to a skinful of raging hormones.

Something has to give. I don't know what I was thinking, assuming we could have the sort of sex we did and then walk away. Because I can't stop thinking about her. And I know it's not one sided. When we're near each other, it feels like all the cells in our bodies align, drawing towards one another in some weird gravitational pull. One way or another, we have to sort this shit out.

The silence has built to a deafening roar by the time we reach the Spit Bridge. I can't think of a single thing to say other than 'I'm taking you home to fuck you senseless'. Which, of course, I can't do. Can I?

I slide a surreptitious look at her as she stares out the window. Maybe it would lessen the tension. Perhaps we need closure after the last time. That might solve the problem. Perhaps I have built the whole thing up in my head. It couldn't possibly have been as good as I think I remember. Fuck. This is self-justification at its worst.

I'm so deep in my thoughts I nearly miss it when Lulu clears her throat.

"You can drop me anywhere along here. I can grab an Uber or a taxi, no problem," she says, careful not to look at me.

And that does it. Her whisky voice pushes me over the edge. I need to silence this noise in my head, or I'll go crazy. Without a moment's thought, I'm swapping lanes and heading straight for my apartment at Milsons Point. There is no way I'm letting her out of my sight until we have resolved this once and for all.

"Where are we ...?" I hear the moment the penny drops and she understands where we're going. She says nothing more, but I can feel her watching me and hear the hitch in her breathing.

"I know what I'd have bet." That's what I say, but the words sound more like 'I need to fuck you'. Which is, of course, what I actually mean.

"Bet?" She looks momentarily puzzled. "Oh, you mean, in the water?"

I nod. "Another opportunity to be inside you." I flick my gaze quickly to her face. She's blushing and her eyes are burning. It could be embarrassment, but it feels more like lust. I recognise it because it's exactly what I'm feeling. She takes a few moments to answer.

"But you didn't win." Her words might be light, but the look she gives me is something else altogether.

"It was a draw."

"So, what are you saying?" Her tone is amused with a hint of anticipation, if I don't miss my guess.

"I've tried to forget what happened. Tried to draw a line under it. But I haven't been able to think straight since the last time. And we need to get past it."

"So, we're going to your place?"

I shoot her another look, taking in the way her breathing has sped up.

"Yes. I'm thinking maybe we need to open it up and let it burn itself out."

"You're crazy. You know that, right?" she gasps.

"I've been *going* crazy since the last time. And then today you got on my damn boat in those bloody shorts. You knew precisely what you were doing."

She starts to deny it but can't get past the first strangled word. "I ..." And it arouses me further to know she was trying to get under my skin. If pheromones were flammable, this car would have gone up in a fireball by now.

"So, I'm suggesting we fuck. Hard and fast. As many times as it takes. Until I can hear your name without my cock standing to attention. Are you telling me that's not what you want?" We come to a red light and I turn to face her, looking directly into those hot blue eyes. "Use your words, Lulu. I need to know."

"This is absolute madness." Her pupils are dilated, hands gripping her knees until her knuckles are white. And then there are those nipples pushing at the fabric of her top.

The lights change and I have to look back at the road. I wait for what feels like a lifetime for her to speak again. I can almost hear the argument she's having with herself in her head.

"I can't believe I'm saying this," she croaks, her voice as taut as my muscles. I don't know if it's excitement or nerves, or maybe both. "Okay. Let's say you're right and I want that. It's just sex. Yes?"

"Yes," I answer, but a small voice in the back of my head laughs, because even now, I know it's not true. I can barely hold back a sigh of relief as she comes to her decision.

"Well then. Let's do this."

We don't speak again as I manoeuvre through the streets to my building, pull into the underground garage and park. We wait for the lift without even glancing at each other. If I look at her, we might not even make it into the lift, let alone my apartment.

It's so quiet I can hear the creaking of the Velcro on my board shorts, straining under the pressure of my swelling cock.

The air is hot and heavy and follows us out into the hallway. I stand back to allow her in my front door first, then turn away to close it, resting my forehead on the cool wood for a moment, trying to control my raging pulse, to no effect. I take a deep breath before I turn to face her. She takes a step back. I take a step forward. The space between us vibrates with unspoken, desperate need.

And then we're both moving. Skidding and crashing together. It only takes a second to realise my memory was lacking. It isn't as good as I remember—it's better.

Her mouth is hot. Demanding and giving. Her hands grip my hair like a vise. Just like the first time, I'm completely out of control. And so is she. I shove her roughly against the wall and push her shorts down her legs without bothering to unzip them. Circling her wrists with my fingers, I hold her hands above her head and press the length of my body against hers, grinding my aching cock against her belly.

"All day. I wanted to do this. All. Day." Which is a lie. I've wanted to do this since I first laid eyes on her.

My lips are moving across her face. Down her neck. Nipping. Biting. Sucking. She tastes of sea and sun and woman, and if I don't get my cock inside her soon, I'll be spilling myself all over her belly. Which is a treat for another day.

There's no time for foreplay. No finessing or luxuriating in her incredible body. There will be time for exploring later. Right now, it's hot and hard and fast and brutal.

Releasing her hands, I ease back, grasp the hem of her top and tug it roughly over her head, dropping it to the floor. Now she's naked except for a tiny lacy bra and knickers. I draw her rosy nipples into my mouth, tearing the delicate lace with my teeth as I suck and bite. She grabs my head, burying her hands in my hair, pulling my mouth harder against her breast. I grasp her knickers, tearing them in half without a second thought before shrugging out of my t-shirt.

The sound of ripping Velcro is harsh as her hands dive into my board shorts, tugging my cock free of my speedos. And then I'm lifting her, pinning her against the wall and shoving hard and rough into her tight heat.

"Jesus. Yes," Lulu gasps, bearing down on me.

Words are beyond me. It's primal and violent and volcanic. My fingers dig into her thighs, and my teeth dig into her throat as my cock digs deep inside her.

She matches me rough for rough. Her teeth are buried in the flesh of my shoulder, nails gripping my back, stinging my skin. Her legs are around my hips, heels digging into my thighs.

We're marking each other with teeth and suction and hard, probing fingers.

"I won't last. I need you to come. On. My. Cock. Now," I pant between thrusts. And she does. Her whole body stiffens, back arching, legs slipping from around my sweaty hips as she starts to tremble, the walls of her pussy gripping me tighter as I keep shoving in and out of her. I hold her up against the wall, not breaking my punishing rhythm as she comes. She's whimpering and gasping. I'm grunting and hissing, and the wet slapping of our sweating bodies and her slick pussy sucking on my cock tips me over the edge. I come with a roar, flooding her with jet after jet of hot cum.

CHAPTER FOURTEEN

LULU

It's long minutes before Nick clears his throat, still pressing me up against the wall, our bodies stuck together with sweat. "Did I hurt you? I lost control. I was rough. Are you okay?" His look is gentle in a way I haven't seen in him before.

"I'm great." My voice is a croak. "You didn't hurt me. At least, not in a way I didn't like." At least, I don't think so. All I can feel is the thumping of my heartbeat in every cell of my body.

He flashes a dirty grin. Without a word, he pushes away from the wall, supporting me with one hand, which is just as well, because I don't think my legs are up to the task. He sheds his board shorts, which had only made it as far as his knees, before lifting me into his arms, carrying me through the apartment, into a massive bedroom and coming to a stop in a marble and glass bathroom. Putting me down gently on a stool, he reaches into the shower and turns on the water while I slip off the tattered remains of my bra.

Taking my hand, he leads me into the enormous shower, where hot water is falling fast from a giant rainwater shower-head. My legs are still a little shaky, but Nick wraps one arm around my waist to support me while reaching for the soap with the other. His hands are gentle as he soaps my body with suds that smell like his skin, and despite the fact I'm still coming down from an orgasm, my body responds immediately. It's the smell of Nick and desire.

His eyes follow the path of his hand across my shoulders, over my breasts and down my belly. He hesitates briefly before sliding his soapy hand between my thighs, gliding across my tender, still tingling flesh. He's already hard again, and I can't help but reach out and stroke his length as his fingers slip through my folds. The dreams and fantasies I've had about Nick float through my mind, and I drop to my knees, my tongue coming out to taste his length. The marble is hard, but all I care about is having Nick in my mouth.

"Christ." His head falls back against the tiles, eyes squeezing shut as I take him into my mouth, circling the head of his cock with my tongue before sliding my lips as far down as I can. "Yes. I've imagined this so many times." His hips begin to move in short, gentle thrusts, his cock nudging the back of my throat. "Look at me. Watch me while you take me in your mouth." His voice sounds like the feel of his stubble on my breasts.

I look up at his face as I continue to work his length, one hand grasping the base, the other cupping his balls, which are already contracting.

Hot water runs down the ladder of his abs and splashes on my face, but our gazes remain locked on each other's faces.

It doesn't take long. "I'm going to come," he groans seconds before he releases in my mouth, so fast I have trouble swallowing it. His legs quiver as I continue to lick and suck him, smiling around his softening length. His breathing is harsh and erratic. "Fuck." He sighs, resting against the shower wall and reaching down to help me to my feet. Nick pulls me into his body, wrapping his arms around me, and I rest my cheek on the hard muscles of his chest, feeling a surge of power I've never experienced before.

The water runs over us until our heartbeats begin to settle; then, without a word, he shuts it off and wraps me in a soft white towel before slipping one around his hips and leading me into the bedroom, where he flicks on a single lamp beside the bed. Nick touches me with so much gentleness, drying my arms and legs, rubbing some of the moisture from my hair before sliding me onto the plush doona on his king-size bed.

"Your turn," he murmurs, dropping to his knees beside the bed, dragging my arse to the edge and pushing my legs wide. "Do you taste as good as you feel, Lulu?" His thumbs slide up and down my seam. He parts my folds. One thumb finds my clit and starts to circle. "I love that your pussy is bare. So sensitive." His nose grazes the inside of my thigh. I hear him suck in a deep breath. "Fuck, you smell good. All soap and sex." And then his tongue is swiping at my flesh, drinking up the moisture that's already gathering. "Ah, yes. So delicious. Sweet and tangy. And so, so wet." His tongue finds my clit, one finger sliding inside me before he begins to suck in earnest, his whole mouth clamped on my flesh, teeth nipping gently. I can feel my release coming already, shooting out in all directions from his clever, clever mouth. He's humming with delight at how wet I am, and I feel the vibrations all the way to my toes.

"I can't hold on. I'm going to come," I manage to gasp.

"Let go. Come on my mouth." And I do. Hard. He only gives me a moment to catch my breath before he's flipping me over onto my belly, hoisting my hips in the air and plunging his beautiful cock inside me.

"I can still feel you coming. Feel your pussy clenching my cock. So fucking good ..." And within a few thrusts of those strong hips, I'm coming again, gasping and gurgling as I pulse around him, unable to control my response.

Nick keeps thrusting through my release, one hand gripping my hip, the other roaming roughly over my back and arse before curling over my shoulder and pulling me back hard against his thrusts. And then he's coming too, filling me for a second time, and the feel of his cum flooding me brings with it yet another orgasm. I collapse to the bed and he follows, his body heavy and warm over mine.

We're both weak and trembling as he slides me up the bed and under the covers. He turns off the bedside lamp before sinking in beside me without a word, taking me in his arms and spooning me from behind. In what seems like seconds, his breathing slows, his body relaxing in sleep, and I follow, exhausted.

I wake in the middle of the night, the glow from the open bathroom door casting a square of light that doesn't quite reach the bed in this enormous room. But I don't need to see anything because I can feel Nick, his hot, hard cock pressed against my hip, his fingers sliding through my slickness. He coaxes me onto my back, taking a nipple into his mouth with tender suction as he flicks the other with delicate fingers. His eyes glitter as he rises over me, and presses the head of his cock to my entrance. My breath catches at the intensity in his eyes, in his touch.

He thrusts, achingly slow. Elegant hands cup my cheeks, trailing over my temples as he lowers his lips to meet mine, searching and soft. He's drawing the breath from my body with his kiss and the steady, deliberate rhythm of his hips. I feel the rise of the wave before we both slide down the other side into release.

This was a different Nick. Gentle and sensitive and unhurried. As much as I love rough and hot and fast Nick, this new Nick could be even more dangerous. Even thinking words like love in the same sentence as his name is a danger I can't afford. I reach out and run a finger over his lips before I roll away, unable to face him. Or myself.

When I wake the next morning, Nick is fast asleep, with his arms crossed under his head, face turned towards me. His long eyelashes and full lips are offset perfectly by the strong jaw and straight nose, saving him from being too pretty. The silvery grey sheet is tangled around one of his legs, leaving his muscular back, his arse and a strong thigh and calf on display. I take a moment to appreciate the view and the softness of the hundred-million thread count sheets. But even now I can feel stirrings of unease. Not because I fucked him again. But because I fear I could be in danger of doing what I had always promised myself I'd never do. Giving my heart wholly over to another. To Nick Pierce, of all people. This is utter madness.

I slide carefully off the bed, my footsteps silent on the plush carpet. I head to the hallway where, in the absence of underwear, I pull on my still-damp swimming costume. Slipping into my top and shorts, I grab my bag and head downstairs, ordering an Uber as I go. Waiting for Nick to wake up is not an option. I need space. Some time to get a grip on what I'm feeling. To take a few deep breaths and think. And if I have to look into those perceptive grey eyes, I know exactly what will happen.

Like the last time I slept with Nick, I head home, shower and drag out a fresh canvas. If nothing else, this whatever-it-is with Nick is good for my art. Unlike the last time there's no anger, just a sense of disquiet that is almost totally smothered by an overwhelming desire to do it again.

CHAPTER FIFTEEN

NICK

F or the first time in what feels like an eternity, I wake up
and reach across the bed, expecting to find warm silky flesh.
Nope. No flesh. Nothing but cold, empty sheets. Fuck. Without even lifting my head, I know she hasn't just popped into
the bathroom. The sheets are too cold. She's gone. It shouldn't
bother me nearly as much as it does. I should be relieved. No
awkward after-sex conversation about 'what this is'. No need to
promise to call or invite her to spend the day together. Nothing
but peace and quiet. The way I like it. Only I'm not relieved. I
feel strangely ... hurt. And a little angry. And confused. All of
which only makes me angrier. At myself.

I could have sworn I said we needed to fuck this out. Maybe
she thinks we have. Well, I've got news for her.

A brief search for a note turns up nothing but another set of
torn underwear, proving I yet again completely lost control. I
take a long hot shower and gulp down a strong coffee.

Heading to my desk, I try to focus on work, but the torn
underwear I dropped in the bin taunts me. Sighing, I head into
the bathroom and fish them out, along with the knickers still
in my drawer from the first time. They're completely ruined,

and my mind wanders to the moment it happened. I feel myself hardening at the memory.

Checking the tag on the ruined knickers and bra, I google the brand and locate where they're stocked in Sydney. Which is how I find myself in an upmarket lingerie store, asking for help. It's the least I can do. After all, I tore them.

I call Mandy as I start my car. "I need Lulu MacLeod's address."

"I beg your pardon? Good morning to you too. And why on earth would you need her address?" Hmm, didn't quite think this through. Plausible excuse needed—and fast.

"I gave her a lift home last night, and she left her, ahh, her jacket in my car. I'd like to drop it off to her in case she needs it."

There's a long silence before Mandy answers. "Her jacket? It's twenty-five degrees outside. Why would she need a jacket?" There's another long pause. "And if you took her home last night, don't you know where she lives?" I can hear the wheels turning in Mandy's head, which is never a good thing. But I'm in too deep to back out now. And I need this address.

"I dropped her off in North Sydney. And you never know, it might turn cold. Anyway. I don't want it lying around in my car, so could you be a dear and cough up the address, please, Mandy." The sooner I get off this call, the less likely Mandy is to twig that I'm up to something, well, not quite professional.

Fortunately, she can log into her files from home, and in no time, I have an address. Which could be a good thing. Or a very bad one. Right now, though, it seems essential. Inevitable.

"That can't be right. Is this her business address? Because it's Saturday, Mandy. I'd like to drop it off today. What's her home address?"

"That's it. She works from home, I think."

"But that area is all factories and warehouses ..." I can't believe she would live there. No. Wait. Maybe I can. It's Lulu, after all.

"What can I tell you? She's an artist ..." Mandy is beginning to lose patience with me.

"Fine. Thank you." I'm not entirely convinced, but since it's all I have to go on, I head off, a bag of sexy underwear on the seat next to me.

I take the time during the drive to call Ben and let him know I won't be racing this evening. Something tells me I'll be busy. He laughs and agrees to act as skipper. I'm sure he'll find someone to crew.

Some of the old warehouses in this part of town have been done up—now housing cafés and designer clothing or home-ware stores—but not the address Mandy gave me. Still unconvinced, I hit the button for the industrial lift. Enormous steel doors clank open and I'm hit in the face with an explosion of colour. Every centimetre of the lift, even the ceiling and floor, is painted in swirls of reds, yellows, pinks and oranges, which somehow resemble flowers without actually looking like them. It's breathtaking. And so unmistakeably Lulu MacLeod, I know I'm in the right place, the widget-making factory on the ground floor notwithstanding.

The ride is short and filled with ominous creaking and clanking. I have no time to second-guess myself before the doors open again on a freshly painted—red—industrial sliding door. It occurs to me I might be unwelcome. I might be intruding. But I can't *not* follow through on my plan. It's as irresistible as she is.

Music drifts out onto the landing as my knock echoes in the small space. Suddenly the door slides open, clanking in harmony with the lift, and I'm hit with simultaneous waves of sound and desire.

"Hello." She looks a little startled to see me.

"Good"—I pause to check my watch—"afternoon. I hope I haven't disturbed you." She's wearing overalls covered in paint, as are her hands. Red, purple and a deep midnight blue.

"Is there something you wanted?"

Yes. Yes, there is. You. Again. Already. But I manage not to verbalise my thoughts.

"Well, yes. I wanted to drop this off for you." I hold up the bag, attempting a charming smile and probably failing. Charming is not my natural territory. "I found your, ahh, underwear." I can feel the tips of my ears burning. Lulu says nothing, so I blunder on. "You left them behind. They were a little ruined. A lot ruined. Completely my fault. I thought perhaps I should, well, replace them."

Lulu steps back, allowing me to enter her apartment. Although apartment seems like an astonishingly inadequate word for the space. Much like Lulu, it's an assault on the senses. As though a fireworks manufacturer, florist and art gallery all exploded together. It's an enormous open space filled with colourful couches, mismatched rugs and furniture, and dozens of paintings hung and propped against bare brick walls. Sunlight pours in through floor-to-ceiling windows opening onto what looks like a small rooftop garden.

"That really wasn't necessary, but thank you." She moves to take the bag and then pulls back, looking at the paint on her hands. "Would you mind putting it down over there?" She waves me towards a deep red velvet sofa, picking up a remote as covered in paint as her overalls. The music drops abruptly to background noise.

I can feel the tension between us like a physical being taking up most of the oxygen in the massive room. I want to ask her why she left without saying goodbye. Want to ask her if she would like to do it again. I want to bury myself in her. But I stand staring at her, mute.

Eventually, I blurt—blurt?—I've never blurted in my life, "I've interrupted. You're working."

"That's ... okay." Her eyes shift to the far side of the room where an enormous canvas is propped on an easel. A work in progress. It's spectacular. I can't help myself. I move closer. I don't know much about art, but I feel the passion rolling off the canvas. The colours, the bold brush stokes, the thick paint, all scream with intensity and lust.

"Wow. That's incredible. It's ..." For a moment, I feel lost for words. And then it hits me. Right in the chest. Like a wrecking ball, as Miley Cyrus would say. "Is that ... is that *us*?" I don't know why I'm asking. I already know, deep in my soul. Lulu has put on this canvas the feeling I haven't been able to articulate, even to myself, all day. Words are inadequate, but the painting says it all.

Her cheeks turn pink as she nods, not looking at me as she whispers "Yes." She must feel my gaze on her face because she looks up and our eyes lock. They say the eyes are a window to the soul, and what I see in Lulu's is what I feel in my own. "I had to get it—the emotions—out while they were still ... fresh."

I have no idea who makes the first move, but somehow, we're kissing again. Lulu grips my shirt with paint-covered fingers, and I drop the shopping bag I had no idea I was still holding to the floor. It's instantly intense. I'm not simply kissing her with my mouth. I'm kissing her with my whole body.

"I need to be inside you again," I growl as my fingers find the snaps on her overalls.

"Yes. Yes. Me too." Her hands are already pushing my jeans down my legs. I toe off my shoes and step out of the pants as my shirt hits the floor, along with her overalls. Sliding my hands under her perfect arse, I lift her against me, her legs wrapping around my waist. It's a big open-plan apartment, and I head for the bed in the far corner, dropping her on top of the quilt and pulling her to the edge before falling to my knees and burying my face between her thighs. There goes another pair of knickers as I push the lace aside and suck her clit into my mouth. Lulu hisses out a breath, and within seconds I can feel her begin to pulse.

"That's it, gorgeous, come all over my tongue, so I can fuck you before I explode."

That's all it takes. She's crying out, her fists clutching my hair, back arched. Before she has a chance to catch her breath,

I'm moving up her body, onto the bed, gripping her thighs and thrusting into her. I can feel the throb of her orgasm squeezing my cock. I won't last long. Her hips kick up to meet me thrust for thrust, heels digging into the bed beneath her, knees wide.

"Faster," she gasps. "Harder."

Somewhere in my lizard brain it registers we're doing this without a condom—again—but there's not a force in heaven or earth that could make me pull out now. I've completely lost my mind to this woman. What's worse is, at this moment, I have no desire to get it back.

I can feel my orgasm bubbling in my balls, rising like a tidal wave. Sweat drips off my face onto her breasts. Breasts bearing the marks I left there last night, with my mouth and my fingers. Those marks ignite me past breaking point; my thrusts become brutal and uncontrolled.

We peak together. I roar my release as she chokes out a garbled 'oh my God', her muscles closing around me like a vise. I collapse over her, barely able to support my weight on my forearms to avoid crushing her. My heart pounds against her breast, my breath coming in heaving gasps. And I swear, I hear Lulu MacLeod purr.

CHAPTER SIXTEEN

LULU

I have no words. No. Scratch that. I have no brain cells. They have all died, gone to heaven, and are now floating on a soft, warm cloud, smoking a metaphorical cigarette and eating chocolate. Or maybe peeled grapes. Those big, fat pink ones.

I have no idea how long it takes, but eventually, my breathing levels out. I feel Nick shift to the side, his arm still over my waist, his body pressed close to my side.

"We seem to be making a habit of this," he murmurs. I turn my head to look at him and snort out a laugh.

"What's so funny?"

"I'm sorry, but you have paint in your hair. And on your face." I reach up a still trembling hand to wipe at the red and purple streak on his cheek, which only makes it worse.

"Hmm. Well, it was worth it." His expression is soft, as it was last night. My stomach does a strange roll I can't identify. "I can't seem to help myself with you. I don't usually lose control like that."

I can't help but smile. "Me either, it would seem." I turn towards him as he shifts onto his back and pulls my head to his shoulder. We're silent for so long I wonder if perhaps he's falling asleep—after all, we didn't get much sleep last night.

"Your painting. It's beautiful. Astounding, actually." I hear his low words and feel them rumble through his chest to mine at the same time. "Do you always paint after sex?"

"No. Not at all. But then I rarely have sex that's so..." I struggle to find the right word.

"Intense? Out of control? Nuclear?"

"Yes. I felt completely ..." Again, I'm lost for words. Luckily, Nick seems to know exactly what I'm trying to say.

"Unhinged?"

I nod.

"I did too. I completely lost control. And I'm not even a little bit sorry." For the first time ever, I see Nick grin. A wide, open, uninhibited grin reaching from his eyes to the edge of his cheeks. It makes him look years younger. And a whole lot more dangerous.

I feel myself grin back. "Me either. And I wouldn't be opposed to doing it again. Maybe after some refuelling?" I get up and grab my robe from the end of the bed.

"That sounds like an excellent plan." Nick follows, stalking naked across the loft to where he dropped his pants and stepping into a snug pair of dark grey boxer briefs which, thank you underwear gods everywhere, do nothing to hide his assets.

I crack open a bottle of the sparkling water I can't seem to get enough of these days and pour us a glass before putting together a share plate of cheese, nuts, fruits and chicken with some lovely crusty bread I picked up on my way home this morning. It's hard to believe it was only this morning I did the walk of shame from Nick's apartment. I've had more orgasms in the last less than twenty-four-hours than I've had in the past year. But it's not only the quantity. The quality has been good. Off-the-charts good. And it looks like there will be more where they came from. I hand Nick his glass, where he is standing, examining the painting I started this morning.

I'm not normally a particularly fast painter, but this morning, just like the last time, inspiration seemed to fly off my brush and onto the canvas. The painting is maybe half finished, and as I look at it, I wonder how he knew this was us. My paintings are pretty abstract, and this one is no exception. There are no human bodies as such. Nothing more than vague shapes hinting at limbs and heads and torsos.

We stand side by side, staring at the painting, sipping our drinks.

"How did you know this was us?" I ask, needing to understand what he sees.

"Honestly? I have no idea. It felt like last night, if that makes sense. Those shapes there"—he waves his glass towards the centre of the painting— "they look something like bodies, and the colours are what I felt—hot, intense, passionate," he says with a sheepish grin. "What we both felt, I think."

The sun has lowered in the sky, and sunlight is hitting the painting directly. I lower the blind on the window in my studio area so the paint won't dry too fast in the heat. With my back to him, I don't hear Nick move until I feel his lips on my neck, his free hand brushing aside the silk of my robe so his mouth can wander across the skin of my shoulder.

"Perhaps we can refuel in bed?" I suggest as I melt against him. I don't need to ask twice.

The sun has set by the time we've devoured the share plate and enjoyed several more atomic orgasms. I drift off, wondering if Nick will be there in the morning.

This time I wake up in my own bed, the small spoon to Nick's big spoon, with no desire to move out of his grip. This is a risk. A pretty big one. Yet I feel like I have no choice but to see where this leads. It's like Nick has a gravitational pull I am powerless to resist. He is the moon and I am the tide. Resistance is futile, as they say in *Star Trek*, and I've never been one to waste time in futile pursuits.

He must sense I'm awake because his lips brush my ear. "Do you have plans today?"

"Nothing specific," I answer vaguely, a little shy to say what I'm thinking, which is, you are my plans. "You?"

"I do, as it happens." I feel a twinge of disappointment before he continues. "Lots of plans. Lots of exceedingly dirty plans."

"Dirty, hmm? How dirty?" I rub my arse against his morning erection.

"Absolutely filthy. We'll need a shower. Maybe even two." His fingers slide over my hips and slip between my legs, where I'm already wet and throbbing. "Does that sound like something you might be able to get on board with?"

"Yes," I moan, already feeling the orgasm building, "that is definitely something I can get on board with."

Nick was right. His plans were filthy. And did involve two showers and four orgasms—each—before we decide last night's refuel is no longer enough. We make it out the door by mid-afternoon, starving and exhausted. Nick's shirt is covered in red, purple and blue paint, but he doesn't seem to care, which surprises me a little. He's always so put together at work. At least I managed to get the paint off his face and out of his hair.

We head to my favourite nearby café on foot, snag a table and order quickly before the kitchen closes. Once the server delivers our coffees, I jump right in.

"So, this"—I wave my hand between us—"what do you think this is? I mean, is it a one-time thing or ...?"

One of Nick's eyebrows lifts towards his hairline, which he does quite often, I've noticed. "It's already been more than a one-time thing."

"You know what I mean." I roll my eyes.

Nick leans back in his chair, his long legs stretched out in front of him. Despite a furrowed brow, he looks more relaxed than I've ever seen him. Not surprising, to be honest. I've lost count of the orgasms, and I can only imagine he has, too.

"Cards on the table? I'm not looking for a relationship. They don't seem to work for me. And I think you'd agree we probably don't have enough in common for a relationship to work. But I do seem unable to resist you, and more to the point, I don't want to. Whether you want whatever this is,"—he waves his hand between us, echoing my earlier action—"to continue is up to you, so long as you understand the limitations. Of course, if you want to call a halt right now, I will respect your position and we need never mention this weekend again."

Forgetting this weekend is precisely what I should do. And exactly the opposite of what I want. Ruh-Roh as Scooby Doo would say.

"So, you'd like to continue sleeping together but no relationship. No dating?"

"Are you serious? Yes, I would definitely like to continue sleeping—or not sleeping—together." He shoots me one of those rare grins.

"Oh. Okay. Well, me too. If you are." I'm in danger of babbling. Taking a sip of my chai latte, I attempt to align brain and mouth. "In the interests of full disclosure, I don't do relationships either. So, no strings works for me." And that's the God's honest truth. I avoid relationships like the plague. But there is an unsettled feeling in my gut I can't place. "I guess we should keep this to ourselves in the office?"

"I think it would be best, don't you? It's nobody's business, and it's not like this is going anywhere. We're simply two people exploring an intense attraction." He breaks off as the server delivers our food, leaving me to wonder if he means when the project is over and we are no longer being thrown together, we'll go our separate ways. We haven't even touched on whether this is exclusive.

I decide it's best not to overthink it. I'm not interested in a relationship, and neither is he. Enough said. I dig into my lunch and push any questions I have out of my conscious mind. I'm just going to relax and enjoy this while it lasts.

CHAPTER SEVENTEEN

NICK

I finally drag myself away from Lulu after a delicious late lunch in a grungy little café near her loft. I was slightly worried about eating there based on the state of the place, but the food was fantastic. Although it could have had something to do with how monumentally hungry I was. Or how relaxed I was feeling. It's amazing what great sex will do for your mood. And it was great. I've never had sex quite like it.

While studying at Oxford, I had a couple of pretty intense relationships, but all my relationships here in Sydney have been pretty lacklustre. I don't know whether it was being so far from home or not having my father's expectations and my mother's judgement breathing down my neck on a daily basis, but I felt more myself there than I ever have. Until now. Not that this is a relationship.

But it's not purely the sex either. Which surprises me a little. Lulu is funny, well read, articulate and incredibly warm. She's great company, and we laughed all through lunch, which is odd because I'm aware I can be somewhat awkward in social situations, and my small talk game is pretty weak. But with her, I feel more comfortable than I can remember feeling with anyone other than my sister. I'd never have imagined we have anything in common, yet we seem to agree on a whole range of things—from the state of politics in this country, to the tragedy of there being only twelve episodes of *Fawlty Towers*.

As I head home, I think about the stark difference between this simple lunch with Lulu and my recent dinner with Eleanor. Even while I was still sitting at the table with Eleanor, I couldn't have said what we discussed, yet with Lulu, I remember every moment. The banter, how she ordered a plate of food bigger than her head and then laughed at herself as she devoured it, offering me tastes and moaning in delight. How we shared a dessert, feeding each other from the same spoon.

None of that changes my position, though. I told Lulu I wasn't interested in a relationship, which is true. You could say I was in a relationship with Eleanor, but in reality, that was just on paper. Neither of us made room in our lives for the other, and there were no actual feelings involved. I don't have the time or inclination for a relationship. Nor, I think, the interpersonal skills required to make a success of one. Frankly, there's too much up in the air for me right now to even consider one. Until I get my head on straight, I don't have much to offer. Especially not to a woman like Lulu. It's a relief she feels the same.

Then there's the undeniable fact we come at life from opposite sides of the brain. I can't imagine this developing into a relationship. But I'll enjoy it while it lasts.

I let myself into my apartment, equal parts exhausted and relaxed, but the peace the solitude of my apartment usually brings eludes me. I work a lot and spend a great deal of time on my own. I find I can only tolerate people for a very short period. Although Lulu MacLeod appears to be the exception. I trained myself out of feeling lonely at a very young age, but I can still recognise it when it happens and it's happening now.

I spend a couple of hours working before throwing an omelette together and falling into bed. My enormous, wildly expensive bed that now feels cold and not particularly comfortable.

I'm in the office early on Monday, still feeling relaxed after the events of the weekend. Mandy arrives right on time at eight am and sits opposite me for our regular start of the week planning session.

"Did you get Lulu's jacket to her?" she asks.

"Jacket?" For a second I'm blank. Distracted by images of Lulu at the mention of her name. I hope I'm not salivating like one of Pavlov's dogs. "Oh, yes. Jacket. Yes, thank you. I did. Delivered safe and sound." So, now I'm rambling. Perhaps orgasms kill brain cells?

"That's good. I'm sure she appreciated it." I look down and try to suppress my grin at the thought of how much she appreciated it. Straightening my face, I look up at Mandy. Am I imagining the glint of speculation in her eyes?

I spend a couple of hours trying, and failing, to concentrate. I know Lulu won't be in the office today, which is a godsend. I need a bit of space. At the moment, the simple mention of her name has my body responding, and I need to get myself under control before I see her again.

I double down on trying to get some work done, but it doesn't last. Giving up, I pull out my phone.

Me: Good morning. How are you? Delete.

Me: Hi. What are you up to? Delete.

Me: Hi. I can't stop thinking about you. True, but no. Delete, delete, delete.

Me: I hope you're having a great day. Are you free for dinner tonight?

What am I doing? Dinner implies dating. But straight out asking for sex doesn't feel quite right. Oh, for fuck's sake. What are you, a teenager? Just send it.

Lulu: Just dinner?

Okay, she went there. Who am I to refuse?

Me: Well, now that you mention it ...

Lulu: As it happens, I am free for *dinner*. And I'm having a *satisfyingly* productive day thank you. You?

Me: Chained to my desk. Which is the opposite of satisfying. But given the situation in my trousers, it's probably a good thing

Lulu: Situation? There's a situation?

Me: Someone mentioned your name

Lulu: Oh. Well, hold that thought until *dinner*

Me: Oh, I will. I'll pick you up around 7

I put the phone down, then flip it face down because I'm in danger of re-reading that conversation like a lovesick teen. I need to get back to work.

Is this sexting? Not quite, I don't suppose. But it's coming perilously close. I've never sexted anyone in my life. Have never even been tempted. But Lulu brings something out in me I didn't even know was there. Like the sex talk. I've never been particularly vocal during sex, but something about her, being with her, opens me up.

I'm not sure how she went from annoying the living daylights out of me to being pretty much my every waking thought. I can only put it down to the incredible chemistry and hope it burns itself out. Part of me already thinks I'm fooling myself. I've never felt this kind of seismic pull before. I need to be careful. Which begs the question, why did I suggest dinner? All my rational thought processes seem to have gone out the window. I need to protect myself. And Lulu. If I let myself get too close, heartbreak is inevitable because this will never work. Our worlds—not to mention our characters—are too different.

I'm running a little late thanks to a lengthy conference call, but I text Lulu and she's fine with it. I've made a reservation at a restaurant Will assures me is 'hip and cool', thinking it might be more her scene than the stuffy restaurants where I tend to take clients. Her door is ajar as I step out of the lift. She's curled on the deep velvet sofa with a Kindle in her lap but looks up as she hears me at the door.

"Hi." Her smile is warm and, interestingly, a little shy. She's so beautiful. Her mad hair springs wildly, framing her face in every shade of blonde. Her blue eyes sparkle above pink cheeks and lips, which seem to owe nothing to makeup. Uncurling her long legs, she stands, and I take in her lush figure skimmed by the sheer black lace dress she's wearing. For a moment, I think she's not wearing anything under it before I realise it's an illusion caused by the flesh-toned lining. Her feet are bare, but a pair of towering heels sit next to the sofa, fallen where she must have dropped them before curling up. "How was your day?"

Whatever happened during the day, I can no longer remember it. "You look beautiful," I breathe, cupping her cheek in my hand and brushing my lips over hers. "Stunning."

She laughs a little nervously. "Why thank you." She drops a little curtsy and a wicked grin. We're both a little nervous, but as my eyes lock with hers, the nerves start to fall away and I can feel the heat building in my blood. In my bones.

"We should go. Now. Otherwise, I'm not sure we'll get out of here at all." I release her cheek and step back, shoving my hands in my pockets to stop myself from reaching out and touching her.

"If you insist. Dinner first, and then ..." Her eyebrows raise. I love how honest she is about how she's feeling and what she wants. No pretence.

"And then... all the dirty things," I agree.

"Promise?"

"Scout's honour." I hold up three fingers.

By the time we reach the restaurant, which, as Will promised, is moody yet modern, we seem to have overcome our initial awkwardness. Maybe it's the dimness in the car. Or maybe it's simply Lulu. She's a conversational gymnast, jumping from topic to topic with ease and grace. By the time dinner is over, I'm left in no doubt about her views on the world—which I'm surprised to find are similar to mine. We jump from climate change to social justice to funding for the arts. We agree, and we disagree. We debate—sometimes heatedly. Sometimes I concede, and sometimes she does. It's cerebral foreplay like I have never experienced before. So many firsts with this woman. I ignore the clanging of alarm bells and relax into Lulu's company.

All throughout dinner, physical tension is ever present. Our hands touch, our knees brush under the table, our eyes lock. All of it is raising my temperature, and by the time we're on our way back to her place, the pressure in my trousers is uncomfortable and every inch of my skin feels tight. I don't want to pounce on her like I did over the weekend. More than once. I'd like to take my time. But I'm not sure that's on the cards.

CHAPTER EIGHTEEN

LULU

Nick is a surprise package. A bit like the kids' game pass the parcel. He's quiet and serious, yes, but every layer I peel back reveals a little unexpected treasure. I've always believed I was open-minded and not judgemental, but it feels like I was judgemental where Nick was concerned. He's not what I had imagined him to be. He's funny—in a wonderfully dry way—and thoughtful and compassionate in his views. Even when we disagree and the discussion turns heated, he listens and appreciates alternative points of view. And the sexual tension is off the charts. By the time we're stepping out of the lift, my knickers are wet, my nipples are hard and my skin is on fire. I hope he doesn't want a nightcap—unless it's a big taste of me.

I tidied up the apartment this afternoon. There are even fresh sheets on the bed and a full box of condoms in the bedside drawer, in case he decides he wants to use them. As it turns out, I can't wait to make it to the bed. No sooner has the door clanged shut than I'm grabbing the lapel of his very expensive suit and dragging him in for a kiss. Nick doesn't seem to mind as I peel his clothes off where he stands and we christen the kitchen bench. We get as far as the shower for round two before finally finishing up in bed.

Nick doesn't say much most of the time, but in bed, he all of a sudden becomes Chatty Kathy. Dirty Chatty Kathy. I can't believe how much the things he says turn me on. As we drowse, spooning in my cosy bed, I can't help but bring it up.

"You have a filthy, dirty mouth on you, Mr. Pierce. It's real a surprise to be honest."

"It surprises me too." He chuckles. "It's not something I've done before. You must bring out the sex fiend in me, I guess. Does it offend you?" His fingers drift lightly up and down my abs.

"Nuh-uh. Quite the opposite. I've never been with anyone who talks like that during sex. I like it. I like it a lot." I can feel his cock stirring against my arse, and push back slightly, encouraging him.

"You keep that up and you'll be getting another filthy, dirty mouthful." His hand slips lower, brushing the flesh at the top of my thighs.

"A *mouthful,* huh? What a good idea."

I turn to face him, pushing him onto his back and straddling his thighs, my lips starting at his nipples and moving down across his ribcage and belly before skirting across his hip, nipping and sucking at the pale skin.

"Jesus Christ," he moans. "For God's sake, stop teasing and suck my cock, woman." His hips are already lifting off the bed, his cock hard and leaking pre-cum.

"Patience, patience," I murmur, my lips brushing close, but not close enough. Shooting him a quick grin, I relent and drop my lips to the tip of his cock, kissing the swollen head before sliding down as far as I can go.

"Fuck, your mouth feels good," he gasps as he scoops up my hair in one hand. I start to suck harder, scraping my teeth gently on his length. I can feel this belly and thighs quivering and know he won't last much longer.

"Yes, yes, yes. I'm going to come in your mouth, beautiful. Will you swallow it?"

I nod, taking him as far back in my throat as I can, and then he's thrusting, his hand tangled in my hair as he shouts, garbled words falling from his mouth as cum shoots down my throat.

"So fucking good. So fucking beautiful."

I wipe my hand across my mouth, picking up the dribble of cum from my bottom lip, and grin. He's boneless on the mattress, face flushed, hair damp with sweat, an expression of complete abandon on his face. I feel a surge of pride. I did this to him. This man, who is so reserved and careful in the rest of his life, completely relaxes and abandons himself to me.

"You've got a bit of a dirty mouth on you yourself." His grin is open and lazy.

"I'll take that as a compliment."

"Oh, it is, beautiful, it is."

I lay down beside him, and he pulls me into his chest. I don't know where we stand on the whole sleeping over thing—especially on a work night—but Nick doesn't seem to be planning to move any time soon.

As if reading my mind, he presses his lips to my hair. "Are you okay with me staying, or would you prefer me to go?"

"No, I'd like you to stay. If you want to."

"Well, this bed is quite comfortable ... not to mention the possibility of morning sex." His hand skims up my belly and across my breast, his fingers brushing the already hard nipple.

"Morning sex is a wonderful way to start the day, I hear. It would be a shame not to take advantage of that opportunity." I can't seem to keep my lips off him. Even as I'm talking, my lips are grazing the side of his chest. The voice in my head whispers another warning, but the pull of this man is too strong. I know it will end, and probably not well, but I can't seem to care.

· ❤ · ❤ · ❤ · ❤ · ❤ ·

Morning sex turns out to be the best way to start the day—bar none. And I'm a bacon and pancakes girl from way back. After waking me up with not one but two orgasms, Nick showers and heads off to the office without a word of when I will see him next. I try not to obsess. After all, this is not a relationship. This headspace is most unlike me, and calls for some girl therapy.

After I organise to meet Rosanna for lunch, I spend the morning working on the painting I started on Saturday morning. I can barely even walk past it without getting the tingles. And it's without a doubt the best work I've ever done. I'd be mad not to include it in my show. But the idea of strangers seeing it doesn't sit right. Before I leave, I take a quick snap of the painting with my phone to show Rosanna.

No sooner have we sat down than Ro is giving me the eye. "Spill." She rolls her hand for me to speak.

"How do you even do that?" I know she knows, and I guess it's because she knows me so well. She shrugs and raises her eyebrows in waiting.

"As Britney once said, 'Oops, I did it again'."

"What? With Nick the Sex God?"

My cheeks burn as I nod. "And it was sooo good." I bring up the picture of the painting on my phone and hand it to her.

"Oh. Oh. My. God," she whispers. We're at a café around the corner from her office since she only has an hour. "That is ... wow. It's even better than the last one you did after sex with Nick. He must be amazing."

I can't even meet Ro's eye, I'm so embarrassed. Although you can't see any bodies, to me it screams sex. Really, really great sex. I don't think I could show it to anyone but Ro.

"Is that how it felt? You know, when you were with him? Honest to God?"

My mind returns to last night. And this morning. And I can't hold back a sigh that sounds somehow both filthy and contented.

"Yes. It is. I can't begin to explain it. Sure, he's gorgeous, but it's more than that. There's something I can't even describe."

"You lucky bitch," Ro squeaks, jumping in her seat when the server puts her lunch in front of her. "Oops. Sorry." He gives her a flirty grin, which sails straight over her head. I can't even with her and the servers.

"Can I get you anything else?" And by that, I feel like he means his phone number, but Ro only shakes her head.

"No. Thanks. We're all good."

"He's cute," I comment as he walks away, tossing a lingering look over his shoulder.

"Who? The server? Yeah, I guess so," she replies vaguely. "But no changing the subject. Are you going to include this in your show?" Ro knows me so well. Already she can sense my hesitation.

"I don't think so. It feels too personal."

"I get it. Has he seen it?"

"Yeah, he called in while I was working on it, and you know what? He got it straight away. As soon as he saw it, he knew. And he said it was the same for him." There's that filthy, contented cat sigh again.

"But? I'm hearing a 'but' in your tone here, which I'm not understanding."

"Well, he's amazing. The sex is amazing. But our lives are so different. I don't see how it could work. And we talked about what this is." I fiddle with the salt and pepper shakers rather than look at Rosanna because I'm having enough trouble with my thoughts, never mind putting them into words. "Neither of us wants a relationship. He was pretty clear. He doesn't have the time or the interest. And you know how I feel about getting involved."

"I do, yes. I don't agree with it, but I do know. It sounds to me like you're both on the same page." She waits patiently while I push my lunch around my plate, trying to articulate my feelings.

"We are. I guess. I'm just confused. He left this morning without saying anything about when we would see each other again. And now I feel, I don't know, nervous?"

Ro's eyebrows hit her hairline, but she remains silent.

"This feels different somehow. To all my other relationships."

Ro snorts at my use of the word relationship.

"Well, I'll leave aside the fact that all your other relationships have been nothing more than extended one-night stands," Ro holds up a hand to stop the interruption she sees on my face. "Yes, yes. I know, apart from Damon, and address the real issue. You like this guy, and you're scared of catching feelings for him. Have I summed it up?"

"Maybe. Yes. I don't know."

"Do you think maybe it's a little too early to be worrying about what this might or might not be?"

"Exactly. It's way too early. So why am I thinking like this?"

"Maybe because, despite claiming the two of you are so different, you can see potential?"

"Perhaps I should break it off now? You know, to be safe."

Her warm hand covers mine "Oh, sweetie." The look she had been skewering me with goes soft. "I get it. I do. But you can't live your whole life avoiding connecting with anyone in case you get hurt. Relax and enjoy it for what it is."

But I have very good reason to be scared.

"You know what happened to Dad. It broke him. For such a long time."

"And I bet if you asked him, he would say he wouldn't give up one day with your mum, despite how it ended. Have you ever raised it?"

"No. How could I even ask him? He never talks about her. I can't bring it up. It would break his heart all over again."

"Maybe. But maybe he'd like the chance to talk. Maybe he doesn't bring her up for fear of upsetting you. And there you both are, suffering in silence."

She's right, of course. I'd be the first to tell anyone to be honest and open. But there are some things too painful to touch. I feel like my mum's memory has been put in Pandora's Box, and if I open it, all sorts of chaos will be unleashed. Dad took years to recover from the loss, and I can't bear to see him like that again.

"None of this is helping me right now. What do I do?" My voice sounds so whiny I wince. I'm not a whiner. Ever.

"I think you already know the answer to that." And she's right. I do. What I think I should do is run far and fast. But this time I will take her advice and enjoy it while it lasts. Because honestly? I don't think I could walk away if I tried.

CHAPTER NINETEEN

NICK

"You're in a suspiciously good mood again today." Mandy gives me the side eye as she leaves my office after our regular morning progress meeting. "Who are you planning on taking down, and for whom?"

"I beg your pardon? I don't take people down. Well, not unless they deserve it. Can't a man be in a good mood without being up to something?"

"Other men, yes. You? No. You're definitely up to something." I can almost see the wheels turning in her head.

"Hmmph. I didn't realise I was that ruthless."

"Yes, you did. You take great pride in it. But this seems different. You almost seem ... No. That can't be it."

"What can't be it?"

"If I didn't know you, I'd say you're, well, relaxed."

"That won't last long if this interrogation continues. Rather than being suspicious, perhaps you should accept I am, in fact, in a good mood and enjoy it while it lasts?"

"Whilst waiting for the axe to fall," she mutters as she leaves, snapping the door behind her. That gets a laugh out of me.

Mandy's comment about me taking pride in being ruthless circles for a while. I know I'm a tough negotiator but have never thought I went so far as to be ruthless. Maybe it's true, but is it my natural inclination or was it bred into me by my father? I feel like I'm late to the party when it comes to knowing who I truly am. My father's death has cast my whole life in a different light, and I'm not sure I like it.

As it happens, my good mood lasts all day, and unlike Mandy, I don't need to wonder why. The only cloud in my uncharacteristically blue sky is I didn't arrange another date with Lulu. Although, given our agreement, I shouldn't call it that.

I'm aware Lulu will be popping in and out of the office from here on out and know I will have to take care to avoid her. Mandy has a suspicious mind, and I feel like if she sees us together, she'll know something is going on.

I spend any spare moment during the afternoon wondering how soon is too soon. By the time I leave the office, my impatience has won out. I drop by my apartment, pack a small overnight bag—yes, it's presumptuous, but a good boy scout is always prepared—and head over to Lulu's.

Me: Are you at home?

Lulu: Yes ☺

Me: What are your plans for this evening?

Lulu: Icecream and maybe some bingeing

Me: Alone?

Lulu: Are you offering to keep me company?

Me: Is that an invitation?

Lulu: If you bring ice-cream it is

Me: Would wine do?

Lulu: You're lucky I already stocked up on white chocolate & raspberry ice-cream

I'm already on the pavement in front of her building with a bottle of wine and my overnighter in hand, so I head inside and call down the lift. I can see her surprise when she opens the door.

"Did you teleport here?"

"I was more or less downstairs when I texted. A little more than less." I can feel the grin on my face. I feel like I'm doing that a lot lately.

"You're very sure of yourself, Mr Pierce." Her eyes are twinkling, cheeks pink, I hope with pleasure.

"Perhaps hopeful is a better word?" I drop my bag to slip my arm around her waist and kiss her.

"And the overnight bag?"

"I think we both know where tonight is headed." I drop my lips to her neck and suck on her silky skin. "No point in playing games."

And then I'm backing her up against the wall and standing the wine on the side table before my hands drop to the buttons of her overalls. She's been painting again, but this time appears to be relatively clean.

"I find myself in need of a pre-dinner fuck," I murmur in her ear. It seems like we're on the same page because her hands are busy unzipping my fly and pushing aside my boxer briefs. This woman knows what she wants and isn't afraid of going after it. "And the bingeing you mentioned? I hope you meant bingeing on me."

Her response is nothing but a gurgle of laughter mixed with a moan as my fingers find her already wet and swollen. "Oh, yes. That's it. Always so wet for me, Lulu." I pull my fingers from her heat and suck them into my mouth. "You taste so good." Then I'm dropping to my knees, my face buried in the smooth flesh at the top of her thighs, tongue sliding into the wet heat.

"Oh, good God. I can't. I can't stand ..." she gasps. I tip her over my shoulder and carry her to the bed, where I can take my time bringing her to the brink with my mouth before burying myself in her with one brutal thrust.

It turns out Lulu does binge on me. And vice versa. We order Thai takeaway and eat it naked on her bed, followed by a shared bowl of icecream. By midnight, we're both physically exhausted and aching all over. I stretch out on the bed with Lulu curled like a cat in the crook of my arm in a deep sleep.

I have no idea what this thing is between us. But it's snug and enveloping and overwhelming in the best possible way. I don't generally do feelings. I was taught from a young age not to express any type of emotion, but it seems like even the idea of Lulu brings with it a warm tide of sensation washing through me. Not to mention a rush of blood to my boxers. Part of me wishes I could attribute it to just that—simple lust. Purely physical. The other part, maybe the bigger part, knows this is something more. And for some reason it all seems tangled up with my feelings of dissatisfaction regarding my life.

I wake up the next morning determined to live in the moment and not worry about what will happen in the future. Lulu makes it pretty easy.

"Is that bacon I smell?" It's not even full daylight, and Lulu is at the stove in her colourful silk robe, frying bacon and scrambling eggs.

"I thought you might need some sustenance after last night." Her tone is as wicked as her grin.

"No one's ever cooked me breakfast before." I slip my arms around her from behind, bury my face in her crazy curls and breathe deep of the ever-present wildflower fragrance.

"Nobody? Not even your mother?"

"Especially not my mother. The housekeeper would make me porridge when I was in primary school, but by the time I hit high school, I was pretty much on my own. A bowl and a box of cereal were left on the bench for me. There was always plenty of food in the fridge if I wanted anything else." I move over to the coffee machine. An old-fashioned contraption I have no idea how to operate. I can feel Lulu's stare on my back.

"Did your mum work long hours?"

"You don't have a pod machine?" I ask, hoping it will distract her.

"No way. Do you know how much landfill those things create?" She follows me and starts the complicated ritual of making coffee the traditional way.

"So, your mum?" It's evident my ploy is not going to work. What I feel about my mother is not something I should put into words, so I skim the surface of that deep, dark water.

"No. She didn't work. She ... Well, I don't know what she did, to be honest. Socialised I guess." I lean against the counter, aware of the message my crossed arms send. I don't want to talk about my family, don't want to bring that toxic sludge into what has so quickly become such a happy space for me.

"What do you have planned for the day?" As a subject change, it's not very subtle, and I can tell by Lulu's face she knows what I'm up to, but she lets it go.

"Meeting with suppliers for the furniture for your offices. I need to negotiate them down on price. They think because I'm young and blonde, they can take advantage of me. What they don't know is they're dealing with a Scot." She rubs her hands together in apparent glee at the upcoming negotiation.

That night over dinner in her loft, she takes great delight in retelling the story of how she beat the supplier down until he was almost giving the furniture away, capitulating to all her demands.

"As my Da would say—'I didnae come doon in the last shooer'." She affects a delightful Scottish accent as she quotes her father.

Who would've thought Lulu would be such a hard-headed businesswoman? My first impressions of her as an arty flake were so far off the mark, I can barely believe it. I'm usually an excellent judge of character. All I can think is I was blinded by unresolved lust.

After dinner, Lulu suggests we catch a movie. I fully expect to be dragged kicking and screaming to some arty, angsty, French film, but we end up at the latest in the James Bond franchise. I wonder when Lulu will stop surprising me.

"Best Bond?" she asks as we settle into our seats with a big box of popcorn between us.

"I don't know. I've never thought about it. Daniel Craig, I guess." I've never had a lot of spare time for movies. Or maybe I haven't made the time.

Lulu gasps in horror and turns wide eyes on me. "Never thought about it? Okay. Well, then, all you need to know is Daniel Craig is good, Pierce Brosnan was acceptable, and Roger Moore was iconic, but the one and only true Bond was, without a doubt, Sean Connery."

"Because?"

"Duh. Because. He's. Sean. Connery. Oh, and it doesn't hurt that he was Scottish. Bless his soul." Her eyes are gleaming as she presses a hand to her heart. I can't help but lean across and kiss her senseless.

It's not a reflection on the film that I spend more time watching Lulu than I do the screen. She watches the movie with her whole body, shifting, jumping and bracing in her seat during the action scenes, scrunching up her face at the villain and going all pliant and soft in the sex scenes. By the end of the movie, I can barely restrain myself. My hand wanders up her leg, skimming her knickers, as I drive her home.

It doesn't even occur to me that what we did tonight was a date. Nor does it occur to me to drop her off and go home to my place, or to leave after the mind-blowing sex. It just seems natural to stay.

CHAPTER TWENTY

LULU

We said we didn't do relationships. We said we didn't want to date. But over the next few weeks we fall into a pattern that feels an awful lot like dating. Nick stays at my place pretty much every night. We spend every spare moment together, waking and sleeping. Half of Nick's wardrobe ends up in my cupboard because we always stay here. He tells me it's because I work from home, so it's more convenient. But I get the feeling he enjoys my apartment. When I called his apartment minimalist, what I meant was cold and soulless. At the time, it seemed to fit him, but now I know Nick better, and it doesn't suit him at all.

What has surprised me most is the realisation that Nick is actually shy. He's smart and ambitious, and when it comes to work, he takes no prisoners. But on a personal level, his abrupt manner hides a shyness I can't help but find appealing. It's a beautiful balance to his work-related arrogance.

We avoid each other as much as possible at the office in case someone twigs to what is going on. Sometimes I see Mandy looking at me with a gleam in her eye, but she doesn't say anything, so neither do I.

Sometimes we go out—to a movie, a play or dinner. But more often we stay in, where touching and nakedness are not frowned upon. Weeks in and we still can't seem to stop touching each other. I had expected it to fade, but it feels like the reverse. Sometimes the sex is so intense it feels like my heart stops, and rather than scare me, it thrills me.

We talk, sometimes for hours. About everything. Except about our families and friends. I don't know what Nick's motivation is, but I feel like this is the last line of defence for me. If he breaches that barrier, I'm done for. And if I'm honest, I'm afraid if I try and broach the subject, he'll shut it down. He was pretty quick to change the subject when we touched on his childhood. So, like a coward, I allow us to continue to exist in a bubble.

Despite that, I feel like Nick knows me better than anyone, except maybe Rosanna. Our post-sex conversations add to a level of intimacy I've never experienced before. I feel like I can tell him almost anything. Which is how he finds out about his many and varied nicknames.

"What did you call me?" he asks as he flops back on the sofa, taking me with him.

"Nothing." I was already red from exertion, and now I'm probably crimson.

"Did you call me Nick the Sex God?"

"No." I bury my face in his chest with an embarrassed laugh.

"Yes, you did." He pushes my hair off my forehead and brings my face up so we are eye to eye. "Spill woman."

"It's embarrassing. It's a nickname I gave you ..."

"It's embarrassing that you think I'm a sex god? You've got to be kidding. It's the best nickname ever. In fact, as far as I know, it's the only nickname I've ever had."

That makes me a little sad and fills in more of the vague picture I have of his lonely childhood.

"Seriously? Well, it's not the only one."

"What do you mean?"

"When I first met you, I had a whole lot of nicknames for you. Nicholas the Tardy. Nicholas the Cranky. Nicholas the Disapproving. There were quite a few." I can't believe he's chuckling after I've called him cranky and disapproving.

"Those I don't like so much. I think I like Nick the Sex God best." He kisses my forehead and tucks me against his chest. "Want to hear something funny?" He waits for my nod. "I had a nickname for you too. Although only the one. I'm not as inventive as you." He sounds surprisingly bashful for someone who was talking dirty to me mere minutes ago.

I sit up at his admission. "You did? What was it?"

"Not as good as Sex God, sadly. I thought of you as The Interloper." He laughs as I slap his chest.

"That's not very flattering."

"At first, I told myself it was because you were invading my space. But in reality, I think it was because you were invading my thoughts."

"Hmmph. I'm not sure that makes it any better." But there is no heat in my words, and I settle onto his chest, strangely warmed by the thought we were both inventing silly nicknames for each other, even when we didn't like each other. And even though The Interloper isn't all that nice, I'll take the sentiment behind it any day.

The next afternoon when Nick calls to check if we have any plans—we, not I—I suggest we spend the night at his.

"Why?" he asks.

"Because we never do. And you have that fantastic view. And there's a swimming pool in your building. Perfect for late-night pool sex."

"There are security cameras in the pool area," he says, but he doesn't sound horrified. Intrigued, maybe. A little thrill runs through me and I can feel my knickers getting damp.

"We'll have to be careful with the angles then." Even I can hear the innuendo dripping off my words.

"You're a dirty girl, Lulu MacLeod."

"I so am. Meet you there at seven?"

"Bring your swimmers." I can hear the dirty smirk in his voice.

"I won't need them—" I sing song and hang up before he can get a word out. My cheeks burn at the mental picture I have of him sitting at his desk, cock straining against his smart charcoal grey trousers. I can't wait for tonight.

Nick lets me into his apartment, and it's exactly as I remember it. Monochrome and not a thing out of place. Which I guess is partly because he has barely been here except to pick up clothes and mail for the past month. But I get the impression it always looks much the same. Sydney Harbour is spread out before the enormous windows, the setting sun turning it pink and gold, lights from the bridge and Luna Park twinkling. But it doesn't quite make up for the showroom feel of the place. Nick lets me wander around with the glass of sparkling water he poured me, watching me take everything in while he pours himself a scotch. The whole place seems to fit the man I thought Nick was when I first met him, not the one I know now. It's as though there's a public Nick and a private Nick. I know which one I prefer.

I wander until I find an alcove off the living room.

"What's this?"

"A piano."

It's not just a piano. It's a beautiful, shiny, black baby grand. I can't believe I didn't notice it the last time I was here, but I guess I was distracted.

"Well, yes, so I see. But why do you have it?"

"Why does anyone have a piano? To play." He looks away, pulling on his earlobe.

"You play the piano? You've never mentioned that."

"Yeah, well. I don't play much anymore. I don't have time."

"Would you play something for me?" I can see the *no* hovering on the tip of his tongue. "Please? I've always wanted to be able to play an instrument, but two weeks into guitar lessons, my teacher told Da not to waste his money, so that was that." I shrug and roll my eyes.

Nick chuckles and reluctantly moves towards the piano. I watch as his hand glides over the curved side of the instrument, "Okay, but please bear in mind I haven't played in months."

He sits down, hands me his glass and opens the lid. For a few moments, his beautiful fingers rest gently on the keys, his eyelids lowered. I wait, almost holding my breath, not entirely sure what I'm expecting to hear. Running his hands up and down the keys, Nick glances at me, then plays a couple of quick scales. Taking a few deep breaths, he positions his hands and starts to play. I've never heard the piece he's playing, but he's utterly lost in the music, body swaying and eyes intent on his hands. As the last notes die away, he turns on the stool to face me. I'm sure my jaw is hanging open, my eyes popping from my head. I have no idea what to say.

The silence draws out, until, seeming embarrassed, Nick clears his throat. "So." His cheeks are pink and he can't quite meet my eyes.

"Nick," it's barely a whisper, "that was magnificent." Another puzzle piece clicks into place. Nick has the soul of an artist.

He reaches out and takes his glass from my hand, swigging a big mouthful. He seems self-conscious and uncomfortable.

"I can't believe you don't play anymore. You're so good. You must have had lessons for years."

"Years and years. Mum insisted. Dad thought it was a waste of time. I was the meat in the sandwich." He hangs his head, as if admitting that is somehow shameful.

"Did that happen a lot? The meat in the sandwich thing?"

"Enough. Too much. It's the same in every family, I guess."

Whoa. There's some deep-rooted family shit going on here. The look of discomfort on his usually self-possessed face breaks my heart. No wonder he doesn't do relationships. He's as fucked up by his childhood as I am by mine. I search for something light to say, to lift the mood.

"You know what this needs to make it perfect?"

"No. What?" he asks eagerly, grasping at anything to save him from further discussion about his family.

"A *Pretty Woman* moment." I kick off my shoes, take his glass of scotch back, and put both glasses on a nearby table.

"A what?"

"You know, the piano scene in the movie *Pretty Woman*."

"Never seen it."

I know you don't get to be a lawyer, or get a scholarship to Oxford by hanging out at the cinema, but it never ceases to amaze me what a small life Nick has led up to now.

"Never seen it? Then you're in for a treat, Mr Pierce." I saunter towards him, undoing the buttons on the front of my dress before sliding between the stool and the piano. "In this scene, Vivienne finds Edward playing piano. And when he finishes, he lifts her onto the top ..." I place his hands on my hips and indicate he should lift me onto the piano. His eyes are molten as he follows my instructions.

"And then?" His voice is low and hoarse with need.

"Then he plays her like a fiddle." And I lie back. Just like in the movie.

CHAPTER
TWENTY-ONE

NICK

L ulu's loft has enormous windows along one wall, opening out onto the flat rooftop of the factory below. It's nothing more than an ugly concrete roof with a wall on one side, windows on another, and her loft on a third, but in typical Lulu style she has painted a mural on the wall and decked the space out with plants, a couple of sun lounges and some fairy lights. On Friday night, I arrive to find her reclined on one of the sun lounges—she never locks her door, much to my exasperation—a glass of wine in hand. She's wearing a short t-shirt dress and, I can already tell, no bra.

I hadn't noticed it before, but in the far corner is a small portable clothesline. Fluttering in the warm evening breeze are several of my shirts, socks and jocks. The scent of the jasmine she has growing up the wall is thick in the air.

"Oooh good, you're home. Perfect timing. I just opened a bottle." She lifts an almost full bottle of my favourite red from the table beside her and pours a glass, pursing her lips for a kiss as she hands it to me. I don't know if she realises she's referred to her place as my home, and I don't correct her, although I can't help but register how nice it feels.

"What's that?" I gesture to the clothesline with my glass while loosening my tie and sitting down on the end of her lounge.

"A clothesline. It's used to hang wet clothes on. Very handy invention. A gentleman by the name of Mr Hill, I believe," she replies, her tone dry.

"I meant my shirts and things."

"Well, I was doing a couple of loads, so I put your things through the machine as well." She looks momentarily nervous. "I hope that's okay?"

In reality, it goes against the whole 'not a relationship' discussion. But then, so does staying over every night and making me breakfast. And all the post-orgasm soul-baring conversations we have fallen into the habit of having. And I find I like it. A lot. It makes me nervous. But it also makes me happy.

"I don't expect you to do my laundry, Lu." But I know she can see by my expression it's more than okay. Ordinarily, I send my suits and shirts out to the dry cleaner and my housekeeper takes care of the rest of my washing. I can't remember anyone, even my mother—especially my mother—doing my washing for me out of the goodness of their heart. I feel a lump form in my throat at the simple kindness of the gesture.

"I know. But it was here, and it was no trouble." It's not often Lulu looks shy, but she's doing it now.

"Well, I guess I need to come up with an appropriate thank you then." Putting my glass on the ground, I slide one hand up her bare leg and under the hem of her dress, surprised and delighted to find her bare.

"What's this? Going commando, Ms MacLeod?" My fingers brush her already wet folds as she drops her legs to either side of the lounge and puts her untouched wine on the table. "And so ripe and ready to eat."

"It pays to be prepared." Sitting up, Lulu whips her dress off over her head, and just like that, she's naked. Closing her eyes, she slides a little further down the lounge as I kneel on the ground at the end of the chair, careless of my expensive trousers, and lean forward, licking her with the flat of my tongue and smacking my lips.

One hand presses her open, while the other snakes up from her hip to her breast and I roll her already hard nipple between my thumb and forefinger. I feel the skin on her belly tighten in response as I slide my hand back to her thigh.

The only windows looking onto this roof are the dirty, frosted, reinforced windows of the factory next door. Maybe someone could see us, but I doubt it. Yet an unexpected thrill runs through me at the thought we might be watched. My hands hold her legs wide apart as I lick and suck her swollen folds. I can feel her thigh muscles straining against my hold, her breathing becoming ragged as I latch onto her clit and suck gently. Without lifting my lips, I let words tumble out. I have no idea what I'm saying, but I know Lulu loves to hear me talk while we fuck, and I can feel her edging closer to release.

My cock is throbbing, thumping to get out of my trousers, so I let go of her legs and pull myself free as quickly as I can without taking my lips off her. Lulu's hands are in my hair, pulling and flexing in time with the pull of my mouth on her clit. Gasping for breath, I rear up, pulling her all the way to the end of the lounge. I want to plunge into her, but I need her to look at me first so, I hesitate. Her gaze finds mine.

"Now," she demands, and that's the signal I need to thrust into what feels like heaven. Not fast and hard, and not slow and sweet, but somewhere in between. Strong and steady and powerful. Her feet have found the floor, and she is lifting her hips off the lounge, meeting my long rhythmic strokes. I bring my hand up from her thigh, pressing and rubbing her clit with my thumb and that's it for Lulu. Her hips buck, her spine stiffening as a furious blush rushes across her beautiful chest and up her throat to her cheeks. I pull out and stagger to my feet, grasping my cock, so slick from her orgasm. It only takes a couple of strokes before a stream of cum spills across her breasts.

"Fuck," I gasp, folding forward until my forehead meets hers, "you are so damn beautiful."

"If that's the thanks I get, I might do your washing more often." Lulu grasps the back of my head and brings her mouth to mine, tasting herself on my lips; then, with a wicked laugh, she runs a finger through the mess on her chest and brings it to her mouth to suck. I'm half-hard again already.

I fall onto the other sun lounge and, scooping up my glass, take a gulp of wine.

Recalling our conversation about pool sex—and making a mental note to fit it in sometime soon since we never got to it after our *Pretty Woman* re-enactment— I gesture to the windows with my glass, but my eyes are trained on her face, watching her reaction. "Do you think anyone can see us from those windows?"

She's momentarily surprised before a wicked grin spreads across her face.

"I don't know. Maybe. Would you like them to?"

"Have people watch me fuck the most beautiful woman in Sydney? Watch me slide my cock into your delicious pussy? Fuck yes." I love the way her post-orgasm blush intensifies with my words. I can tell it's only part embarrassment. The thought of being seen turns her on, too.

It crosses my mind how far off my previous path I have gone. A man with serious ambitions for politics, or law for that matter, wouldn't even be considering what amounts to indecent exposure. This is the exact opposite of what I said to Claire about avoiding future scandals. These days, it feels like there are two of me. The lawyer me and the personal me. Right now, I don't know which one is more real, although I have my suspicions. But the sight of Lulu so aroused is enough to get me hard again. I'm keen for round two, but Lulu insists we clean up.

"Hold that thought, Nick the Filthy." She laughs. "We have plans."

"Oh, have no fear. I'll hold the thought alright."

We eat dinner at a Vietnamese diner with Formica tables. A month ago, I'd have been more likely to call the health inspectors rather than eat there. But the food is sensational, and the staff knows Lulu by name. Predictably, they love her, and we get far more food than we actually paid for.

After dinner, we end up in a bar in Marrickville, and the place couldn't be more Lulu if she had designed it herself. The walls are covered in memorabilia, the tables and chairs mismatched and worn, and I have never heard of any of the craft beers they have on tap. But the grizzled old guy playing the piano is doing an incredible job of sliding out some of my favourite obscure jazz tracks. I'm touched that she arranged for us to see a pianist after finding out I could play. Her thoughtfulness is humbling.

As with the restaurant, the staff all know Lulu, and so do half the disreputable-looking patrons. I wonder again how I could have missed her overwhelming charm when we first met. People are drawn to her. I watch, mesmerised, as she chats and laughs with strangers and acquaintances alike. She radiates warmth and an authenticity I have rarely seen in my life. And I'm starting to wonder if, even though this is not what I thought I wanted, perhaps it's what I need.

As we listen to the melted chocolate notes of the performance, it occurs to me Lulu is someone who grabs life with both hands and squeezes everything she can out of it. I'm incredibly lucky she's bringing me along for the ride.

I've done more real living in the past few weeks with Lulu than I've done in the previous thirty-three years of my life.

CHAPTER TWENTY-TWO

LULU

"**A**m I ever going to meet this man you're practically shacked up with?" Rosanna asks as we sit side by side in our favourite pedicure salon, one foot each in a foot spa, the other being massaged with hot stones.

"No. I don't think so. And we're not shacked up. It's not even a thing. I told you that. It's ..."

"A thing?"

"No. It's not a thing. It's just casual."

"He spends every night at your place. Seems like a thing to me." Rosanna squirms as her pedicurist hits a ticklish spot.

She may have a point, but I'm not ready to admit it to her yet, or even to myself, although I don't know how much longer I can go on fooling either one of us.

"No. Really. It's just the sex is soooo good. I mean off-the-charts good. I'm grabbing all I can get while I can. It'll be over soon enough. So what's the point of introducing you? You know how you are. You'll get attached, and then when we break up, you'll be sad." I don't realise my misstep until Ro responds.

"Aha! You can't break up from a not-a-thing. So, it must be a thing."

"It's not. And you know what I mean. When we both move on is what I should have said." I wave my hand as though none of this means anything.

"Would it be so bad if it was a thing?" It feels like Ro is accusing me of something.

"Yes. You know I don't do love."

"But you do, though. You love me. And you love your dad. You let us in."

"That's different."

"I don't see how. If something happened to one of us, you'd still be heartbroken. I hate seeing you waste your life. You have so much love to give, Lu. And what about children? Don't you want kids one day?" I've never had a panic attack, but I think I might be on the verge of one right now.

"You know, I don't think children are on the cards for me. I mean, I love them, and I can't wait to be Mad Arty Aunt Lulu to yours, but for me? I don't think so."

"Seriously?" Rosanna manages to look sceptical and disappointed at the same time.

"Seriously. It's hard to juggle kids and creativity. With kids, you have to be present, in the moment. And when I'm painting, I'm all up in my own head. I can't see how it would work." It's a story I've been working on in my head ever since I started hearing the faint ticking of a clock.

"I feel like you're making excuses to fit the narrative you've told yourself. Don't throw away a chance at being happy because you're scared." There's that accusation again.

"I'm not scared, and I'm not making excuses. And once and for all, the thing with Nick is not a thing. It's great sex. Period." That's my excuse and I'm sticking to it, whether Rosanna buys it or not.

"Right. You keep telling yourself that. Meanwhile, I'll be watching with the popcorn." Ro mimes shovelling popcorn into her mouth.

I laugh, but something inside me flutters. I know Rosanna is right, and I'm fooling myself. We do spend every night together.

The key I had cut for him today seems to be sniggering at me from inside my bag.

I pretend to be engrossed in the toffee-apple red being painted onto my toes.

"We're spending this weekend on his company boat," I drop, hoping for casual. That gets a snort.

"Yeah. Not a thing. I've never known you to delude yourself like this before." Ro leans over and squeezes my hand. She's certainly laying it on thick here.

"Well, it can't be a thing because neither of us are interested in having a thing. And you'll feel silly when it's over and he's gone."

"Hmm. I feel like it might not be me feeling silly. Please be careful you don't shoot yourself in the foot, Lu."

Rosanna's warning from earlier in the week echoes in my mind as I get ready to head to the marina on Friday afternoon. Even though Nick said I wouldn't need anything but a toothbrush, I pack shorts and swimmers. He can't be serious that we'll be naked all weekend. Although I wouldn't complain.

Part of me wants to bring up the conversation I had with Rosanna with Nick. Not the kid's part. The 'thing' part. But the minute he walks in the door, all those thoughts fly out of my head and I fall into the moment. Just the sight of him. Or the spicy smell of his cologne, or the sound of his voice, has the power to completely derail any rational thought I might be attempting.

Nick left work early, but it's still dusk by the time we climb onto the boat. I'm surprised when I open the fridge to put in the cheeses and wine I had brought. "The fridge is full of food."

"Of course it is. I got the club to stock it for us. We'll need to keep our energy up." Nick gives me a flirty grin as he heads for the cabin in the front of the boat with our bags.

"Is that so?"

"Damn right. I'm going to devour you on every flat surface of this boat and maybe some vertical ones. You'll need sustenance." My belly clenches in anticipation as Nick's powerful arms come around me from behind. I try to squeeze the cheese into the already-packed fridge as his hands slip into the waistband of my shorts. I suck in a deep lungful of his delicious smell and run my hands along the muscles of his forearms.

"And here I thought you were going to teach me to sail."

"That too." He kisses my neck and moves away up the galley stairs, giving me the opportunity to ogle his fine arse and legs. "First lesson is casting off. Then I know a nice private spot we can anchor for the night." I can tell by his expression why he wants privacy, and I can already feel the heat building between my legs.

On deck, Nick explains what I need to do with the ropes, then quickly and expertly steers the boat away from the dock.

"We'll motor tonight since there's not much light left."

The engine is throaty, and the smell of diesel lingering at the dock gives way to fresher, salty air. Now the sun has gone down, the air is cool and damp, but feels wonderful after a week of hot weather in the city. As we motor across the water, I watch the colours of the sunset bleed into the night, the tones soft at first, then deepening to bright oranges, pinks and purples. I have a set of pencils and a sketch book with me, and before I know it, I have pages and pages of rough sketches and colour patches clamouring to be worked up into paintings.

While Nick manoeuvres us to the spot he has chosen to anchor for the night, I open a bottle of wine and pull out a beautifully laid cheese platter. My strange aversion to the taste of wine hasn't gone away, so I pour a glass of the sparkling water I've become addicted to.

"I'm glad there's plenty of food. I was scared you would make me fish for my supper." I hand him a glass as he lets down the anchor.

"Not a fan of fishing, Ms MacLeod?" He sits on the broad cushioned bench and pulls me onto his lap.

"Ugh. No. Nasty smelly things. I even threw up a little in my mouth during *Lord of the Rings* when Gollum ate that fish." I shudder in revulsion.

"What a shame. I had a whole afternoon planned out tomorrow."

At my look of horror, Nick laughs long and loud, his grey eyes twinkling. I love that sound. Especially because it is so rare. "I have much more interesting ways to spend our time planned. Which reminds me." And he starts making good on his promise to christen every flat surface of the boat. Who knew sex on the deck of a boat in the moonlight would be so delicious?

By the time we motor into the dock late on Sunday afternoon, we're both a little tanned in places that have not seen the sun before and we've done a pretty good job of meeting Nick's challenge. Stella was right—sleeping on a boat is fantastic. Waking up on a boat is even better. The water in the early morning is like glass under the mist, and the sound of the bird calls echoing off the cliffs is some of the most beautiful music I've ever heard.

She was also right about it being inspiring. I have dozens of sketches my fingers are itching to turn into paintings, so many colours and shapes whirling in my head. As we come back into mobile phone range, Nick's phone starts to chirp with a sound I now recognise as his email alert.

"Sounds like you'll have some work to do tonight," I say as we load the bags into the boot of his car.

He looks apologetic. "I'm afraid so. The price I pay for skiving off for the weekend."

"That's okay. I have work to do too. Those paintings aren't going to create themselves, and I have so many ideas. I can't wait to get them all on canvas."

We're both quiet on the first part of the trip back to the city. I can't help but think about the last time we made this trip and, glancing over at Nick, I think he is too. He stops at a red light. Our eyes meet and we grin at each other.

"Do you recall ..." he begins, at the same time as I say, "The last time ..." and we crack up laughing. It's strange to remember how humourless I thought Nick was when we first met. The Nick I know now—the one who sunbaked naked on the boat and danced with me in the moonlight—is not the same man I met in the lift. Or maybe not the man I'd thought I met.

Back at my place, Nick sets up his laptop on the dining table and I head to my studio corner. The only sounds are Nick's furious typing and the faint scraping of my pencil on the canvas. We do this a lot in the evenings, both working on our own stuff and it feels so peaceful, yet, at the same time, the air seems charged with awareness of each other. Nick and I are so comfortable together, and if I'm honest with myself, I can't imagine a time when I won't want to jump his incredibly well-put-together bones. I need to take a step back and think about what we're doing here, because every day is proving this is more than a purely physical thing.

I've always been a bit of a fly-by-the-seat-of-my-pants kind of girl when it comes to romance, or if I'm being honest, sex, since I don't do romance or relationships. So far, those pants haven't steered me wrong. But the voice that whispered quietly at the beginning of this adventure with Nick, the one I ignored, is now shouting at me to beware. As a matter of fact, she's jumping up and down and waving her arms. I'm taking a big risk here. Because this is the first time flying by the seat of my pants has had the potential to include my heart as a passenger.

CHAPTER TWENTY-THREE

NICK

I've been dodging mum's calls since I broke up with Eleanor. The voicemails she leaves have been becoming more and more strident, so I finally agree to have dinner with her. It feels odd not spending the evening with Lulu, which scares me. But I rationalise it away with the excuse I'll miss the sex. I told her I'd probably stay at my place tonight, but I'm not even fooling myself, never mind Lulu.

My head says there's no other option but for this to end, but I can't seem to stay away. I know I'm being selfish, and I need to stop. But I keep thinking maybe I can have one more night? One night has turned into two. Two days to a week, a fortnight, a month. Every day I wake telling myself I should end it, and every day a selfish voice whispers, *not today*. Right now, I'm having trouble remembering why ending it is a good idea at all.

As I let myself into the house, the strong smell of beeswax and lemon remind me it was the maid's day to polish the furniture. I pull down the emotional shutters Lulu has opened and prepare myself for Meddling Mary's barbs.

Mum greets me with the usual tepid cheek kiss, despite not having seen me for weeks, which is such a contrast to the enthusiasm with which Lulu greets me, even though we are rarely apart for more than twelve hours.

The kiss might be tepid, but the look in her eyes is like dry ice. Hot and cold at the same time. She wastes no time getting to the point as we each sit down with a drink.

"I had lunch with Eleanor and Angela last weekend. She tells me you suggested calling it off last time you met." And there goes the eyebrow.

"Yes. I did. Although it was more than a suggestion." I find myself running a finger under my collar. "Not that it's any of your business, but I have no interest in pursuing a relationship with Eleanor. It was always more your idea than mine." Being with Lulu has thrown the shortcomings of my relationship with Eleanor—and every other woman I've ever dated—into stark relief.

"Eleanor seems to suspect there might be someone else involved." Disapproval drips from mum's tone like acid.

I think back to the day a few weeks ago when Eleanor arrived unannounced in my office, ostensibly to return a couple of books I had loaned her. She was still operating under the assumption I would 'come to my senses', and there was a veiled threat she would not continue waiting for me to wake up to myself much longer. I dismissed the whole episode. But we did pass Lulu in the corridor as I was escorting Eleanor to the lift. Is it possible she picked up on something when Lulu caught my eye? Are we that transparent? We try and avoid each other at the office for this very reason. But surely a passing glance wouldn't give us away?

"Perhaps Eleanor is looking for excuses. Someone, or something, to blame. When the reality is the relationship has run its course. It's as simple as that."

"She's under the impression it's some woman in your office. And I must say, she sounds highly inappropriate. Eleanor said she appeared to have a tattoo on her arm. And a stud in her nose."

Damn. It seems we are that transparent.

Mum barely takes a breath before she continues. "Is this about sowing your wild oats? Because if that's the case, a discrete affair will take care of it. There's no need to upend your entire life, your very future, for a bit of fun, Nicholas." I can't suppress the shudder of distaste at her words. I have long suspected this was the arrangement she had with my father and she's all but confirmed it. But it's not the life for me.

"This is about nothing more than Eleanor and I not being suited." I'd give anything to get out of here right now. I'm grateful for my years of legal training. I know my face is an unreadable mask, but I can feel myself shifting in my chair, my knee starting to jiggle, which will piss mum off even further. I wish Claire was here.

"You must be joking. She's the perfect match for you—smart, beautiful, well-connected. She's precisely the sort of woman you need on your arm. Particularly when you enter politics."

"Again, more your idea than mine. Yours and Dad's. And to be frank, I'm no longer convinced it's the right path for me." I don't address her comments about Eleanor. One battle front at a time, and I'd rather discuss her ambitions for my political career than Eleanor. That takes me too close to Lulu, and if Mum gets the idea she and Eleanor are on the right track, she'll make it her business to interfere, I have no doubt.

Mum couldn't look more horrified if I'd told her I was joining the circus.

"Now I know you're joking. I won't have it, Nicholas. It was your father's dying wish. We worked on this plan for years. You can't simply change your mind on a whim. And Richard has already spoken to people in the party. They're very keen to have you. All you have to do is say the word and the seat is yours. Yet here you are, breaking it off with his daughter. I can smooth it over with him right now, but you'll have to call Eleanor and ..."

I cut her off with a raised palm before she can continue. "No. Absolutely not. Eleanor and I are over. Apart from anything else, you and Richard might be surprised to learn my political views don't reflect yours or those of the party. They would be sadly disappointed by my position on a whole range of issues." This is the first time I have fully articulated—even to myself—that I don't want to go into politics. I can almost see the wheels turning in Mum's head.

Mum's lips are pursed, eyes narrowed, and her damn eyebrow is up again.

"There's something afoot here, and believe me when I tell you, I will get to the bottom of it. Apart from anything else, Angela and I have been friends for years. How am I supposed to tell her you've dropped her very eligible daughter like a hot scone?" I have to suppress a laugh. As usual, it's all about external appearances for Mum.

"You don't have to tell Angela anything. I think I have made my position clear to Eleanor, and it is nobody else's business but ours." I shudder at the thought of going back to such a cold-blooded relationship.

"Well, I think you might be wrong about that. I told Eleanor this is simply a hiccup. You need to wake up to yourself and put things right. Immediately. Before it's too late."

I can feel my entire body tensing, and I'm in danger of crushing the glass I'm holding. A large part of me wants to tell her I've moved on, but if she gets wind of my relationship with Lulu, there's no telling what ends she might go to. Despite the fact Mum is an art lover, she would never countenance me being in a relationship with someone like Lulu MacLeod, and it would be entirely in character—and not the first time—for her to poison any relationship that did not suit her agenda. It may have worked when I was a kid, but it won't work now.

"I said it's over and I meant it. I will not have you dictating my life. One more word and I will be out the door." She looks disgruntled at the granite in my tone.

From behind me, I hear a slow clap. It can only be one person, and thank God she's here.

"Well done, Mum. Trying to tell a grown man how to live his life. Classic." Claire stalks into the room, dressed as usual in artfully distressed but wildly expensive clothes.

"Telling him how to live his life? You're being melodramatic. I am merely pointing out the foolishness of his behaviour," Mum answers with an exasperated sigh. I give Claire a thank-God-you're-here look, and she responds with a silent 'I've got your back'. We may be almost polar opposites in personality, but we've always been close. Two lonely children being brought up in an emotional wasteland.

"I missed the first half of this conversation. Is she trying to foist The Ice Princess on you again?" Claire pours herself a generous glass of wine and plops down next to me where I've made room for her on the sofa, kicking off her shoes and propping her feet on the coffee table because she knows how much it drives Mum crazy, as does any physical display of affection, so I throw an arm across Claire's shoulder and hug her to my chest.

"Don't call her names," snaps Mum, at the same time as I reply, "Yes." Claire and I laugh. Mum purses her lips and attempts to change the subject.

"It's nice of you to grace us with your presence, Claire. I had begun to forget what you look like."

"Well, take a quick picture. I'm only here for dinner, then I'm out. Won't be back tonight." My sister is the wild child in the family. Being the youngest and a girl, my father had little interest in her, so she was largely left to her own devices.

I know virtually nothing about Lulu's family, but I have overheard her speaking to her father on the phone once or twice. The warmth in her tone and the teasing way she talks to him suggest a closeness Claire never had with Dad, or Mum, for that matter.

And there I go again. I'm thinking about Lulu. It must show on my face because Claire elbows me in the ribs.

"What's put that smile on your face?"

"I can't be happy to see my baby sister for the first time in weeks?"

"You can, but something tells me that's not it." Under her breath, she adds, "Fill me in later."

After a frosty dinner, during which we all avoid any personal topics of conversation, I offer to give Claire a lift to the city and she heads upstairs to change, leaving me alone with Mum again.

"Don't think this is the last of this conversation, Nicholas." Again, with the eyebrow.

"Which conversation would you be referring to, Mum?" She's going to have to work for it.

"Your future, Nicholas. Your career in politics, and your relationship with Eleanor. There is nobody more suitable. She's patient, but she won't wait forever, and well you know it."

"Not going to happen, Mum." I turn and call up the stairs, "Hurry up, Claire." I need out of this house. Now. Before I say something I might regret.

On the short drive to the city, Claire gets straight to the point. "What are you up to? You seem—well, I'd almost say happy. But I'm not sure I know what happy looks like on you." Which reminds me of Mandy's recent comment.

"I'm not up to anything. Life is going well right now, that's all."

Claire turns in her seat and studies my profile. "It's her, isn't it? Lulu the decorator? You're seeing her!"

I'd almost forgotten I had confided in Claire after the first time Lulu and I slept together.

"Yes." I frown as we pull up at some lights. "We're ... well, I'm not entirely sure what we are, to be honest."

"Whatever you are, it seems to be agreeing with you. I can't wait to meet her."

"Don't get excited. Whatever it is, it's just casual." Which doesn't feel right. Things with Lulu feel anything but casual, despite what we've both said.

Claire sees something on my face which gives me away. "Hmm. I'm not buying that."

"She's been very clear she's not interested in a relationship. She's also not the right woman for me."

"The smile on your face earlier suggests maybe she could be."

"Lulu is different. She's warm and open-minded and passionate. I can't begin to picture her as the wife of a partner at CPM. It's not even that she couldn't fit it. Buy why would she want to? I can't imagine Lulu wanting that life for herself. *I* don't even want that life." Well, that slipped out without me intending to say it. I put it down to the Lulu effect.

"If you don't like your life, then change it. You're more than what Mum and Dad wanted you to be. Dad isn't here anymore. You don't have to keep living up to his legacy and that stupid promise or whatever bullshit you're telling yourself."

"Don't pull any punches, Claire—tell me what you really think."

"Oh, I will. I hate seeing you try to live up to the impossible standards of a man who isn't even here to see it. You've succeeded. You've proved yourself. Isn't it time you started doing what makes *you* happy?" She pauses only long enough to suck in a ragged breath. "And if Lulu makes you happy—go for it. Fuck what Mum thinks. And fuck what Dad would've said. This is your life. Not theirs."

"I wish it were that easy, Claire. I have responsibilities. I can't simply walk away and reinvent myself."

"Yes. You can." We drive in silence for a few blocks, the only sound being Claire's occasional loud sighs. "I only say this because I love you, Nick, and I want you to be happy." The scary thing is, right now I am happy—with Lulu.

"I know, Claire-Bear." I use the nickname I gave her as a child, letting her know I'm not angry. "And I appreciate it. Let me think about it, okay? Anyway, enough about me—how are you? I'm not buying all the sanitised shit you gave Mum earlier about how hard you're working at uni." She appears tired and a little down.

"You know me. I'm great. Always the life of the party."

"Yes, I do know you, which is why I'm asking." Claire has struggled to find her place in the world. "Are you even still at uni?" Last time we spoke, she was struggling through the first year of the third degree she has started, none of which have been completed.

"Well, no. Not as such. It just wasn't me, you know? But don't tell Mum. At least until I work out what it is I'm going to do."

"Of course I won't tell Mum. But I worry about you not having any direction." Dad left us both with a sizeable trust fund, so Claire doesn't need to earn a living. But she's bright and smart and full of energy, and she needs somewhere to direct her talent other than clubbing.

"I know. But I'm fine. Honestly. I'll work it out. Eventually." A rueful grin crosses her face.

"You know I'm always here if you need a sounding board or a shoulder, don't you?"

Claire drops her head to my shoulder, patting my upper arm. "Yeah, I know. Gotta love a dysfunctional family, huh?"

We laugh as I let her out into a crowd at the front of a thumping, pulsing club in Kings Cross. We've had the conversation about her hanging out in places like this, but she's an adult, and I don't want to ruin the mood further, so I let it go.

Without a second thought, I head to Lulu's loft. Tonight has been unsettling, to say the least, and maybe I should go home and process what Mum said. But Lulu is like a drug, and I'm a hopeless addict.

CHAPTER TWENTY-FOUR

LULU

Nick comes in from dinner with his mother in a strange mood, and maybe I'm in a strange mood too. Part of me is relieved he didn't ask if I'd like to go with him. Meeting his mother would take us into actual relationship territory.

But another part of me is a little hurt. We've spent almost every night together since this started, so if it's not a relationship, I don't know what is. Maybe for him, this is purely physical. Or maybe we're both using our sexual chemistry to hide behind. But sometimes, when I catch him looking at me, his expression all soft, I just don't know. Having a conversation about it would be the right thing to do, but I don't know how to bring it up. And I don't honestly know what I want his answer to be. I've spent my whole life avoiding getting involved. Putting a label on this feels very scary. So, I don't ask.

I've been feeling unusually emotional lately. I think the pressure of having my first solo exhibition is getting to me. And since

Sebastian called me this afternoon, my emotions have been on a roller coaster.

"By the way, I have a date for my exhibition," I tell him after we've exhausted ourselves and lie sweaty on my sofa. "It's the twelfth of November."

"That's great." His voice is sleepy, his hands skimming lazily up and down my back.

I screw up my courage. "Would you … I mean, if you want to, you could maybe come …" Wow—so articulate.

"Hmm. I think that might be the night of the partners' dinner, actually. I'll check with Mandy and let you know. Is that okay?" I feel his body stiffen next to me.

Now I'm in full retreat. "Oh, no, don't worry about it. I know how busy you are." I'm equal parts disappointed and relieved. I wait for Nick to respond, but the silence stretches on. I get up, and in a strange reflection of the first time we had sex, I fill a couple of glasses of water.

"The work on the office is almost finished. Another couple of weeks and it will all be over. The tradies have pulled out all the stops to get it done quickly." As a diversionary tactic, it's not great, but desperate times call for desperate measures.

"Yes, I noticed things seemed to be winding up." He grabs the change of topic and runs with it. "I expected we'd be in for a much longer process. What you've achieved is quite stunning."

"Even your office?" I'm trying for light-hearted. I even throw in a poke in the ribs, but I'm not sure he's buying it.

His answering laugh seems forced. "Especially my office."

I curl into him and feign sleep, all too aware we might soon reach our expiry date. For the first time in my life, that's an unwelcome thought. Which is, in itself, an unwelcome thought.

The very next morning, I'm hit with another unwelcome reality. I'm having trouble focussing on anything today. Nick's reaction to my invitation last night is going around in my mind and I can't see any other explanation than he's beginning to feel like he's had enough. And it scares me.

I'm in Will's office trying to concentrate on what the painter is saying about tints and stains when Nick's office door, which is right beside me, opens. Nick can't see me, but I can see him, and his body language is screaming tense and uncomfortable. With him is an older woman I can only see in profile, but even from a distance, warm is not a word you would associate with her. She's all hard angles and cold colours.

They're obviously in mid-conversation.

"I've bought you some time for now, Nicholas. But she won't wait forever so whatever is going on, sort yourself out quick smart so we can move forward with our plans."

Nick replies, his voice so low and gravelly I can't make out his words. But he puts his hand on the small of her back and leads her towards reception.

Mandy appears out of nowhere and sees me watching Nick and the woman round the corner into reception.

Gesturing towards them with her ever-present iPad, she grimaces. "Glad I was away from my desk when she arrived."

I raise my eyebrows at her, asking without asking.

"Nick's mother. Lovely woman. If you have a thing for cacti."

I try to make some sort of vague noise of disinterest, although even to my ears, it sounds like the cry of a wounded animal. Which is how I feel. Wounded.

What I heard was vague, to say the least. But is it possible they were talking about me?

This evening is my regular boot camp date with Rosanna. And when I say regular, I mean we drag ourselves there once in a blue moon, although if anyone asks, we definitely go every week.

The class is held in the park at Rushcutters Bay, a short walk from Rosanna's apartment. You'd think exercising with uninterrupted views of the harbour would be a little less painful. You'd be wrong.

I get to the park early and find a bench in the sun to watch the beautiful yachts moored at the Cruising Yacht Club. The breeze is fresh with salt and carries the clink of rigging and cries of seagulls, while the afternoon sun is sliding towards a golden glow. Sights, sounds and smells which would normally relax me, have no effect.

Yet again, I'm reminded of the perils of eavesdropping. I can't quite make sense of the conversation I overheard this afternoon, but I can't shake the feeling it was about me. I know we said this wasn't a thing at the start. But lately, I've felt like maybe that's not entirely true. And if there's someone else waiting in the wings until he gets tired of me, well, I'm not okay with that.

Ro turns up at the last possible minute, just as the class starts.

"Why does it never rain on boot camp days?" she grumbles, laying her towel out on the grass and dropping onto it for some stretches.

"Because one of us did something terrible in a previous life," I answer with a groan as I grip my ankles and lower my head to my knee.

"I hate this. I mean. I. Really. Hate. This," she grumbles.

"Focus, girls," shouts our torturer. I mean instructor. "If you've got enough breath to talk, you're not working hard enough."

We make it to the end of the class. Barely.

"Christ, I hate that class. Remind me again why we do it." Ro gasps as she lies spreadeagle and sweaty on her towel.

"So we can go to that Mexican place and eat our body weight in nachos."

"Oh yeah. So, what's got your face looking like someone stole your favourite handbag?" Rosanna sits up, taking a massive gulp from her water bottle.

I spit out the thought that's been torturing me all afternoon.

"I have to break it off with Nick."

"How can you break it off if it isn't a thing?" Her sarcasm isn't just biting, it's mauling. So mauling my eyes fill with tears and all I can do is shake my head.

Watery though she is, I can see the shock on Ro's face. "What happened, Lu?"

I tell her about his response to inviting him to the exhibition, and what I heard his mother say this morning. Her face is a picture of confusion.

"Umm. Did I miss something?"

"What do you mean?"

"Well, this evil mother. Did she mention your name? Did she even say she was talking about a woman? Or an affair? Or a not a thing?"

I think back over the conversation. "Well. No. But it's obvious she was talking about me. Us."

"Yeah. Not obvious to me, sweetie. Did you ask him?" Ro is shaking her head. I can see how exasperated she is with me. But I'm too far gone to reel it back in.

"No. I legged it out of there, and I turned my phone off. I can't talk to him right now. Not until I work out what to do. But I think I have to break it off. Before it's too late." And then I'm crying. Bawling, sobbing, ugly crying. In public. This is not who I am, and I'm furious with Nick for putting me in this position. But most of all, I'm furious with myself. I knew an end was inevitable, and not only should I have known better, I *do* know better. I watched my father fall apart after losing my mum. I've always vowed it was never going to happen to me. Yet here we are.

"Looks to me like it's already too late," Ro says, wrapping me in her still-sweaty arms. She warned me. More than once. Yet I sailed right on in there and broke my own heart. To her credit, there's not even a hint of 'I told you so'. She lets me wallow for a few minutes before she hands me a tissue to wipe under my eyes and nose.

"Do you think it's possible you misunderstood?"

"I don't see how. She was telling him to sort himself out so they could get back to their plans. It seems pretty clear I'm his bit of fun on the side before he settles down." I blow my nose and accept another tissue from Rosanna.

"Wow. What are you? Eighty? Bit of fun on the side." Ro passes me her water bottle for a swig.

"Maybe when he said he didn't want a relationship, what he meant was he didn't want one with me." I sniffle.

"And yet here we are, with you in the middle of what, it is clear to anyone with eyes, is a relationship. Are you sure this isn't just you being you?"

"What is that supposed to mean?"

"I love you to bits. You know this. But I also know as soon as anyone starts to get close, you find a reason to run. Are you sure that's not what this is?" Ro smooths my hair back off my face. And cups my cheeks.

"No, it's not. Well, maybe. A bit. I don't know. What I do know is I'm not okay being some kind of placeholder, or experiment or, or ..." The idea that maybe she's right sets me off all over again. "I promised myself I would never end up like Dad. And now look. Even if there is an explanation, which I doubt, I have to break it off."

"Argh. Talk to him. Find out what they were really talking about before you do a mic drop on the whole relationship. Either way, I'm here for you. And you know what? You have much more important things on your plate right now. You need to concentrate on getting your exhibition sorted. You've been working towards this for too many years to let some guy mess it up."

I nod, hiccupping as I mop my face with still more tissues. She's right. And it is entirely possible they weren't talking about me. But my reaction speaks volumes. Nick has got too close for comfort. And I realise I've left it too late to let him go without a world of hurt. For both of us.

Ro waits till I'm calm again. "So, when are you going to talk to him?"

"Tonight, I guess." My belly clenches at the thought, but the sooner I do this, the better.

·❤·❤·❤·❤·❤·

As luck would have it, I don't get to follow through on my plans because when I turn my phone on again, I find a message from Nick saying he's been called to some urgent client meetings in Melbourne and will be away for three or four days. I can't do this over the phone. It will have to wait. In the meantime, I decide to spend as much time as possible in the office, trying to get ahead of the work there so that when he comes back I don't have to be there as much.

Unfortunately, the Nick-shaped hole he leaves in my life throbs like an infected tooth the entire time he's gone, which gives me a taste of LAN—Life After Nick. I'm completely overwhelmed by my feelings and hardly know what to do with myself. Rather than facing it head-on, I avoid his calls, which become more frequent as the days go by. I can tell by the tone of his messages and voicemails he knows something is up, but I can't bring myself to talk to him. And then he goes and ups the ante.

As a rule, I don't answer calls showing as 'private caller', but I have a few balls in the air with the exhibition and finishing the office, so I make an exception. But it's Nick. He doesn't waste any time.

"You've been avoiding my calls." The sound of his voice weakens my knees, and I drop onto the floor in front of the painting I've been working on, leaning against the wall.

"No, I haven't. I'm very busy, Nick." If he wasn't so right, I wouldn't be so defensive.

"Right. I see."

"Was there a reason for your call? I'm kind of in the middle of something."

I can hear the leashed impatience in his voice. "Yes, actually. Firstly, I wanted to check on you—"

"I'm fine. I'm a big girl, Nick. I was fine before I met you, I'll be fine after you're gone."

There's a sharp inhale from Nick. And a long pause.

"Gone. Okay. Well, secondly, I wanted to suggest you come down to Melbourne to meet me for the weekend. I thought we could have a mini getaway." My breath catches. If he had asked me this a few days ago, I would have jumped at the idea. Now? Not only do I not know what we are, but I feel too raw.

"As I told you. I'm busy, Nick. I don't have time." Even I can hear what a complete bitch I'm being. Another lengthy silence on the other end of the line speaks volumes.

"What's going on, Lulu? Is this about me not going to your exhibition?"

"No. Of course not. You're not obliged. I know how busy you are." Liar, liar, pants on fire. And I don't think I'm fooling either of us.

"If I could get out of the partners' dinner, I would. But I can't."

"Sure. I know that." And now I'm the petulant teenager. Very mature.

"And what did you mean by when I'm gone?"

"Well, I'll be finishing up at CPM at the end of next week. So ..." I can't even bring myself to say the words. Tears are streaming down my face and I'm struggling not to alert him by sniffling.

"So, what? That's it then, is it?" His voice is sharp, but I'm not sure if it's hurt or anger I'm hearing.

"Well, it would make sense." Nick is quiet for a long time. I pull the phone from my ear to check he's still on the line when he responds.

"Not to me, it wouldn't." Now it's my turn for silence. "I don't see why we can't go on as we have been," he adds eventually.

"Is that what you want? Don't you have a life you want to be getting on with?" Now would be the time for him to fess up about his plans. I hold my breath as he answers.

"I am getting on with my life. We said at the beginning we'd carry on until we'd had enough. Have you had enough? Because I haven't."

My stomach flips. I don't want to do this on the phone, but I don't want to lie either. Who am I kidding? Every word coming out of my mouth is a lie. And maybe every word coming out of his is too.

"I … I don't know. It just seems like the right time …"

"This is not a conversation we should be having over the phone." He hasn't used this tone with me since we first met, when he was still Nicholas the Disapproving. "I understand you don't want to come to Melbourne for the weekend, so I'll get a flight home on Saturday morning. We can talk then."

Nick hangs up without another word, and I cry myself into a coma.

Over the next couple of days, Ro keeps up a steady stream of calls and texts and stupid cat memes, trying to distract me. I don't have the heart to tell her it's not working. She knows me well enough to see through my half-hearted responses, but is kind enough not to call me out on it. I honestly don't know what I'd do without her.

Everything I paint looks like misery on canvas. So much so that Sebastian, who calls in to see my progress, looks concerned and suggests maybe I should take a break.

By the time Nick returns from Melbourne, I'm beside myself. It's clear he wants us to keep seeing each other, yet he still hasn't suggested we become anything more than casual. And none of that negates my fears.

"What was all that about, Lulu?" he asks as he drops his overnight bag by the door, having wasted no time coming straight from the airport.

I go to speak, but he holds up a hand. "And don't insult my intelligence by saying it was nothing."

I'm grasping at straws. My head is screaming, tell him; my heart is screaming, tell him. But what they each want to tell him is not the same thing.

I have to come clean. Rip the band aid off. "I heard what your mother said. In the office. About your plans."

He looks momentarily confused, and then the lights start to flicker on.

"I see. Refresh my memory? I have a habit of forgetting conversations with my mother. What, exactly, did you hear?"

"About how she won't wait forever and you should sort yourself out quickly so you can move forward with your plans." I can feel my hands shaking, and I cross my arms tightly across my body and put the mass of my ancient dining table between us.

"Right. And what did I say?" I feel like a hostile witness being cross-examined. Nick's face is like granite.

"I don't know. I didn't hear that bit." When I say it out loud like this, it sounds ridiculous.

Nick nods. "Well, if you had, you'd have heard me tell her in no uncertain terms to mind her own business and stay out of my affairs."

The heaviness in my chest lifts for a moment. Until I realise his words are not a denial.

"So, who is this *she* your mother was talking about?"

"She's my ..." He looks uncomfortable, which is a red flag I don't even want to think about. "I guess you could say she's my ex-girlfriend. Eleanor. And before you ask, we broke up before you and I started ..."

"Sleeping together?" Nick flinches as though I've slapped him.

"Yes. And frankly, I'm disappointed you didn't simply talk to me. We could have avoided all this drama." Frustration is starting to creep into his tone.

Great. So, his mum wants him back together with his ex. And I still don't have an unequivocal denial that he's planning on getting back together with her at some point. But I was also very clear I didn't want a relationship. I know I'm on shaky ground here.

"Well, I guess I thought maybe you were ready to call it quits." My voice cracks and I can't continue.

"You know how this feels, Lulu? It feels like you've got one foot out the door." Nick starts around the table. Stalking towards me like the panther I once compared him to.

I know he expects me to deny it, but he's hit the nail on the head. I do have one foot out the door. It's how I get the second foot out the door that's presenting the problem. I feel like a fox with its foot caught in a trap of its own making. And I'm about to gnaw my leg off to escape.

"We always said this was no strings, Nick." I can barely hear my voice.

"We did. But it doesn't mean we can't be invested while it lasts."

There it is again. No commitment for anything more. Which should make me happy. Because that's what we agreed. But it hurts.

We're facing off now. Silently. My arms crossed. Nick's hands on his hips. I can almost hear the synapses firing in his brain. I can't speak past the prickly mass of fear, regret and grief caught in my throat.

"Well. I'm not ready to call it quits. But the question remains, are you? Are you in or are you out?" Nick asks.

I hadn't counted on how hard it would be to break it off with him face to face, with those sharp grey eyes seeming to see right through me to the hidden thoughts even I don't understand. And when push comes to shove, I can't do it. I know I have to break it off, but I'm in so deep already. Whether it ends now or in two weeks is irrelevant, so I trade tomorrow's pain for today's happiness. I can only nod.

His hand comes up and, with gentle fingers, he pushes a curl off my face. And then I'm in his arms. His touch has such power over me. I can't do it. I can't.

"Well?"

"I'm in."

In the days that follow, I sometimes catch Nick watching me. He's noticed how strung-out I am, but he doesn't say anything. I hope he puts it down to the stress of the upcoming exhibition. Luckily, because we're both so busy, we don't have much time to talk. I'm tired and headachy, which is to be expected, I guess, with everything I have going on.

Once my exhibition is over, I'll work out how to extricate myself from the mess I've created. I try not to think about the fact Nick might actually do it for me. Until then, I don't have the bandwidth to deal. At least, that's what I tell myself.

On my last day at the CPM offices, Harry surprises me by throwing a cocktail party. By now I'm so tense, the smell of the hors d'oeuvres makes my stomach flop like a dying fish in the bottom of a boat, and I hate fish. Even the idea of champagne makes me shudder, and I go with sparkling water. Harry makes a beautiful speech about the work I've done and how much they'll all miss me around the office, and everyone is incredibly merry.

I excuse myself as early as possible, pleading how busy I am with work for my exhibition, which opens in a few days. Harry walks me to the elevator, his arm draped affectionately across my shoulders.

"I'm sorry we won't be able to make it to the opening of your exhibition." He seems genuinely disappointed. "But the partners' dinner has been in everyone's diary for months. Still, Stella and I will call in over the weekend. We might be lucky enough to pick up something if it hasn't all been sold." The lift doors open. "Don't be a stranger."

"Thank you, Harry, for everything. I enjoyed working with you all so much." I give Harry a tight hug, and then I'm in the lift, feeling like there's a good chance I've left a large part of my heart behind.

CHAPTER TWENTY-FIVE

NICK

The four days I spent in Melbourne seemed endless. Despite the twelve-hour days, there was a constant emptiness where Lulu belonged. But what made the whole trip a nightmare, made my blood run cold, was when she blindsided me with the suggestion we end things. I all but hung up in her ear. But my stomach was bottoming out, and I needed to get off that call and gather my thoughts. When it comes to legal matters, I have no trouble thinking on my feet, but hearing Lulu float the idea of ending things? I needed a plan.

When I arrive back in Sydney, things are tense. It all starts to make sense when she tells me she heard my mother's comments. It was pretty clear my mother came to the office that day on a fact-finding mission. At the time, I was grateful there was no sign of Lulu. I thought I had dodged that bullet. Turns out I hadn't.

The timing of all this couldn't have been worse given my trip to Melbourne, and the fact I can't go to her exhibition. It seems like things are all going belly up at once. What hurts is she didn't trust me enough to call and ask me to explain. How she imagines I could be thinking about anyone else is beyond me.

I try to make it clear I'm invested in the relationship—because that's what this is—without freaking her out. Lulu is clearly on edge, and I'm reluctant to push too hard. I know she's under a lot of pressure and doesn't need me to add to it by asking for things she's not ready to give. Because she's sticking to the 'no-strings' story, despite her freak out over Eleanor. Years of working in the law has taught me when to advance and when to wait things out. I know we can't go on like this forever, but if we can get through the next couple of weeks, we'll have the headspace to sort it out. It's a band aid on a gaping wound, but somehow we muddle through the next few days.

It occurs to me her mood changed after our conversation about me going to the opening of her exhibition, but there's no chance of me getting out of the partners' dinner. Or maybe it's because I hadn't invited her to the dinner. I did consider it. But as the widow of the managing partner, my mother will be there. And given the way Mum is behaving at present, I don't want them anywhere near each other. Especially when things are not settled between us. It was a stroke of luck the dinner clashed with the exhibition. Problem solved. Or so I thought. Now I'm not so sure.

On Lulu's last day in the office, Harry puts on a cocktail party for the staff and makes a gushing speech about the hard work Lulu has done. Her cheeks are pink, and she seems delighted, but she also appears tired. She's been running herself ragged the last few weeks. Honestly, I'll be relieved when her exhibition opening is over and we can sit down and have an honest conversation about us.

As Buddha said—resistance to change is painful. I've been torturing myself by resisting the inevitability of a future with Lulu since the moment we first met, but if my four days in Melbourne and our first argument have taught me anything, it's that I don't want to be without her. At all. Ever. Because being without her, even for a few days, bled all the colour out of my world.

I need to find a way to make this work—awful partners' wives, manipulative mother and all. I know it's selfish, but I can no longer imagine a life without her. She brings a joy and warmth to my life that I didn't even know I needed. I've changed, thanks to Lulu, and I don't want to go back to the old me.

We were both clear at the outset we weren't interested in a relationship, but I feel like that idea is a long way behind us in the rear-view mirror. For me, at least. And sometimes I catch Lulu looking at me in a way that suggests perhaps it is for her too. I certainly hope so. If not, I have some serious work ahead of me because I'm not walking away from her without a fight.

Her exhibition opening is on a Thursday night, so I book us a romantic getaway to the Southern Highlands for the weekend. Complete with massages, a spa bath and dinner at a two-hatted restaurant. I'll lay all my cards on the table then and hope she does too.

I leave the farewell party half an hour after Lulu. I'd intended to leave straight away, but was cornered by the most boring of partners and couldn't get away. Letting myself into her loft with the key she shyly gave me weeks ago, I expect to find her watching television or painting, but all the lights are out except for the bedside lamp. Lulu is curled on her side, her Kindle clutched in one hand, sound asleep. With the way the light is hitting her face, I can see the shadows under her eyes. It should feel creepy watching her sleep, but instead, it feels like, in this moment, everything is right with the world. I'm right where I was always meant to be.

I undress quietly, turn off the light, put her Kindle on the bedside table, and slip into bed beside her, even though it's not much past ten pm. Lulu sighs as she squirms back against me and I wrap an arm across her body, taking her hand in mine and burying my face in the wildflower hair I adore.

"I love you," I whisper, even though I know she's too sound asleep to hear me. Those words have been circling in my head for a while now. It feels good to have said them out loud. I can't wait to be able to say them when she can hear them.

* * *

Over the next few days, Lulu becomes increasingly exhaust-ed, and it's no wonder since she's working furiously to finish everything for the opening. I wish there was something I could do to help, but other than making sure she eats a decent dinner and trying to coax her to bed at a reasonable hour, there's not much I can do. Her appetite seems to have vanished along with her energy, and I find myself worrying about her to the point I order food to be delivered in the middle of the day in the hope she'll eat.

She's a little crabby too. No. Not a little. Quite a lot. It's not directed at me, though, but at herself. Every one of the paint-ings she was previously happy with comes in for criticism. I'm grateful for Sebastian, the gallery owner, who calls in to collect the paintings she's still fussing over. They have a tussle over whether they're ready, but he insists if they aren't photographed 'tomorrow, my darling' they won't make it into the catalogue, which was due at the printers yesterday. I'm glad to see the paintings go. The less work she has around her, the less likely she is to stress over whether it's good enough.

The series of paintings she did after our weekend on the boat are breathtaking, but neither Sebastian nor I can seem to find enough superlatives to convince her of their worthiness, although his enthusiasm can sometimes coax her out of her anx-iety. I understand why she's fretting. For Lulu, this exhibition is about establishing herself in her own right. We haven't discussed it much, but I understand her father is also an artist, and she wants to stand on her own, not ride on his coat-tails. If anyone understands the need to prove yourself worthy to your father, it's me.

I couldn't be prouder of her. She puts her heart and soul into everything she does. She's talented and professional and deter-mined, and those qualities shine so brightly that I can't believe it took me so long to recognise them. Somehow, someway, I will find a way to have her in my life. And if it means turning mine upside down or reinventing myself to do it, then so be it. Claire's right—it's my life and it's time I started making choices based on my happiness.

"Are you putting our painting in the exhibition?" I ask—bravely, I think—one evening as she fusses over a painting she picked up from the framers today. She had been unhappy with the frame and insisted on having it redone, even though it had already been photographed.

"No." Well, that told me. I can't help but feel relieved. I would never ask her not to include it, but for me, it's an intensely private and special piece. If she had included it, I would have called Sebastian and arranged to purchase it before the opening because there's no way it wouldn't have sold. And there's no way it should belong to anyone else.

Taking my life into my own hands, I continue. "Why not?"

"Because ..." She sighs, closing her eyes and scrunching up her face as if in pain. "Because it's personal. Private. And it doesn't fit with the rest of the body of work."

I kiss her forehead, hope blooming in my belly. "Would you like me to make you a cup of tea?"

It seems coffee has gone out of favour, and just as well since the last thing she needs is to be any more strung-out. I can't help but smile as I remember our conversation at lunch the day she took the job at CPM. I get it now.

As I boil the kettle, it occurs to me I have never had the urge to take care of someone the way I do with Lulu. Well, apart from Claire, I guess. If I didn't already know how much Lulu meant to me, this would be a dead giveaway. A cup of tea seems such an inadequate thing to do for someone who has taken me over, body and soul.

I put the steaming cup on the work table next to her pot of brushes and wrap my arms around her from behind, wishing I could infuse her with some of my strength. For the first time, she feels frail in my arms and I realise how much weight she has lost in the last couple of weeks.

"It will all be over soon, and you'll be able to relax and enjoy your success."

"Thank you," she whispers, but her answer is distracted, her mind back on the work, leaving me to watch and worry.

Hours later, I tip the cold tea down the sink and put the cup in the dishwasher, counting the days.

CHAPTER TWENTY-SIX

LULU

B y the morning of the opening I feel like I've been trampled by a herd of Highland cattle. I've spent the last few mornings clutching the toilet bowl, and I don't like it one little bit. Luckily, Nick has been super busy, leaving for work at the crack of dawn. So I haven't had to suffer the indignity of an audience.

I've no sooner finished cleaning my teeth—for the second time—than I hear the front door rumble open. Rosanna's boss might not be great at career development opportunities, but she makes up for it with her willingness to be flexible about Ro's work hours. So, she's been able to take the day off to keep me calm before the opening.

"In here," I call out. Ro knows I've been a wreck the last week or two and is aware the nerves have travelled to my stomach and set up camp there.

"Well, isn't this handy? You're right where I need you." She's smirking.

"Honestly, Ro, I'm in no shape for games this morning." My hands are still shaking from the violence of this morning's upchuck.

"No games. Hop on the toilet and pee on this." And from a paper bag, Ro pulls a white plastic stick. It takes me a shocked moment, but I've seen enough rom-coms to recognise it for what it is.

"Don't be ridiculous. What for?"

"Tired. Headachy. Emotional. Throwing up." Ro ticks the points off on her fingers. "Can you join the dots? Have you had a period lately?" I'm having trouble wrapping my head around what she's saying.

"No. No, no, no. I am *not* pregnant. I have an implant. And you don't get a period with an implant. So there."

"Uh-huh."

"You're being melodramatic. This is all just nerves and stress and worry and ..."

"Fine then. If you're not pregnant, you won't mind peeing on the stick. Because it will be negative. No harm done. Right?"

I plop down on the side of the bath, suddenly dizzy. I can't be pregnant. Implants are so reliable. And just because I feel ...

Oh crap.

I snatch the stick from Ro. "You had to do this to me today, didn't you?"

"I'm sorry, sweetie. But I can't watch you go on like this another day. If it's negative, then you have nothing to worry about. If not, well, we'll work it out later. But best to know one way or the other—yes?"

Ro stands at the bathroom door while I pee on the stick.

"How long until we know?" I hand it to her while I wash my hands.

"Hmm. Ummm. It says on the box one minute, but ..." She holds the stick up and there in the window are two undeniably dark pink lines. Already.

"Well, that can't be right. It's only been twenty or thirty seconds. If we wait a minute the line will go away." We both stare at the lines. I reach out blindly to turn on the bathroom light, just to make sure.

"I think it's getting lighter." I suggest hopefully. Willing it to go away.

"No, I don't think so." She could at least have the manners to look doubtful.

"Maybe it's a faulty test?"

"Maybe. The box says over ninety-nine per cent accurate. But there are two sticks in there, so do you want to do it again?"

I'm back on the toilet in a flash as Ro pulls the other stick from the bag. This time I don't get up. My eyes are glued to the stick, and Ro peers over my shoulder. Within seconds those two dark pink lines fill the window.

And just like that, my whole life takes a one-eighty-degree turn. If Ro says something sympathetic now, I think I might break.

"Well, on the bright side, it will be the world's most beautiful baby with you and Nick as its parents." Ro sits on the side of the bath to face me, still sitting on the toilet with my knickers around my ankles.

It crosses my mind how lucky I am to have a friend who knows me so well and thinks nothing of watching me pee and holding my hand before I've even washed it. But I can't even form words to answer her.

"Ginger tea for Mama?" she asks, and we both start to laugh until I'm crying and laughing at the same time.

Rosanna has me settled on the bed, propped up on pillows with a cup of ginger tea before either of us say another word.

"How could this have happened? I have an implant. What am I going to do?" My voice is barely a whisper. I remember my plan to check when my implant needed replacing. The plan I didn't follow through. And the conversation with Nick where I assured him he didn't need to worry he'd end up being my baby daddy. Shit.

"I don't know, sweetie. No birth control is one hundred per cent foolproof. And you have been giving it a good workout. But you have enough to worry about today. For now, you're going to finish your tea, get dressed and hightail it down to the gallery to make sure everything is perfect for tonight. Then you're going to bask in the adoration of the crowd and sell a shit ton of paintings. Everything else can wait until tomorrow." Ro perches beside me.

"Can it?" I don't know how I'll be able to think about anything else. At all.

"Well, you're no more pregnant today than you were yesterday, are you? So yes, it can. And whatever happens, whatever you decide, you know I'm in your corner. Always. Unless you make someone else godmother. Then you're dead to me." Ro makes a face as she sips the ginger tea she made herself in solidarity. "Erk. Hope you don't need nine months of this stuff."

A hot shower, another cup of ginger tea and some dry toast and I'm as ready as I'll ever be. The Black Gallery is in the trendiest section of Oxford Street. Ro and I arrive to find Sebastian in a flurry of colour and movement, and half a dozen tradies up ladders hanging paintings and adjusting lighting.

"Ohh, here she is." I'm air kissed to within an inch of my life before he turns to Rosanna. "And who have we here, darling? Oh my, you could be mistaken for a nineteen-fifties Italian film star, my love. I'm Sebastian. Delighted to meet you." Ro gets the same air-kiss treatment before Seb sashays off ahead of us, waving his hand in his wake. "Come, come, come. What do you think? Are you happy with the placements? The lighting? Oh, and the catalogues arrived last night. Thank God. Cutting it way too close for my liking. You *must* have a browse. They're *stunning*."

Sebastian's energy and enthusiasm are contagious, and I'm swept up in deciding last-minute details, leaving me no time to dwell on this morning's revelation. By mid-afternoon, everything is as ready as it can be.

"Off you pop, darling. You know I love you, and I think you're beautiful, but it won't do to have those bags under your eyes tonight. I want you to pop some cucumber on them and have a nap and I'll see you back here at seven pm sharp." Sebastian sweeps the door open, as a courier arrives with the biggest flower arrangement I've ever seen.

"Delivery for Lulu MacLeod?"

"Ohh—aren't they divine," Sebastian coos, directing them to be placed on the entry table, signing for them, then looking at me expectantly.

I know they must be from Nick, but I'm surprised to see his own bold and angular handwriting on the card:

'You deserve every success in the world. Can't wait to hear the story of your triumph. N xx'

"Are these from the delicious man I keep seeing at your loft?"

"Yes." I force the word through the lump in my throat, touched he must have taken the time to visit the florist himself.

"Well. He's a keeper. Now off you go. We'll leave these here in the foyer to greet the guests." And with that, Sebastian floats away, leaving Ro to take me home.

Neither the nap nor the cucumber slices do much for the bags under my eyes. Largely because the nap is spent tossing and turning, wondering how to break the news to Nick. When Ro comes to wake me, I'm staring at the ceiling.

"I can't see him tonight. I need time to ..."

"Yeah, I can imagine. Why don't you stay at mine tonight? Tell him we're going out after the opening and you'll see him tomorrow."

"I'm not sure tomorrow will be enough time." I sigh.

"It doesn't have to be. It only has to be enough to get through tonight. Tomorrow you can work out what to do next. Why do today what you can put off until tomorrow, right?"

She's right, so I text Nick:

Me: I'm going to stay at Rosanna's tonight after the opening. We're going out to celebrate.

Nick: OK. If you get a chance, give me a call and let me know how it went?

Me: If I can

Nick: I should be finished with dinner around 11. If you decide you want company, let me know where you are and I can join you. Or pick you up.

Me: That's fine. You have a good time at the dinner. I'll see you tomorrow

Nick: OK—well the offer's there. You know where I live if you want to come over after you're finished celebrating.

Me: Sure

It's only afterwards I realise I forgot to thank him for the flowers. Never mind, I'll thank him tomorrow. Before I drop a bomb on his life.

People start arriving at the opening right on time, and within half an hour, the space is packed with people and chatter. Rosanna keeps me supplied with sparkling water and whatever hors d'oeuvres she thinks won't jump right out again. Despite my pounding head, I think I manage to be somewhat sparkling and a little bit engaging. At least nobody seems to notice the bags under my eyes, except for Sebastian, who tsks and whisks me off to his office where he dabs something that smells vaguely medicinal on the puffiness. He can see the question in my eyes. "You don't want to know, darling. Now go. Be charming. I'm going to count all the lovely numbers with dollar signs in front."

"You've sold something?"

"Lots of somethings, darling. I'm kicking myself for not going higher on the pricing. I must get back—that woman from Mona is circling, and there's someone interested in a commission I need to lock in. So shoo, darling. We'll talk later."

By the time the last of the guest has left, there are only a couple of paintings left unsold, and even those have people interested in them. I have complete faith Sebastian will get them over the line.

"What did I tell you?" Rosanna clinks her champagne against my glass of sparkling water. "You are on your way, Lu."

I look around, taking in all the red dots next to the paintings. "I can't believe all the fantastic things people were saying about my work. Only a couple mentioned my father, and even then, they were saying I'm as talented as him."

"Well, of course you are, darling." Sebastian's eyes pop up from his iPad where he has been adding up sales, and he turns the screen to us in triumph. "And here's the proof."

I almost spit my water at him when I see the amount of money I made tonight. "Halfway through the night, I upped the prices." He giggles at my expression of horror. "We are not a charity, darling." My dad would love Sebastian.

As we climb into a taxi, my phone starts to ring—Nick. I hesitate, shooting a pleading look at Ro. "Don't answer if you're not ready to talk to him. You told him you were going out. Maybe the music was so loud you didn't hear your phone."

Feeling guilty, I let it go to voicemail.

We settle onto Ro's big bed, me with another ginger tea, Ro with a glass of her dad's homemade Limoncello.

"Well, at least this explains why wine has tasted weird for the past couple of weeks," I say, sipping the hot tea as I send my dad a long text about how the opening went, and telling him I'll call in the morning.

"I guess it does. Do you want to talk about it?" Rosanna tucks the covers around us.

"No. I don't think so. Not tonight. You were right. Time enough to worry about it tomorrow."

"Absolutely. Get a good night's sleep, and we'll work out a plan in the morning." She picks up my phone, puts it on silent and turns out the light. We sip in silence for a while before she whispers, "I'm so proud of you."

"Thanks, Ro. Don't know what I'd do without you." I squeeze her hand in the dark.

"Lucky you'll never have to find out."

And with that, I drop into the best night's sleep I've had in weeks.

The next morning, after another round with the toilet bowl, I find Rosanna checking out the paper on-line.

"Is there a story about the exhibition?" I ask. But something about her body language alerts me to a problem. I look over her shoulder, and right above the article on my exhibition is a story announcing Nick's engagement and plans to stand for a seat in parliament.

"What the actual fuck?" Ro whispers.

I can't even formulate words. Because along with the article is a picture of Nick with the very beautiful, very poised woman I saw with him in the hallway at CPM only weeks ago. And her name is Eleanor.

CHAPTER TWENTY-SEVEN

NICK

L ulu's texts have unsettled me. It's not that she's going out after the opening. It's that she hasn't asked me to go too. Or maybe it's because she's going to stay at Rosanna's and not come home to tell me all about the opening. I know she and Rosanna are close. They talk every day, and catch up for coffee or lunch a couple of times a week. But with things as unresolved as they are between us, it feels like she's pulling further away from me.

I had imagined Lulu would want to come home. Celebrate with me. It hasn't escaped my notice that the unsettled feeling in the pit of my stomach reminds me of a childhood spent hoping for approval and never quite getting it.

I haven't mentioned the weekend getaway I've booked. My plan is to surprise her, pick her up mid-afternoon tomorrow and not tell her where we're going or what we're doing. I push my doubts to the back of my mind. Over the weekend, I'll open up and tell Lulu how I feel, and ask her to do the same. Come Monday, these insecurities will all be history.

The partners' dinner is, as always, at one of the most exclusive restaurants in the city. Personally, I think the food is sub-par, particularly for the prices they charge, but most of the partners wouldn't know a good meal if it bit them on the arse, and are more concerned with the location, décor and who is eating at the other tables.

I offer to pick my mother up on my way, but she assures me there is no need, and when I arrive at the restaurant, I understand why. Standing next to her, sipping a glass of no doubt expensive champagne, is Eleanor.

I can feel my blood pressure spiking as I take in the scene. The woman I love is having the most important night of her life, and I'm not there. I'm here at what will no doubt be a very boring work function. With the two women in the world I would pay good money to avoid. My instinct is to turn and leave. But I can't do that to Harry.

"Nicholas, darling." Mum air kisses me and misses by a country mile. "As always, you're late. It's lucky I suggested Eleanor come with me; otherwise, she would have been cooling her heels at home waiting for you."

"Mother. A word?" I take her arm and lead her away with barely a glance at Eleanor.

"That was rude, Nicholas. You didn't even acknowledge Eleanor, let alone greet her properly." She throws a smile over her shoulder at a irritated Eleanor.

"What is she doing here?"

"Well, I mentioned the dinner and asked what she would be wearing, and she said you hadn't said anything about it. Which, I assured her, must have been an oversight. So, I suggested she come with me and meet you here. You're welcome."

"How dare you interfere in my private life? Not to mention I believe I made my position on Eleanor crystal clear—to both of you, Mother." A glass of champagne is thrust into my hand, and I can barely contain the urge to hurl it across the room.

"Nonsense. You can't have been serious. What would people say if you were to attend without Eleanor? Once you get these ridiculous ideas out of your head, you'll thank me. It's past time you started making public plans for your future."

"As it happens, Mother, I am making plans. But not with Eleanor." It's a struggle to keep my voice down and an expression of pleasant disinterest on my face.

"And what do those plans entail, may I ask? Shacking up with some tramp who will only hold you back? I will not have it. Now pull yourself together and do the right thing." Mum's tone is nails on the blackboard of my soul, raising childhood memories I've fought to forget.

My heart is pounding, and I can feel my ears burning. I'm having trouble not losing my temper hearing her refer to Lulu so rudely.

"No, you may not ask. You have proven yourself incapable of respecting any boundaries in my life. This relationship is important to me, and I *will not* tolerate your interference. Nor will I tolerate you speaking about her in such terms." I realise this is the first time I have admitted to my mother there is, indeed, a relationship happening, and it feels like a new beginning.

"I see. You imagine yourself in love, do you?"

"Again, none of your business. But she is someone I very much hope will be part of my future, and I won't have you trying to manipulate me—or her."

I watch as Mum processes this. I begin to hope the message has been received.

"It's very evident to me, based on both your behaviour and Eleanor's description, this woman is highly unsuitable. I will not countenance any more of this silliness."

"She's perfectly suitable. For me. And that is all I care to say on the matter. Now I will be polite to Eleanor because she doesn't deserve to be humiliated in front of the entire restaurant, but I warn you, if you *ever* pull a stunt like this again, I will rain down hellfire like you have never seen. Do I make myself clear?"

She leans forward and whispers in my ear. "This is neither the time nor the place. We will discuss this later." And with a monumental display of arrogance, my mother walks away in a drift of expensive perfume. Freeing me, at last, from any regrets I might have been harbouring.

I do my best to avoid Mum and Eleanor during pre-dinner drinks, but of course, as Eleanor is my *partner*, we are seated together at dinner.

As the night drags on with no word from Lulu, my leg begins to jiggle, drawing irritated glances from my mother. Between the main course and dessert, a photographer arrives. Harry is always on the prowl for public relations opportunities, so I assume he organised this to promote the anniversary of the founding of the firm. Groups of us are herded together and somehow, I find myself with Eleanor clinging to my arm, which is beyond a shadow of a doubt my mother's doing. "Cut it out," I whisper and push her hand away, earning yet another eyebrow from Mum.

No sooner do I think things are starting to wind down and I can escape than waiters appear en masse with bottles of very expensive champagne, pouring glasses for everyone at the table. My mother stands and taps her glass with her unused dessert spoon.

"I would like to take this opportunity to make an exciting announcement."

A cold dread settles in the pit of my stomach I begin to rise from my seat to stop her, knowing I'm not going to like what I hear. I register Eleanor is also rising beside me, moving close as though to take my arm again. I'm about to tell her to sit down when my mother continues.

"My son, Nicholas, and the beautiful Eleanor Whitford are engaged to be married, which will coincide with him running for a seat in parliament at the next federal election."

The table erupts in cheers, and I'm frozen to the spot. I know my mother will stop at almost nothing to get what she wants, but this went further than I could ever have imagined possible. My mind returns to our earlier conversation. The woman is completely out of control. It takes me a minute to realise Eleanor is clinging to my arm, accepting the congratulations of those around us.

Making a scene goes against the training that's been drilled into me every day of my life. But I can't let this stand. I step away from Eleanor's clinging hand.

"Actually," I begin, in a voice loud enough to be heard over the hub-bub, which brings everyone to silence, "I'm afraid my mother is very much mistaken. There is no engagement, and I have no plans to stand for election, now or in the future. Good night."

I don't stop to see how my words land. I walk out of the restaurant without a backward glance, leaving my mother and Eleanor to deal with the explanations.

I call Lulu from the cab, but it goes to voicemail and I don't leave a message. She'll call me when she can, I'm sure. I ask the cab to detour via the gallery, but the lights are all out, so I'm guessing she's in a bar somewhere with Rosanna.

My blood feels like it's been carbonated, and not in a good way. I need to talk to Lulu. Tell her what happened tonight. Feel her calming presence. But then I think about her exhibition. She deserves to have the night to celebrate. It would be cruel to bring her down with the shitfuckery my mother pulled tonight. There will be plenty of time to fill her in on our weekend away.

The upside of tonight's mess is I am finally done with my mother and her controlling ways. What she did tonight was unforgiveable. Not only for the position it put me in, but for the unnecessary embarrassment to Eleanor and upset to Harry, who was undoubtedly blindsided by the idea I would no longer be working at the firm. And I feel not a shred of guilt or remorse when I say I'm not sure if I'll ever feel ready to speak to her again.

I prowl restlessly around my soulless apartment for a while, checking my phone for messages before eventually climbing into a cold bed to toss and turn for the rest of the night.

The next morning there's still been neither a call nor text from Lulu, and I'm really starting to worry. I've left half a dozen messages and texts and still nothing. I swing by her loft on my way to the office, but she's not home. I guess she's still at Rosanna's. If they had a late night, they're probably still asleep.

I know I need to speak to Harry and explain what happened last night, but he's not in his office so I leave a note for him to come and see me and retreat to my office to wait.

There's no point trying to concentrate, so I stare out the window. Waiting. Until Mandy comes in and unceremoniously dumps an updated contract on my desk, giving me a death stare.

"Is there something you'd like to say, Mandy?"

"Nothing whatsoever," she spits, turning to leave. But as she reaches the door, she turns back. "You know, I always thought that hard exterior was a façade. I guess maybe I was wrong." And with that little gem, she's gone, passing Harry with a glare as he comes in. I guess word has gotten around. Although it doesn't entirely make sense because I know Mandy despises Eleanor. But I have bigger problems today.

"Well, would you like to explain what happened last night, son? Because I think I speak for all of us when I say we're rather confused." Harry settles into one of the lush velvet visitors' chairs so carefully chosen by Lulu.

"I'm so sorry, Harry." I scrub my hands over my face. "I hardly know what to say. I had no idea my mother had any of that planned, and there is not a shred of truth to anything she said. In point of fact, Eleanor and I broke up several months ago."

"Thank goodness. Humourless woman if ever there was one. Never could work out what you saw in her. But I have to admit I was surprised to discover one of my senior partners, and I like to think somewhat of a mentee, would make the decision to leave the firm without at least discussing it with me."

"Of course I wouldn't. I hope you know that." Harry is the second last person on earth I would want to hurt. "It's true she and Dad had plans for me, as you know, but lately, I've come to the realisation their plans might not be what I want."

"Can an old man give you some unsolicited advice?"

"I don't see why now would be any different than usual," I say with a smile.

"I've known you all your life, and I've watched you grow into a good man and a great lawyer. But what I haven't watched you become is happy. You only get one shot at this life, Nick. Don't waste it on trying to impress others. The only person you need to impress is yourself." Having dropped his wisdom bomb, Harry hoists himself up and leans forward to pay my arm.

"Do you want to know what happened after you left the restaurant?"

"Absolutely not. And for the foreseeable future, I don't want to hear Mary's name, if it's all the same to you."

"Understandable." He turns at the door. "By the way, have you seen the social pages today?"

"No, Harry, I don't typically check the social pages, surprisingly enough." I don't have much patience left for anything today.

"You should. There's a picture of you and Eleanor, so you might need to do some damage control. Oh, and there's a great review of Lulu MacLeod's exhibition opening."

I may be sluggish today, but that one wakes me up pretty damn quick.

"What? Photo of Eleanor and me?"

My fingers shake as I bring up the newspaper on my laptop. Right there, front and centre, big and bold, is a photo of Eleanor and me. Everyone else has been cropped out, and I'm gazing down at her, my hand over hers on my arm. Fuck. Fuck, fuck, fuck. The photographer must have caught me just as I was pushing her hand away, but that's not how it looks. It looks as though I'm holding her hand. It looks intimate.

And then I read the caption:

'*It appears on-again-off-again power couple Eleanor Whitford and Nick Pierce are on again, and he's finally put a ring on it. Sources close to the couple have also indicated he will be parachuted into a safe seat at the next federal election, courtesy of his new fiancée's well-connected father, Richard Whitford. Lucky for some.*'

I don't need Sherlock Holmes to tell me who the *sources* were. I'm not shaking anymore. I've turned to stone.

"I'd get onto it quickly if I were you. Wouldn't want anyone misunderstanding." Harry saunters out with an evil chuckle. Somehow, even he knows about Lulu. Looks like we were far more transparent than I thought if both Eleanor and Harry picked up on our connection.

It takes a good couple of minutes for my mind to start functioning again. All I can hope is Lulu hasn't seen this photo. And why would she? She's not the sort of woman who checks the social pages.

Fuck. Why wouldn't she?

Right below the incriminating photo of Eleanor and me is the piece about her exhibition, with a beautiful photo of her in front of one of her paintings. She's stunning, but as I blow it up on the monitor, I can see the signs of strain on her face and the slight puffiness under her eyes.

Still no answer when I call, so I leave another voicemail. Mandy must hear me because she's back in my office door, hands on hips. "You'll be lucky if she ever speaks to you again. I certainly wouldn't."

It dawns on me that somehow Mandy also knows Lulu and I have been seeing one another. I guess I shouldn't be surprised. "How did you know?"

"Oh, please. I'm not blind. Or stupid. Unlike the other person in this conversation."

I stand up, grabbing my jacket from the chair behind me as the door opens. It's Lulu. Her face is like thunder, and she's lugging a parcel and an overnight bag. I don't need to ask what the parcel is. I know. It's my heart on a canvas.

"Lulu. I can explain—" I choke out.

"Can you? Is now the best time to explain about your girlfriend? Oh. No. Wait. Your fiancée. Did I get that right?" She fires the words like bullets.

"No. You didn't. She's not my fiancée." I start towards her, but she stops me with a look.

"Well, whatever she is, Nick, we're done, so she's welcome to you." Lulu dumps the painting against the wall, along with the bag.

"She's my ex-girlfriend. Emphasis on ex. We've discussed this."

"Yes. But what you left out of your carefully crafted narrative is she was here—in your office—only a few weeks ago. I recognise her from the photo. Why was that? And if she was such an ex, why not tell me?" There's venom in her voice I've never heard before.

"Because it didn't matter. She was here returning some books I'd loaned her. It didn't occur to me to mention it because it wasn't important." I can feel my hands clenching and unclenching, almost as though I'm trying to hold on to her by will alone.

"How very convenient. Even though I asked about her, she slipped your mind."

"Yes. Because I never gave her a second thought. We broke up before you and I started ..." I trail off, knowing what I want to label us, but unable to get the words out in the face of her anger. Now is not the time to tell her how I feel. I don't want to say those words for the first time in anger or frustration.

"Started fucking?" For the first time, the word sounds obscene on her lips. "Because that's all this was, Nick. A casual, no-strings arrangement. We said so only a few weeks ago. When I asked you if there was anything going on. Which you never fully denied."

Her words hit me like that wrecking ball I'm becoming familiar with, but this time, not in a good way. Her use of the past tense hasn't escaped me, but I'm starting to get angry now too. "Yes. That's exactly what we both said, isn't it? And wasn't it you who tried to end it a few weeks ago? So why are you getting so worked up?" I know the words are a mistake as soon as they leave my lips, but my anger and fear have taken the wheel.

"Because you lied. You lied. How am I supposed to believe anything you said? And now I'm kicking myself. I should have ended it then. Because regardless of what *we* were, what *I* am not is a liar or a cheat." She's heading for the door, and I'm frozen in place.

"Neither am I."

"All evidence to the contrary. But at least it all makes sense now. If you're going to be a successful politician, you need the right kind of wife. One, I'm guessing, with the right pedigree. And the right look. Which is evidently not me. So now seems like as good a time as any to put an end to it. Goodbye, Nick." Lulu snaps the door sharply shut behind her, leaving me breathing in her wildflower scent for what might be the last time.

CHAPTER TWENTY- EIGHT

Lulu

It's been thirty-six hours since I woke up in Sydney. Not much less since I broke it off with Nick. I tried to sleep on the plane, but all I did was cry with my eyes closed. My face must look even worse than I think, because Dad takes one look at me and bursts into tears of his own. And there we are, in the middle of Inverness Airport, both of us crying like babies.

"Let's get you home, hen." Dad hefts my carry-on bag and takes the handle of my suitcase, leaving me to struggle into my coat before braving the sleety rain falling outside. Bless him, he doesn't ask a single question on the long drive home, just keeps up a quiet commentary on the state of the roads, the weather and the prospects for the farm and the new distillery. His soft burring voice and the rumble of the car lull me into a half-sleep and before I know it, we're pulling up in front of the house Dad now calls home. It's too cold and miserable to stand outside admiring the ancient stonework—Scotland in November is not a place to be outdoors with my thin Australian blood.

Dad takes me and my bags upstairs and runs a deep bath for me.

"You'll be exhausted, *m'eudail*. You hop in the bath, then into bed with you. We'll talk when you've rested."

By the time I drag my sorry arse out of the bath, there's a steaming hot cup of tea and a scone sitting on the bedside. All I've eaten since I left Sydney is a dry bread roll—who wants to be hurling in a plane toilet?—and I inhale both before falling into bed.

It's well and truly dark by the time I wake up, but then again, it's winter in the Highlands—it's dark most of the day. I feel marginally better than when I arrived. Now it feels like I've been run over by a herd of sheep—not cattle.

Dad is in the parlour with one of the farming magazines he's taken to reading since inheriting this pile from my grandfather a couple of years ago. The creaking of the ancient stair treads has given him advanced warning, and he shifts over on the worn old sofa to make room for me.

"Feeling more yourself now?"

"Yes, a little. Thanks, Da. Thank you for picking me up and not quizzing me, and letting me sleep. Thank you for being you." I snuggle into his side, my head on his shoulder, breathing in his familiar smell.

"You've nothing to thank me for, hen. I'm your da. Simple as that. Are ye ready to talk about it yet?"

"No. Not even a little bit. But I will." He takes my hand with a gentle squeeze and waits.

I clear my throat nervously. "Well, Da, you're going to be a grandad."

"Och, what wonderful news." He kisses my forehead without a moment's hesitation. "Not what I was expecting to hear, but a wonderful blessing nonetheless." He waits for me to continue, and when I don't, he steps in. "But I'm sensing you're not entirely sure how you feel. Would I be right?"

"Yes. And no. I don't know." I can feel the unshed tears building and will them away. "It's complicated."

"Of course it is. Why else would you be here in such a lather? Start at the beginning, then."

And so the whole sorry story comes out. By the time I'm finished, I'm crying and so is Da.

"Well, *mo ghradh*, however they come aboot, babies are a blessing, and this one will be loved, as it should be. But tell me, are ye sure ye can't work things out with your man? It sounds to me like perhaps you ran off without so much as a by-your-leave."

"What's to work out, Dad? He lied to me. We always said it was no-strings. The last thing I want is a relationship. And now ..." I don't even know how to finish my sentence.

"I see. So did you run off because ye saw the photo, because it seems he lied to ye, or because ye gave yourself a fright with your feelings?" he says with a sad smile.

I hate that maybe he's right.

"Because ..." Ugh. Dad and Rosanna are singing from the same hymn sheet. That's pretty much what she said as she dropped me at the airport. Only not as politely. She might have included references to heads and arses, convenient excuses and cowards. "All of them maybe."

He says nothing but raises an eyebrow. Which reminds me of Nick. So, the tears start again.

"I just need a little time to process, Da."

"Aye, I can see that. Well, you take some time. But you need to be honest with yourself, hen. And don't take too long. You do have to tell him about the bairn, and the sooner the better, regardless of what you feel."

"Yes, I know. But not right now. Right now, I just want to ... well, I don't know what I want. Other than to not feel like this."

"I have every faith you'll make the right decisions, my darling. And what better place than here in the fresh air with people who love you to help settle your mind?"

"Yes, that's what I need. Some good clean air and a bit of time to work out what to do."

I'm starting to feel much more like myself within a few days. I'm glad I turned my phone off when I left Sydney. I'm not ready to speak to Nick. I'm not ready to hear excuses. Or maybe worse, a deafening silence. And right now, I don't know what to believe. Dad gets me a new one from the village, and the only people I give the number to are Rosanna and Sebastian, and they've been threatened with death if they pass it on.

I spend a lot of time walking the fields, despite the cold. Even the nausea is more bearable, usually only hitting first thing in the morning. Morag, Dad's housekeeper, works out pretty quickly what makes me sick and what settles my stomach.

But the nights are hard. An electric blanket is no substitute for the warmth of Nick's body, and crying myself to sleep has become a sad ritual.

The exhibit at the gallery finishes with every piece sold, and I'm able to Skype Sebastian and a couple of potential clients to discuss commissions. Dad is happy for me to use his supplies, but he works with watercolour, so I hit the internet and then do a daytrip to Inverness to stock up on what I'll need. Dad has converted a room at the top of the old tower into a studio. The light is great, at least when the sun is out, and it's plenty big enough for us both to work in there. It reminds me of when I was small and we'd stand side by side, me with my tiny little easel, painting for hours. It strikes me that in not too many years, this might be my baby and me, and my hand goes to my ever so slightly rounded belly.

By the time I've been in Scotland for a couple of weeks, Dad and I have settled into a soothing routine. I have no idea if Nick is still trying to contact me as I haven't turned my old phone on since I got the new one. Dad hasn't once asked what I plan to do or if I've spoken to Nick, but I know he sees my puffy eyes in the mornings for what they are.

"I was wondering if you had given any consideration to seeing a doctor, hen." Dad drops casually into the silence while we're painting early one afternoon. Normally Dad would be out on the farm at this time, but the rain has turned sleety today, so he has holed himself up with me.

"Oh. Um. No. Not yet. But I guess I should. Is there someone in the village?"

"I asked the GP—he's happy to take you on, but there's no' an obstetrician. You'd have to go further afield for that. Although there is a midwife. Morag's sister, Lydia. Would you like her to make you an appointment?"

This is making it all too real. But I know it can't be avoided.

"That's okay, Da. I'll talk to her."

The village GP is old enough to be my grandfather, but kind and knowledgeable. He books an appointment for an ultrasound in Inverness and introduces me to Lydia. My belly is already starting to round out and both of them cluck sceptically when I tell them how pregnant I think I am.

"Och, hen. Are ye sure?" Lydia chuckles when I nod. "Perhaps it's twins. You've quite a belly on you for ten weeks."

I burst into tears when Da asks me how it went. I'm surprised I'm not dehydrated with all the leaking I'm doing.

"Don't fret, hen. Your mother was the same. Why, even before she knew she was pregnant with you, her belly was popping." His eyes go glassy as he says this. It's the first time Dad has mentioned Mum in years. I want to ask him about her, but the last thing I want to do is upset him any more than coming home pregnant already has. Although, to be fair, he seems more excited than upset.

Rosanna laughs long and loud when I tell her. "That'll teach you for being so damn irresistible. He got you pregnant twice."

"It's not funny, Ro. It's hard enough to imagine taking care of one baby all on my own, never mind two. And we don't know if it's twins—we have to wait for the ultrasound."

"I'm sorry." She sounds anything but. "In the meantime, have you come to your senses and decided to talk to Nick yet?"

"No, not yet. I'm still too angry. And confused." I break off in frustration. "This is not all about him."

"Oh, believe me, I know. I wish I could say this is not like you, but we both know it's exactly like you."

"What's that supposed to mean? I should ignore him lying to me?"

"Oh, please," Rosanna says with a three-exclamation-point sigh. "You can try fooling yourself all you like, but you're not fooling me. This has nothing to do with the photo or the career plans he didn't tell you about, other than as a convenient excuse. This is you cutting and running because someone got too close."

"It's not." But even I can hear there's no conviction in my voice. "Well, not entirely."

"Three words for you. Grant. Neil. David." I can picture Ro counting off on her fingers. "I could go on."

"I'm trying to protect myself, Rosanna. And my baby."

If you could hear an eye roll, hers would be deafening.

"This is not going away, you know."

I know she's right. But this is scary stuff. I've gone from being able to walk away from relationships unscathed to a quivering wreck. A quivering wreck with a baby on board.

"I just need a little time to get my head together." She can hear the tears building in my voice and backs off.

"Okay, okay. I won't mention him again. So, how is my godchild doing? Still making you sick?"

"Most mornings, yes. But at least now it's not all day—only first thing in the morning. Once I barf, I'm usually good for the day."

"Delightful. Precisely what I wanted to hear as I'm eating lunch."

"How are you and Marco?" I desperately need to talk about something other than me and my problems.

"Ugh. Same, same. Next."

"Maybe you should take a break—come over and visit me? Getting away might give you some perspective."

"Scotland in winter? No thanks. Besides, I want to save my holidays and come over when the baby is born, in case." She leaves the idea I might not return to Australia hanging.

"I miss you so much, Ro. So much. But I can't be in Sydney right now. And Dad is so excited to be a grandfather. I think it would break his heart if I left."

"He could always come to Australia for the birth."

"It's not so easy for him. He has a lot of responsibility now. He's in the process of setting up a new distillery, so he's incredibly busy."

"Of course. I forget what his life is like since your grandfather died. And you have to do what works for you. I miss you, that's all."

A couple of tears escape. "I love you, Ro."

"Love you too. Think about what I said. Please. You deserve to be happy. And your baby deserves a daddy."

"I'll think about it." But I can't let myself dream about how it would be sharing this with Nick. So I push those thoughts right to the back of my mind. It's the only way I can get through the days.

CHAPTER TWENTY-NINE

NICK

The days after Lulu storms out of my office are a blur. I spend the weekend alternately raging and moping around my apartment. It feels like I work through the five stages of grief in twenty-four hours. Except for acceptance. That's never going to happen. Her phone is either out of range or turned off, and none of the texts or emails I've sent have been opened. I go to her apartment and when she doesn't answer, I let myself in to find most of her clothes missing. Mine, I discovered, were in the overnight bag she'd left on my office floor.

My mother has called a couple of times, but hell will freeze over before I answer a call from her. No doubt she'll spout some crap about how she did it for my own good and I'll thank her one day. I'm furious with my mother for setting this situation up. I'm furious with Eleanor for colluding with her. But most of all, I'm furious with myself for not telling Lulu how I feel.

I've spent my whole life avoiding getting involved. I've always told myself I didn't have time for a proper relationship, but lately, I've realised that wasn't the reason at all. It's far more complicated than that. Part of me didn't believe I deserved love, because I sure as hell never got any as a kid. But I also never wanted to end up like my parents. Ironically, it hasn't escaped my notice my few-and-far-between girlfriends all have been little more than a convenience for both of us. Someone to escort to corporate functions, making our—I don't want to call them relationships—carbon copies of my parents. Subconsciously, I was choosing partners I was in no danger of getting attached to. Probably because a large part of me didn't want to risk getting hurt. But Lulu crept under my guard.

No, that's not right. She simply breezed through it like it didn't exist. Lulu actually sees *me*. Not the wealthy lawyer, not the potential politician, not the ticket to a cushy or powerful or well-connected life. Me. And now here I am—more than hurt. Destroyed.

On Monday I'm late to the office. Late for me, at least.

Mandy is already at her desk as I pass. "My office. Now." She leaps out of the chair, grabbing her iPad on the way in.

"Oh, my god. Are you alright?" I can see the worry on her face. I must look worse than I realised, but I ignore her concern. There is only one thing that's important right now. Finding Lulu. If she doesn't want me, I'll accept her decision. Well, not gracefully, and not without a fight. But I will accept it. Except I have to find her first. Explain what happened.

To my horror, I feel heat behind my eyes.

"Lulu has disappeared." I don't know how else to start.

"Disappeared? What do you mean, disappeared?"

"She hasn't been home. Most of her clothes are missing. She hasn't answered her phone. Or text. Or email." That's what I mean, disappeared.

"So, it was serious, then?" I know she means our relationship, not the disappeared part.

"Yes. It was. For me it was. For her too, I think. And then, the photo happened."

"What were you thinking then? Taking The Ice Princess to the dinner?" Mandy has picked up Claire's nickname for Eleanor. There's no love lost there.

"I didn't. Take her, I mean. My mother organised for her to be there. The photo and the announcement ..." I scrub my hands over my face and realise from the feel of the scruff that I haven't shaved since Friday. "She just jumped in there. I wasn't holding her hand. I was pushing it off my arm and telling her to back off."

"Oh, because it looks ..."

"I know how it looks. But it wasn't like that. And now Lulu has seen it. I can't blame her for breaking it off. Except now she's gone and disappeared. And I need to find her."

Mandy is beginning to look as mournful as I feel.

"Maybe she needs a little time to calm down?"

"No. No time. Did you not hear me? She took most of her clothes. And there's that." I gesture towards the painting—I can't even look at it—still leaning fully wrapped against the wall. "She's not coming back." My throat closes over. I feel panic starting to build and struggle to contain it.

Mandy jumps in her chair at my tone. "So, you want me to help?" I can only nod. "Okay—well, have you asked her friends?"

"I don't know them. Her best friend is Rosanna. I think she's a costume designer, but I'm not sure where. That's all I know. The only person I've met is the owner of the gallery hosting her exhibition. His name is Sebastian Black. I think the gallery is called The Black Gallery."

"Right. Well, it's a start, at least. Do you want me to contact them, or do you want to do it?" She's all efficiency now she has a task.

"No, if you could just find their numbers, I'll call them."

"Sebastian Black will be easy." She's already tapping at her iPad. "But it might take a bit of work to track down Rosanna the costume designer."

"If you need to call Steve Piper, get him onto it. Oh, and her father lives in Scotland. Maybe get him to see if he can find him. They're close. He's bound to know where she is." It doesn't even occur to me that asking a private investigator to track down Lulu might be going over the top until I notice Mandy's wide-eyed stare and gaping mouth. "Just do it. Please. Whatever it takes."

She turns when she gets to the door and gives me a look of such compassion I nearly break. "We'll find her, Nick. One way or another."

I can only nod in response, the lump in my throat too big to swallow.

I can't believe I have so little knowledge of Lulu's life, yet I feel as though I know her right down to her soul. I know her dad lives in Scotland, but she never mentioned her mother. There was a picture of a beautiful woman with a toddler on her bedside table. Based on looks alone, I'm sure it's her with her mother, but we silently agreed not to get deeper into each other's lives. Damn 'not-a-relationship' conversation. How I regret it now.

We existed in a bubble, and nobody else was given entry. I don't know what Lulu's motivation was, but for my part, it quickly went from self-preservation to protecting a relationship that had become so important to me. As it played out, my instinct was spot on. If only I'd been able to protect us a little bit longer.

Calling Sebastian doesn't work. I've spent two days calling the gallery and, like my messages to Lulu, my calls to Sebastian Black go unanswered. I'm beyond frustrated. It doesn't help that I'm snowed under with work. But at least work helps to take my mind off Lulu. At the moment, work is the only thing keeping me from completely losing my mind.

On Wednesday afternoon, I finally carve out a free hour to call in at The Black Gallery. Sebastian recognises me straight away and is friendly to the point of obsequious.

"Oh, no. I have no idea where you could contact her. Other than her email, of course. Her exhibition was *such* a success. She has several commissions. I expect she's working on those. She's the big thing right now. I wish I could clone her to keep up with the demand."

"So, you're telling me you have no idea of her whereabouts?"

"None whatsoever. I'm sorry." He shrugs his shoulders, throwing his hands out palms up, looking not the least bit sorry. "But if I hear from her, I'll be sure to let her know you called in and asked after her."

I've been a lawyer for a long time. I know when I'm being lied to. There is no way a man with his reputation in the art world—yes, I Googled him and he's well known as a sharp operator—doesn't know where his latest sensation is. But short of stringing him up by his skinny ankles, there's nothing more I can do. Other than hope he tells Lulu I'm looking for her.

Steve Piper is interstate on a job for another client, so it's two weeks before he's able to start searching for Lulu's father. In the meantime, Mandy is narrowing down the search for Rosanna. Needles in haystacks. I have no idea what Rosanna's surname is. Thank God her name isn't Jenny or Kathy—how many Rosannas can there be? And I have no idea what Lulu's father's first name is. She always called him Dad. Or Da. I'm assuming his surname is MacLeod. I google it. There are hundreds of thousands of MacLeods in Scotland. All I know is he lives on a farm.

"Steve said it may take a while. There are lots of ..." Mandy starts once she's briefed him.

"I know how many MacLeods there are in Scotland." My temper is fraying. It's now been three weeks. Still no word from Lulu, and I'm no closer to finding her.

I do nothing but work, sleep and chase the ghost of Lulu.

Mum calls every few days, and I let it go to voicemail. I can't even bring myself to listen to her messages. Her interfering might have cost me the best thing I have ever had in my life. I'll be damned if I let her get away with it.

Will catches me at the lifts one evening as we leave work.

"Are you okay, Nick? You don't look too good."

I sigh. I seem to be doing a lot of that these days. "Yeah. All good. Crazy busy."

"So I hear. That merger is huge. But it's nearly finalised, I understand?"

"Yes, final documents will be signed by the end of next week, with any luck."

And what will I do with myself then? It's a matter of days until Christmas, then the entire country shuts down for a good month. Without the crippling workload to keep me sane, I don't know what I'll do.

"Are you going away for Christmas?" Will is cheerfully oblivious to my angst. It would seem Harry hasn't filled him in on the situation with Lulu, although he was there to witness the debacle at the partners' dinner.

"No." And then it occurs to me. "Wait. No. Yes. Yes, I am going away."

I'm going to Scotland. I don't know how I didn't realise it earlier. She's in Scotland with her dad. I have no idea where exactly, but if I'm in the same hemisphere, the same time zone, on the same piece of land, when we do finally track her down, I'll be able to get to her quickly. At last, I have a plan.

CHAPTER THIRTY

LULU

D ad comes with me to my ultrasound appointment in Inverness. We head over early to do a bit of Christmas shopping before the appointment. Christmas is a little over a week away. Dad isn't particularly subtle and takes off on his own for a couple of hours, leaving me to pick a present out for him. I wander past a baby shop and stop to look at the display in the window. A winter wonderland of baby equipment. There are a few couples inside choosing prams and cots, and it makes me sad—and guilty—I'm standing here on my own.

Dad and I meet up for lunch, then head to the clinic. I'm so grateful for his presence, but I'm also sad it isn't Nick holding my hand and telling me not to worry. I'm fidgeting in my chair in the waiting room. Drinking a litre of water and holding it in while you have a baby starting to take up room in your belly is a challenge. My bladder is the size of a pea at the best of times. But Dad sits patiently, flicking through the ancient magazines.

At last, when I feel like I might burst, it's my turn and Dad holds my hand as the technician squirts gel on my little bump. It's only a second or two and we hear a whooshing thump, thump. A surprisingly fast thump, thump.

"Hear that? It's the baby's heartbeat. You can see it here." The technician points to the screen where there's a little blinking sepia dot.

"It sounds awfully fast. Is that normal?" My own heart starts to race as I worry there's something wrong.

"Aye. Perfectly normal. A baby's heart beats much faster than ours." She's pressing hard and moving the wand around. An image starts to take shape. At first, all I see is a cashew with arms and legs, but as she clicks on the keyboard and adjusts the wand on my belly, I begin to see little dots that might be fingers, and a nose.

"Oh, hen, look. A beautiful little bairn." Tears are leaking from Dad's eyes.

A wave of love so physical it leaves me speechless rolls over me. Suddenly, this is all real. The tiny life that has derailed my own is not just an idea anymore. And I'm more in love than I could ever have imagined. Fear of getting too close, of leaving myself open to hurt, isn't even a consideration.

"Well, based on these measurements, you are eleven weeks and five days along, Lulu, which is what you estimated. You're certainly big for those dates, but everyone's different. I canna see anything out of the ordinary. Baby looks perfect." Perfect. The one word I needed to hear.

I do the maths in my head as the technician wipes the gel off my belly. Yep. As I suspected, I got pregnant on the first night with Nick. Rosanna is going to laugh her head off.

It's not twins, but now, seeing the little life growing inside me, twins don't seem the worst thing in the world like they did yesterday. More of this overwhelming feeling of love could never be a bad thing.

But I do have one worry.

"Are you sure the baby is perfect? Because I didn't know I was pregnant. And I did have a few glasses of wine before I knew." Another thing I've been torturing myself about. At least my aversion to wine kicked in pretty early, so maybe it'll be okay.

The technician takes another, closer look at the images she recorded while she asks how much and how often I had drunk.

"Well, it's not ideal, but I don't see any cause for concern at this stage. We'll keep an eye on things though, and let you know."

That puts my mind somewhat at ease. All I want is a healthy baby.

Dad and I are both quiet on the way home, me clutching the printouts the technician gave us, unable to look away from the image of the tiny body. She has emailed me a video of the ultrasound, but the internet being what it is in the Highlands, I'll have to wait until we get home to watch it.

It's after seven before we get home, and Morag has left us a big pot of chicken and leek soup for dinner, along with a loaf of crusty bread she baked this morning. Dad heats the soup while I slice the bread, and we eat at the kitchen table, loving the warmth of the Aga and the delicious smells of the kitchen.

"That ultrasound was amazing, wasn't it?" Dad sops up the last dribbles of his soup with a chunk of bread. "When your mum was pregnant with you, they weren't nearly as detailed. It all just looked like a grey blur, but now. Now you can see everything." He pulls the printed shot towards him, tracing the shape of the head with a shaking finger.

This is my opportunity. I don't know whether it's the exhaustion, the emotion, or the comfort of a warm stove and full belly, but the words seem to fall out of my mouth. "Was I planned, Da? Was Mum excited to be having me?"

"Planned? Well, no, not planned as such. But excited? Oh, hen. She was beside herself. We both were." He doesn't look up from the photo.

"My memories of her are so patchy. Sometimes more like feelings than memories. And you never talk about her."

Dad looks up from the ultrasound, eyes watery, sad, and a little reddened. "I'm sorry. So sorry, hen. I should have kept her memory alive for you. But I couldn't ..." His voice breaks.

"It's okay Da."

"No, no, it isn't. I lost the love of my life, and I still grieve. But you lost your mother, and I should've been able to put my pain aside for you."

"Could you ... do you think you could talk about her now?" I whisper, scared to push too hard, but desperate to know—anything. Anything at all.

It takes Dad a moment to answer. "Of course. Yes. What would you like to know?"

I mirror my thoughts of a moment ago. "Anything. Everything."

His eyes are full of pain as he nods. "Well, where to start? Of course, she was incredibly beautiful. You look so much like her. You have her colouring—from her Danish family, I expect, although you got my mad curly hair." He chuckles and rubs a hand over my head. "We had both travelled to Australia for an adventure. It was the thing to do in those days. Finish university and backpack around Australia, picking fruit and working in bars. Although your mother wasn't picking fruit. She was modelling. I was working in a bar in Bondi, and she came in one night with a group of friends. I took one look at her, and that was it. I just knew, and she always said the same, despite my wild red hair."

He runs his hand through his still thick thatch of fiery hair, softened now by a little silver, but only a little.

"We were inseparable from the start. We fell in love with each other and with Australia. Neither of us had any plans to go home. Then we discovered we were pregnant. It wasn't planned. We weren't the planning types. But we were overjoyed. Of course, your grandfather was apoplectic. I was supposed to come home and help rebuild the family heritage, take up my rightful place—especially later, after your Uncle Robbie died. But I was so happy in Australia with your mum and then with you." Dad reaches over and squeezes my hand, holding it in both of his big, work-roughened, paint-stained ones.

"We were so blissfully happy, hen. Vibeke loved you with everything she was. She was so proud of every little thing you did. We both were. It was like living in a little bubble of sunshine. For years. Until it wasn't." His face clouds and he's silent for a long time.

"What happened? When she got sick?" I ask.

"At first, well, at first we both believed, assumed, I guess, she would get better. The survival rate for breast cancer is so good. Was even then. But she had what they call triple negative cancer, which is more aggressive. We did everything. Traditional treatment, natural therapies. We even went to a shaman." His voice breaks, along with the tears he's been holding in. "But nothing worked. Thirteen months and six days after she was diagnosed, she was gone."

I can feel the tears on my cheeks, and I turn my hand in his and squeeze back.

"Afterwards ... I couldn't bear to think about her. So, I shut her up in a box and tried to get on with life. But I was broken, and what I got on with wasn't life; it was existence, and it wasn't fair to you. I can see that now. And I will regret it until my dying breath. As I'll regret the loss of her."

"Do you regret meeting her? Having me?" I can see in his face and hear in his voice the pain it's causing him to remember. But he doesn't hesitate.

"No. Not even for a second. I wouldn't trade those years with Vibeke for anything in the world. Because I was *living,* hen. That was when I was most alive. No amount of pain or regret will ever eclipse it. Never shy away from love, Lulu. Nothing else in this world matters." The passion and pain in his voice crack something open inside of me. It's small, but it's there.

I lie awake in bed most of the night, thinking over Dad's advice. I've spent my whole life avoiding letting anyone get too close because I lived through what it did to my father to lose my mother. And now I've gone from not wanting to be in a relationship at all to the most committed one of all. Motherhood. Maybe I've been looking at this all wrong. Maybe letting someone in isn't dangerous. Maybe keeping them out is. Because you're cheating yourself of those little bubbles of sunshine that make life worthwhile. And despite all my efforts to avoid hurt, I've hurt myself the most by refusing to let Nick in.

Rosanna is right. I love Nick and I used the photo as a convenient excuse to run. I should have at least given him a chance to explain, because, right up till the end, he never once gave me a reason to suspect he was anything but honest. Now I have to at least hear him out. For all of us.

Nick would be well within his rights to be furious with me. And there's always the possibility he won't want a baby. We never talked about children because we deluded ourselves into believing it was all no-strings. I think about the way I'd catch Nick looking at me sometimes, with such warmth it turned his eyes to molten silver. The way he took care of me when I was stressed, sending me food and making me tea. The flowers he sent before the exhibit. If he was not interested in a relationship, what was all that about?

I was angry because I thought he lied. About Eleanor and his plans for the future. But I did too. About my feelings. And that's not fair. To Nick, or me, or our baby.

I sit up and fish my old phone out of the bedside drawer, crossing my fingers as I turn it on. The battery is completely dead, so I swap it on the charger with my new phone and wait for a flicker of life.

As the screen lights up, a melody of notifications bounces into the room. My heart is thundering. As recently as two days ago, Nick was still messaging and emailing. I scroll through them without opening any, checking dates. Not a day has gone past that he hasn't sent something. My heart stops. Until two days ago. There's been nothing for two days. Has he finally given up? Decided I'm not worth the trouble? Gone back to Eleanor? No. No, no, nope. That can't be. I love him. And I think he loves me. No. I *know* he loves me. And I'm having his baby. A baby he knows nothing about. Crap. Crap, crap, crappity crap. Time to sort this mess out.

CHAPTER THIRTY-ONE

NICK

The morning after my chat with Will, I have Mandy booking a one-way flight to Glasgow, and then I bury myself in getting this merger over the line. I can work twenty-six hours a day if it gets me to Scotland faster. And that's what I do.

The final paperwork for the merger is eventually signed, and the client insists on a celebratory dinner. Tomorrow, all the rumours swirling in the media concerning this deal will be confirmed, but I'll be on a plane to Scotland. Dinner is a raucous and boozy affair, but I stick to water. I have work to do when I land and can't afford to waste time on hangovers.

My flight leaves in the early evening, and I head home at lunchtime to pack after wrapping up a few loose ends. I have no idea how long this will take. I've told Harry I don't know when I'll be back, and the couple of small matters I had scheduled for when we return from our summer break have been fobbed off on one of my associates. And despite the fact I'm leaving him short a partner, he's completely on board with me chasing what I want. What I need. As long as I promise to keep him in the loop, because the drama of the last couple of months has been, according to him, better than Netflix.

I take Lulu's painting home with me. I haven't been able to open it, but I don't want to leave it in the office. It might be all I ever have left of her, and I need to keep it safe. As I prop it against the wall in my bedroom, I give in to the need to see it again and rip the brown paper off. The emotion—the joy, the passion, the intensity—jumps off the canvas, galvanising my decision to go to Scotland.

I'm putting the last of my clothes into my suitcase when the doorbell rings.

Claire is shouting, "Let me in," before I can even speak.

"Claire. What are you doing here?" It's a measure of how distressed I am that I have forgotten to tell Claire I'm going to Scotland. I'm ashamed to say I've been avoiding her too.

"I called the office and Mandy told me you're flying out to Scotland this evening. I've been trying to call you for weeks. What's going on? Mum is beside herself." I buzz her in and hug her as she bustles through the door in a flurry of overwrought energy.

"I'm sorry I didn't let you know. I'm afraid I'm a bit of a mess." Claire knows me well, and I'm sure she can tell at a glance I'm not myself.

"What happened? Mum isn't saying anything, except that you're a selfish, ungrateful, foolish man. But I saw the photo of you and The Ice Princess in the paper. And then Will told me what happened at the partners' dinner. I can't believe it. What did Lulu say?" Her words tumble over each other as she follows me into the bedroom.

I check my watch and realise we have time for a quick chat before I have to head to the airport. She sits on the bed as I zip up my suitcase and check my passport while I fill her in on what happened at the Partners' Dinner and everything since. She's unimpressed.

"Christ, our mother is a menace. And so now you're going to Scotland to find Lulu? Are you sure she's there? And what are you going to do about Mum?"

"No, I'm not sure of anything. As for Mum, I was hoping by now she might have got the message I want nothing to do with her. That stunt she pulled might well have ruined things with Lulu, maybe irreparably. So, I'm done."

"About time. I take it you didn't tell her who it was you were seeing?"

"No, actually. I kept it to myself so Mum wouldn't have the opportunity to chase her off the way she did whenever I made a friend at school or university she didn't like. Which happened anyway. Now, thanks to her interference, I don't know if I'll be able to salvage things." The very idea makes me sick to my stomach.

"You love Lulu though, yes?"

"Yes, I'm in love with her, and I think perhaps she's in love with me. But then she was hit in the face with a photo of me in the paper that looked like I was holding hands with another woman and an engagement announcement. No prizes for guessing who the 'source close to the couple' is. What on earth was she to think?"

"I can't say I blame her for breaking it off with you. But once you explain everything, I'm sure she'll understand." Claire gives me a reassuring hug. That's when she spots the painting leaning against the wall, still surrounded by the brown paper I ripped off earlier. She gets up and goes over for a better look.

"Did Lulu paint this?" At my nod, she whistles. "Wow. It's incredible. So intense. You know Mum has some of her father's work in the hallway upstairs at home, don't you?"

It takes me a minute to register what she's said. Finally, I connect some of the dots. Mum is an avid art collector. If she knows of Lulu's father, perhaps she would know where to find him. I hear myself actually growl. It's beyond frustrating I can't ask her because that information could lead me to Lulu so much faster.

"I don't suppose you have any idea what his name is or where he lives, do you?"

"No, I don't. But I'd bet Mum does. You know how she fangirls over her favourite artists."

"Right. But there's no way I want to speak to Mum. So how do I get that information out of her without tipping her off as to who I'm involved with? I don't want to risk any more interference from Meddling Mary."

Claire's expression takes on an evil gleam I'm familiar with from our childhood. "Hmm. Well, leave this to me. I'll squeeze it out of her without her even realising it."

I wrap my arms around my sister, grateful beyond words.

"Claire. I love you. You're a lifesaver. But right now, I have to go. I have a flight to catch."

"You do indeed." She swings her keys in the air. "Would you like a lift to the airport?"

As I'm disembarking in Glasgow, I get a message from Claire. I don't know what she said or how she did it, but she's pretty confident Duncan MacLeod lives in the Highlands, somewhere near Inverness, and Meddling Mary is none the wiser as to where I've gone. I shoot a message to Mandy with the new information so she can pass it on to Steve.

I decide to take a chance and get straight on a connecting flight to Inverness. By the time I exit the airport, with no real plan other than to find Lulu, I'm exhausted, rumpled and smell like airline food. Business class may give you more legroom, but nothing can save you on the long haul from Australia. I book into a hotel, order room service, take a long shower and fall face first on the enormous bed.

I'd like to say the sun is shining and the birds are chirping when I wake, but this is Scotland. The clouds have gathered, and a freezing rain is falling. Still, I'm a man on a mission and like the American postman and Santa, neither rain nor snow nor heat nor gloom are going to stop me.

Powering up my laptop, I google art galleries in Inverness. There are a quite a few, but only eight look likely to house the type of work Duncan MacLeod creates. I fire off an email to Mandy to let her know my plans, slide into my coat, stuff my hat, gloves and scarf into my pocket and head out.

All the galleries are familiar with Duncan MacLeod. Some even have his work on display. It's hauntingly beautiful, although not at all like Lulu's work. None of them will give up his address or even a hint of where he might live. It's three o'clock and almost dark already by the time I start to make my way back to the hotel. Down but not out.

Standing at a crossing, waiting for the lights to change, I find myself face to face with a jewellery shop window. It occurs to me to wonder what I'm going to say to Lulu when—not if, *when*—I find her. Of their own volition, my feet take me into the welcome warmth of the little shop.

"Gude afterrrnoooon." The tiny man behind the counter greets me with almost unintelligible English, putting far more letters into the words than they require. "How caan I help yeee today?"

"I need a ring," I blurt. This blurting is becoming a habit, and not a good one.

"A ring, yee say?" he asks, rolling the r for what seems like a full minute.

"Yes. A ring. An engagement ring." I need to show Lulu I am serious about a relationship with her. Even though I have no real idea what her feelings on the matter are, I need to put myself out there. If she says no, well, I'll work out my next move then. But as Will would say, go hard or go home.

The little man looks me up and down, then holding up a finger to indicate I should wait, disappears behind a curtained doorway, returning moments later with a black velvet tray glittering with stars.

"This is our special selection. I don't keep them on display because they're no' for the faint of heart. But you look like this ring is serious business, so here we are." He reverently slides the tray onto the glass counter in front of me. There are only a dozen or so rings, all of them enormous. I scan them quickly, and right away, I know the ring for her. It's not the biggest, but it is by far the most beautiful. Heavy and worked in white and yellow gold, it has an almost medieval feel. A dark oval sapphire sits in the centre, with a diamond and a ruby on either side. The jeweller sees where my gaze has stopped.

"I see ye have excellent taste, lad. That there is an Australian sapphire. Best in the world they are. Diamonds there beside, and a little cabochon ruby to finish it off. Of course, should it no' fit, we'll be happy to resize it at no charge."

Moments later, I walk out of the shop with a ring I hope to have on Lulu's finger within days.

As I cross the hotel lobby, my phone chimes with a message from Mandy:

We've found him.

And attached is a Google Maps link. I reverse my steps and head to the reception desk.

"I'd like to book a rental car for tomorrow, please."

"Certainly. For how long, sir?"

"Honestly? I have no idea. I'm hoping for the rest of my life."

The girl behind the counter smiles. "I see. Well, how about we start with a week?"

"Yes. That would be fine. By the way, I'll be checking out in the morning."

CHAPTER THIRTY-TWO

LULU

The morning after my talk with Dad, I feel a nervous energy I've been missing since I left Sydney. There's an anticipation in the air I can't quite put my finger on, except to say my mindset around a lot of things has shifted.

Dad is already out on the farm by the time I get to the kitchen for breakfast after my regular morning barf. But Morag is there, peeling vegetables for tonight's dinner.

"How did your appointment go, hen?" she asks.

"Oh, Morag. It's incredible. The baby has little arms and legs, and even the start of fingers and toes, and ears and a nose." I point them out on the little photo we were given.

"I should hope so." She laughs. Then she turns serious, wiping her hands on a tea-towel and placing her hands on her generous hips. "But what it doesn't have, hen, is a father. I know it's not my place to say, but you're so precious to me and I want to see you happy. Don't you think it's time you let the father know what's going on? If not for you, for your wee bairn?"

I know I've been robbing Nick of some incredibly special milestones—like the first ultrasound—by not telling him. But all that stops as of now. I'm booking a ticket to Sydney to sort this mess out. One way or another.

I sigh and flop down onto a kitchen chair. "I know, Morag. I just needed some time. I know I need to tell him. But it's not an over-the-phone type of conversation."

"Well, no, you're quite right. It's no' ideal. But we are where we are, and no' telling him isna' right."

Morag makes me a big bowl of porridge and a strong cup of tea before I head out for my usual walk in the hills. The clouds are heavy and dark, but there's no rain, just an icy wind. I settle down on my favourite protected ledge at the top of the cliffs and look out at the dull grey water. Half a dozen seals are dozing on the rocks below, ignoring the sea birds scuttling around, picking tiny fish from the rock pools exposed by the low tide. The occasional bleating of a sheep breaks up the calls of the seabirds and the roar of the wind. Life here goes on as usual, with no consideration for the turmoil surging through my veins.

This is a beautiful place to raise a child. I didn't grow up here, but we did visit quite often, and walking the hills with my grandfather, listening to his stories of family history, are some of my most cherished memories. It would be a good life for my child, living here. And I know Da would be a brilliant grandfather.

But what I want is Nick. And he's in Sydney. In reality, until I tell Nick, and find out for sure what he wants, I can't make any decisions.

What I don't want is for Nick to feel trapped. I want him to want me, not feel obliged to take me on because of the baby. And I need him to understand I'm not there because of the baby but because I've finally figured out it's too late to run—I'm already all in. All the way. And I wouldn't run even if I could.

I head back to the house, working out the time difference as I go. It's evening in Sydney, and not too late, so I prop myself up on my bed and video call Rosanna.

"Hey, lovely," she chirps. I can see from the background she's in the workroom she has set up in her spare bedroom, surrounded by a colourful explosion of fabrics and trims.

"Hey, Ro. How are you?"

"Doing a little off-books work for myself," she cackles. She's not supposed to design for anyone else, but she can't seem to help herself, and the drag scene in Sydney would be the poorer for it if she did. "Move the phone down—let me look at your big fat pregnant belly."

I do as she asks. "Thanks. Like I'm not feeling fat enough as it is."

"Whoa. You're not kidding. You have an actual belly. Are you calling to tell me it's twins?"

"No, only one bun in this oven, as it turns out."

"Well, that's good. Is it normal to be so big at this stage? I imagined it would be weeks before you started to look like that."

"Apparently, I'm big for my dates. Da says Mum was the same with me."

"Well, it's only a belly—you don't look fat anywhere else. Wait. What? You talked to your dad about your mum?" Her eyes threaten to pop out of her head. Rosanna knows how unusual this is.

"Yep. We had a great talk. He brought her up, so I ran with it and asked. He really opened up."

"Aww. That must have been so tough for him. And for you. Tough but great. How do you feel?" I can see tears in her eyes, even though she's smiling from ear to ear.

"Well, it sucks it took an unplanned pregnancy to get there, but I'm glad we've finally knocked a hole in the wall. It'll take more work, but we're on the right track."

"Speaking of unplanned pregnancies, how are you feeling?"

"Still hurling every morning." I grimace at the memory.

"Yeah. No. I meant, how are you feeling about Nick? Have you made any decisions yet?"

"I have, actually. I need to come back to Sydney and face the music. It's just so complicated. I don't know where to start."

"At the risk of sounding trite—you could start by asking him for an honest explanation."

"I guess so. But it's not just him who has some explaining to do."

"Based on the size of your belly, maybe you won't have to explain much of anything."

I ignore her jab. "I don't want him to think I've only come back because I'm pregnant. I want him to know I'm there because of him. How I feel about him."

"Right. Well, unlike some people we could name, cough, cough, he might be prepared to take you at your word."

"Yes. Okay. I realise I didn't handle this particularly well. I was emotional. Irrational. Hormonal." I grouse, even though I realise these are nothing more than sad excuses for giving in to my fear.

"Particularly well? It's been a monumental, and totally unnecessary, clusterfuck. He turned up at work, you know."

"What? When?" I can't believe she didn't tell me this.

"About a week ago. He'd left a few messages, and when I didn't return his calls, he turned up unannounced, demanding to see me. I had to see him to get him to go away. I lied and told him I had no idea where you are. Which he didn't believe, by the way, despite my Oscar-worthy performance. So put your big girl panties on and work this shit out. It's not all about you anymore. And time's a wasting."

"I checked my phone. He stopped messaging two days ago. What if he's decided it's all too hard?"

"He's been messaging all this time? Can you hear yourself? If I was the one knocked up by a gorgeous, smart, successful man, what would you be saying to me?" She throws the fabric she's been fiddling with up in the air.

"I'd be telling you to ... I don't know."

"Oh, I think you do. You'd be telling me to get on a plane and tell him. What did all his messages say?"

"I don't know. I haven't read them or listened to the voicemails."

"Oh, for fuck's sake. I can't even stand it anymore. Get your head out of your arse and listen to them."

"What if he's angry with me?"

"Angry? Based on the way he looked when he came to the office, I'd say he's furious. And heartbroken. With a side order of guilt and remorse. And maybe that's not unreasonable. What *is* unreasonable is you continuing to stick your head in the sand and pretend this isn't happening. Because it is—one giant belly being exhibit A."

"It's not giant."

"Don't change the subject. The longer you leave it, the angrier he's going to get. And with good reason. Maybe he'll want you, maybe he won't. But either way, it's his decision to make. Not yours. And whichever way it goes, it's better than this limbo."

I sigh. "I know. You're right. But if this all goes to shit, I'm blaming you."

I laugh, feeling hopeful for the first time in weeks.

"Sure. You can blame me. But something tells me going to shit is not what this will do. Except maybe when you're in labour. I watched a doco on childbirth, and when you push–"

"Lalalalala." I interrupt, putting my fingers in my ears. "I don't want to hear it." And now we're both laughing. When we eventually stop, I wrap my hands across my not-giant belly. "Okay, Ro. I'll let you know the details once I've booked the ticket."

"Love you. Say hi to Duncan for me." She signs off with a kiss.

Over dinner, I fill Dad in on my plans.

"Well, *mo chridhe,* I'm glad you've made a decision at last. As much as I'll miss you, I think you're right in doing this face to face."

"Dad. You're supposed to tell me a short email—or a text message even—would be enough." We both laugh. "I'll book a ticket tonight. Open-ended, I guess. And then we'll see."

"You do what you have to do. For you and the bairn. But never forget, whatever happens, darling, you always have a home here with me." Somehow, Dad manages to look sad and happy at the same time. I guess for both of us, this is a bittersweet moment.

"I know, Da. I love you."

CHAPTER THIRTY-THREE

NICK

It's still dark as I put the strange address Mandy gave me into the satnav of my hire car. Thank the satnav gods, the car seems to understand and I head out of Inverness before the morning traffic starts.

In no time, I'm deep in the countryside, towns and villages becoming smaller and further apart. Gloriously green hills bordered by low, dry stone walls are dotted with a motley collection of woolly sheep and shaggy Highland cattle. The sun rises into a perfect pale blue sky, yesterday's clouds having blown away overnight. Everything seems to sparkle and glow. If the dashboard didn't tell me the temperature outside was two degrees, I could almost believe it was summer.

The road takes me south along Loch Ness and then west towards the coast. In less than two hours, I'm crossing the bridge onto Skye. On any other day I might be able to appreciate the wildly beautiful scenery, but my mind is consumed with plans of what I might say to Lulu. In the end, I settle on starting with the most important thing. I love her. Nothing else matters. Except the possibility she might love me back.

If she didn't love me—or at least have feelings for me—would she have reacted the way she did to that photo? I might be obtuse when it comes to feelings, but Mandy isn't, and even she could see no other explanation than Lulu was hurt.

Once I'm on the island, the roads are narrow and winding. Glimpses of glittering sea leap out at me as I roll around corners, only to disappear again on the next bend. Signposts with strange names like Camastianavaig and Flashader pass by, and eventually, the satnav tells me I'm there. A tiny but beautiful stone cottage with smoke blowing from its chimney sits beside an enormous, ancient-looking stone and iron gateway, the elaborate gates standing open on a wide gravelled drive. I'm assuming it was once the gatehouse for a manor house. I park in the small space beside the cottage and take a couple of deep breaths. This is it.

I've hardly had time to get out of the car before the door to the cottage whips open to reveal a small round woman with a mop of steely grey hair and a spotless apron.

"Can I help ye?" she asks in a broad Scottish accent, her smile friendly.

She's not what I was expecting to see, but years of working as a lawyer allows me to keep my cool. "I hope so, yes. I'm looking for Lulu MacLeod. Or her father, Duncan. Would they happen to be home?"

Her eyes widen and her mouth drops open for a moment, almost as though she's shocked to be asked such a thing. But she gathers her wits quickly.

"Och, I expect so, pet. But ye'll need to go on down the drive aways yet. Take care as you do, himself likes to let the sheep roam in the home pasture and they do have a habit of getting onto the drive. If you happen upon one, just drive right up and tip the horn and it'll be out of your way in a trice. Usually."

"So, down this driveway? How will I know which house?" I can feel myself squinting down the driveway, where not a single house is visible, while wondering who 'himself' might be.

"Och, ye canna miss it, pet. They'll both be home at this time, I expect." And with that, she smiles brightly and snaps the door shut in my face. Okay. At least I know Lulu is here.

She's right, there are plump black-faced sheep all over the drive, which meanders for a couple of kilometres down towards the sea. Occasionally I get a glimpse of tall chimneys and once a stone pier jutting out into the water. But no sign of a house. Until there is. I cross a tiny stone bridge over a little stream, round what turns out to be the final bend, and meet with a wide gravel courtyard watched over by a massive stone house. Well, more of a castle, to be honest. Houses don't have turrets. This place has turrets. Three of them. Along with dozens of chimneys and an enormous wooden door, blackened with age and banded with iron. This can't be right. There are no other houses nearby, although away to the left, there appears to be a collection of outbuildings—barns and stables around a broad courtyard.

It's precisely the kind of house, I mean castle, my mother would love, but I can't quite make the mental connection to Lulu. Still, the woman in the cottage seemed sure, so I park the car and get out.

Climbing the half-dozen wide stone steps to the door, I feel confused and out of place. The word interloper crosses my mind, a reminder of my feelings about Lulu when we first met. Despite our current circumstances, I can feel a small smile tugging at the corners of my lips.

I drop the giant doorknocker, and from somewhere deep in the bowels of the house, I hear a loud bark, followed by the scrabbling of claws and a steady footfall. None of that sounds like Lulu.

The door swings open on an enormously tall, enormously broad, enormously weathered man with wild red hair and grubby trousers, tucked into long, striped woolly socks.

"Ah. You're here. I was wondering if you would make an appearance." He somehow manages to make a smile look stern.

"I beg your pardon? You seem to have the advantage of me."
I have no idea how he'd know who I am, or why I'd be here.
Perhaps he's a little mad. Certainly his clothing and hair suggest
it. But then I notice the paint stains on his hands. And the
familiar wild hair. "Are you Duncan MacLeod?"

"I am indeed, lad. Come in, come in. We're letting all the
warm air out."

As he steps back, I take in the hallway. Cavernous is the only
word that comes to mind. Worn stone flagging sweeps away
towards a curving wooden staircase, which rises through two
stories, softened by a faded red Persian runner. On either side of
the staircase is an honest-to-god suit of armour. Pocket doors
sit closed on either wall, flanked by an eclectic collection of
watercolours and oils. I recognise both Lulu's work and her
father's. Along with much older paintings of the castle and the
coast.

Two brown and tan kelpies sniff at my legs, tails wagging
madly until Duncan moves away, and without a word from him,
they're following him down the hall beside the stairs.

"We'll sit in the kitchen—it's much warmer there, aye?" It's
very clearly not a question. We head down a set of worn stone
stairs to another cavernous room, this one much warmer than
the hall upstairs. "It's no' easy to keep a house this size warm in
the winter, so we do spend a lot of time in the kitchen."

"I can imagine," I answer as he busies himself at an ancient
Aga stove, moving a gently steaming kettle onto the heat.

"Tea." Again, not a question. I'm not easily intimidated, but
I can't imagine ever contradicting this man. He wears a natural
authority suggesting years of being obeyed, and he is so far from
what I was expecting I find myself tongue-tied. Unsure of what
to do, I stand awkwardly near the table as though I'm waiting
for permission to sit in the principal's office.

"I should introduce myself. I'm Ni ..."

"Oh, I know who ye are, lad," he interrupts. "You're here
for Lulu. She's out for a wee walk at present. Should be home

shortly." I briefly wonder what Lulu has told him. The lack of open hostility gives me hope.

As he finishes speaking, three things happen at once. The kettle starts to shrill, the dogs let out a happy and piercingly loud yip, and the door on the other side of the room crashes open and closes on a gust of freezing air, depositing a dishevelled Lulu in the kitchen.

"Did I hear the kettle, Da? I'm gasping for a cuppa and some toast. This bairn will make me pay if I don't feed it soon."

She's rugged up for the weather. A thick woolly cap clings to her head, her wild mane of blonde curls springing from beneath it. A waxed coat covers her to the knee, almost meeting the thick socks her jeans are tucked into. Her cheeks are pink from the cold and I've never seen anything more beautiful. And then my mind screeches to a halt.

"Bairn? Bairn?" My eyes drop from her cheeks, which are now white with shock, to her belly, almost hiding beneath the wax coat. Her not-so-small, no-longer-flat belly. Her hands wrap over the bump as though to protect it.

Neither of us speaks as we stare at each other across the now too-hot room. Duncan says nothing but continues to clatter around making a pot of tea, finally thrusting a chunky mug at each of us. The silence stretches on. It's so quiet I can hear my heart thundering.

"I'll go and leave you two to talk. You'll have a lot to say, I expect." Duncan and the dogs slip out the door Lulu came in, leaving a bellowing silence behind them.

"Nick. What ...what are you doing here?" She sinks onto a chair by the table. Tea sloshes over the rim of her mug because her hands are shaking so much.

I struggle to latch onto something coherent to say. "I came to get you back. You're pregnant?" Not my most articulate moment.

"Oh. Yes." It seems Lulu, too, is having difficulty with words.

"Were you ever going to tell me?" It doesn't occur to me that the baby isn't mine.

She sighs. "Yes. Of course, I was. I just ... I needed some time."

"Time? It's been over a month. How much time did you need?" I'm pacing now. Unable to contain the energy coursing through my body.

I watch as her hackles rise. "Over a month, apparently."

"So you *just needed time* to tell me you were *carrying my child* because ...?" I'm trying to keep my cool, but my voice rises to a shout anyway.

"Because? Because?" The only word for her tone is incredulous. "Because you didn't want a relationship. You made that crystal clear. And you never talked about it being any more than what it was. No strings. Casual."

"That's a pile of steaming bullshit, Lu, and you know it. Whatever we were, it was never casual. Not for me anyway. And I don't think for you either." I can feel my blood pressure rising with every word. "You were the one talking about ending things, not me."

She manages to look contrite and angry at the same time. "Yes. I was. But you convinced me not to. And look what happened." I can see her tears threatening to fall, but I'm so angry and hurt I can't seem to dial it back.

"What happened is not what you saw in the paper." I'm in danger of pulling all my hair out. "It was all lies. Concocted by my mother. Who, by the way, is a controlling narcissist. But you never gave me a chance to explain. You just took off. Is this your idea of punishing me? Because it worked."

"No. I'm not punishing you. I needed time to think. I wasn't expecting this. I had an implant. I had no plans to have a baby. And I was confused. And angry. And scared." By now, she's yelling too, and those tears are threatening to overflow.

The tears finish me off, and I sink onto a chair on the other side of the table, as desperate to calm down as I am to have answers.

"When did you realise you were pregnant?" It's barely more than a whisper.

"I found out the morning of the exhibition opening. And then the next morning, there was that story. I saw the pictures, Nick. You were holding her hand. It said you were engaged. I asked you about what your mother said at the office that day, and you made out like it was nothing. But you never talked about there being anything more between us. You never told me you were planning on going into politics. What was I to think?" Tears are rolling unchecked down Lulu's cheeks, sobs choking her words. The last of my anger drains out of me, leaving behind frustration and regret.

"Jesus, Lu. You didn't have to *think* anything. You just needed to listen. I would have explained everything. You could have trusted me. What did you think all those weeks we were together were about? How could you ever imagine I might want someone else? You were the only one I wanted. You *are* the only one I want."

"How was I supposed to know that? You never told me. You never said anything, and I never wanted anything more either."

That stings like a slap in the face. Guilt and fear and hurt churn in my gut.

"No. You made yourself pretty clear during my trip to Melbourne."

"I was scared. It was all getting too ... too ..." Her hands flap, like birds searching for a word to land on.

"I could see that. And maybe I didn't make my feelings clear. Because I didn't want to scare you off. But couldn't you feel it, Lulu?"

"I don't know. I didn't know what to think. Or how to feel. And then I found out about the baby."

"I can't believe you kept something like this from me." I can see how my words are landing in her already stressed heart, but mine is stressed too.

"I didn't know what else to do. I needed time to think about what I wanted." All the fight has drained out of her, but the tears keep flowing.

I need to lay it all on the line.

"Right. Well, I came all the way here. To fucking Scotland. In winter. To find you." I dig around in my pocket, find the velvet box and hold it up. "I came here to get you back. To ask you to marry me. To take you home."

She stares at the box but makes no move to take it. Or speak. Or look at me. My heart breaks.

"I see. I guess I wasted a trip. Because it seems like whatever you do want, it's not me." I throw the box on the kitchen table, along with my broken and bleeding heart. Taking the steps two at a time, I make it out to my car. I'm about to climb in when Lulu appears on the front steps.

"Nick ..."

I glare at her across the roof of the rental car, feeling hollowed out and cold. "You know what? The ball is in your court, Lulu. I love you. But there's no point if I'm the only one in it. If you don't love me back."

Gravel spits from under the wheels as I speed up the drive. The sheep I had approached so cautiously on my way down scatter, and I nearly collect the sweet old lady who helped me as she walks down the drive, basket in hand. But I'm too worked up to care.

When I make it onto the road, I hit the accelerator, desperate to put some space between me and the pain of the past few minutes. What I don't expect as I careen around the hairpin corner is a herd of massive, shaggy red cows. All over the road.

CHAPTER THIRTY-FOUR

LULU

I love you. But there's no point if I'm the only one in it. If you don't love me back.

And then he gets in his car and screeches away. The velvet box is warm and firm in my hands. I'm shaking as I flip the lid, opening it up to the most beautiful ring I have ever seen in my life. It's then the silent tears turn to sobs.

"Come inside, *mo chridhe*." Dad appears from nowhere and, with a gentle hand on my shoulder, guides me into the parlour and onto the sofa. "There now. All this sobbing is not good for the bairn, hen."

But I can't stop. Hours, weeks, months go by before I can get myself under control.

"He didn't even let me explain," I wail.

"Hmm. Seems to be a recurring theme, no?" he says dryly.

"What? I ... you ... Oh, Da." He's right. Nick might not have given me much chance to explain, but he certainly gave me more than I gave him. And he came. All this way. With a ring. It suddenly occurs to me to wonder how he found me. Dad has always kept his private life private. Only a small handful of people know where Duncan MacLeod lives. So, Nick must have gone to considerable trouble to find me.

The front door bangs, and I leap from the sofa—he's back. But it's Morag's curly grey head that appears around the door, and my heart plummets.

"What happened here, hen? I just passed the lad, tearing up the driveway like a bat out of hell. The bairn's father, I'm thinking?"

I can feel Dad nodding, his cheek resting on the top of my head.

"Good-looking lad. Lovely manners. But from the looks of you, I'm guessing things didn't go well?"

"He was unhappy I kept the baby news from him, Morag."

"Oh, aye. Well, he would be, I daresay. But no doubt he'll cool off and come back." She puts her basket on the floor by the door and sits in the chair opposite us.

"I don't think so. He said he couldn't do this."

Dad clears his throat. "No, hen, that's no' what he said."

I give him the side eye.

"Don't look at me like that. I wasn't eavesdropping. Everyone in a ten-mile radius must've heard you both yelling. What he said was, he couldn't do it if he was the only one in it, if you didn't love him back. That's no' quite the same thing, is it?"

And like a bolt from the blue, I realise Nick still doesn't have any idea how I feel about him. I've completely bollixed this up.

Morag makes a typically Scottish tsking noise and turns to go as I leap off the sofa.

"Did you see him pull into the road? Which way did he go?" I'm heading for the door, grabbing the Range Rover keys off the hall table as I go.

"Turned right towards the village," Morag calls after me, which I barely hear, as I start the engine and race up the drive. I have to catch him. Have to tell him I love him.

·♥·♥·♥·♥·♥·

I put my foot down as soon as I'm out of the drive. But I know the dangers of taking the corners of these narrow country roads too fast and force myself to slow down. And as I come out of the first hairpin bend, there's Nick's car, in the middle of the road, surrounded by a herd of Mr Gordon's prized *Heilan' coos*.

I skid to a stop, narrowly missing a couple of the shaggy beasts, and fling myself out of the car. Despite how distraught I am, the ridiculousness of the situation almost makes me laugh.

"Nick. Can you hear me?" The window slides down and Nick's head emerges.

"Are you alright?"

"Yes. I'm fine," he replies as his shoulders follow his head out the window. Good Lord. He's climbing out.

"What are you doing?"

"Getting out. Obviously. I can't drive through them. I might hit one of them."

"Don't get out. They have horns."

"I can see those myself, thank you." But he continues to climb, unable to open the door with the cows pressed against the side of the car. There's no sign of Mr Gordon, who will be furious if one of his cows gets hurt.

"Be careful. They're very gentle. But can be quite bolshy when spooked," I call, trying to keep my voice calm to avoid a stampede.

Finally, Nick has managed to slide onto the roof of his rental and is clearly looking for the least crowded place to get down.

"Please stay on the roof. I'll try and get them moving." I gently pat the nearest cows on the rump, hoping they'll shift. As a rule, they're docile creatures, but they can be stubborn when they want. And I have some things I want to get off my chest, so I realise having him as a captive audience, albeit on the roof of his car, is perfect.

"There's something else I need to tell you." I have to shout over the mooing that's started up.

"Something else? Let me guess. It's twins?" From this distance, I can't tell whether Nick is bitter or making a joke. I can only hope it's the latter.

"Well, no. Although, at one point, there was a school of thought … No. Sorry. Don't distract me. Let me get this out."

"Please. Be my guest. I'm all ears." Looks like it's bitter.

I fear I'll only get one chance at this, so I take a deep breath. "I love you. I should have told you sooner, but I was scared. Scared of loving you. Scared you didn't love me back. So, I ran. And I shouldn't have. I should have stayed. And been honest. But I'm being honest now. I love you. I know you have no reason to believe me … except I bought a ticket. I bought a ticket to Sydney. I was leaving tomorrow to come and tell you. About the baby. About loving you."

"Well, why didn't you just say so back at the castle?" He has his lawyer mask on, so I can't tell what he's thinking.

"You didn't give me the chance," I answer. And up goes his eyebrow.

He's quiet for a long moment. If I was sitting down, my leg would be jiggling with nerves. All at once, even from this distance, I can see his face morphing from closed off to the Nick I fell in love with. Thank God. He starts sliding towards the back of his small hatchback, looking for a space to get down.

"Ow. Jesus. Fuck," he mutters, as he lands on his feet, narrowly missing a horn. The cows start to shift nervously, and Nick yelps before letting out a belly laugh, hopping on one foot. "It stamped on my foot. My boot is ruined."

"Oh. What a shame. I hope they weren't your favourites." And we both crack up laughing, remembering our first meeting. The sound of our laughter echoes in the narrow space between the dry stone walls.

"Don't move," I gasp as the cows start to part, spooked by the noise.

"I don't think so. I've spent a month wanting to hold you. I'm not waiting another minute."

But just as Nick starts to edge his way slowly through the shaggy beasts, one swings its head. It all happens in slow motion. The enormous horn catches Nick right in the chest and he stumbles into another cow, cartwheeling his arms to regain his balance. His injured foot lands smack bang in the middle of a fresh cowpat. Cows scatter as Nick's legs fly up and he hurtles backwards. Even over the panicked mooing I can hear the crack as Nick's head connects with the asphalt.

It's not until I'm racing across the wet road, careless of the cowpats myself, I realise I never even stopped to put boots on.

"Oh my god. Are you alright?" But even as I say it, I can see he's not. He's unconscious, the front of his shirt is torn, and there's a gash in the top of his very smart leather hiking boots.

I pull my phone out of my pocket. Teddy, the local paramedic, answers on the first ring. "Teddy. It's Lulu MacLeod. There's been an accident. On the sharp bend at Gordon's. His *coos* were on the road again. He's unconscious but breathing. No Teddy. The man, not the *coo*."

"Nick? Don't move. The ambulance is coming. They'll be here in a minute. It will all be alright. Just hold on." My sobbing breaths join the disappearing moos of the cows and the distant wail of a siren as I sink down on the wet road, gripping his hand.

If something happens to Nick now ... I can't finish the thought. It feels like all my worst fears are coming true, and I did this to myself. I think I hear him mumble, but I can't be sure over the wail of the siren as Teddy pulls up.

"Don't you dare die on me, Nick Pierce," I whisper.

Teddy laughs when I fill him in on what happened as his offsider opens up the rig and slides out the gurney. I'd laugh at the absurdity, too, if Nick wasn't unconscious on the road.

"Oh, Teddy. Please be careful. It's Nick. I think I heard him groan. I think he might have fractured his skull. Will he be alright?" I can feel the hitch in my breath as I start to hyperventilate.

Teddy takes me by the shoulders, pulls me to my feet and moves me out of the way.

"We've got this. Stay out of the way."

The ambos fly into action, talking to Nick and each other the whole time, serious but calm. I don't understand most of what they're saying, but I do hear the occasional moan from Nick. It's impossible to stand still, and I pace on the narrow road until I realise Dad won't know what's happened. Calling him at least gives me something to do.

"Da. Nick has had an accident," I gasp out.

Dad and Morag arrive as Teddy and his partner are getting Nick onto the gurney, with a brace around his neck and some sort of board at his back. His eyes are rolling around in his head, but at least they're open.

"I'm going with him."

Teddy looks like he might argue but thinks better of it.

Dad moves Nick's rental to the side of the road. "You go. I'll follow in the Range Rover," Dad says, climbing into the car I've left in the middle of the road, the door hanging open.

There's no hospital in the tiny village nearby, so we head down the coast to a little hospital near the mainland. It's not far, but it seems to take forever. At least they let me hold Nick's hand, until they rush him out of the ambulance and into emergency.

Dad arrives only minutes after us, and I fall into his arms.

"Oh, Da. I only just got him back. What if ..." I can't even give voice to the words. This right here is why I don't do relationships. But it's too late now. I'm in. Pain and loss and all.

"Now, now. Don't be thinking like that, pet. He's young and strong. He's going to be fine. You'll see."

I can feel the tears leaking from my eyes, running hot and fast down my cheeks and disappearing into the cashmere scarf I have wrapped around my neck. Dad wrestles my wet socks off my freezing feet, cajoles the nurse into giving me some of the blue booties they wear on their shoes in theatre and puts me in a chair.

It feels like hours, although the clock on the wall tells me it's only been twenty minutes, before a young doctor I don't know comes through the doors to the emergency department. Da appears to know him though.

"Mr MacLeod. I understand you're here to see Nick Pierce. Are you a relative?"

"Oh, give over, Malcolm. You know who I am. He's from Australia. There are no relatives here, ye *amadan*."

"Yes. I'm his fiancée." I jump up. I have no qualms about telling the lie. I will be his fiancée. As soon as he wakes up. I squeeze the ring box I dropped into my pocket before leaving home.

"I see. Well, we've a concern he's fractured his skull, so we want to do an MRI to rule out a brain bleed. We can call you when it's over if ye like."

My heart plummets. "Fractured skull? Brain bleed?" The panic I had almost managed to get under control starts to build again, and I can feel my breathing and heart rate ratcheting up.

"The MRI is a precaution. The fact he's conscious suggests a bleed is unlikely. Probably more like a grade three or four concussion. Otherwise, there's a couple of cracked ribs from the coo horn and a few cuts and bruises. Nothing too serious."

My knees buckle and I feel a strong arm around my shoulders, as Da gently pushes me into the nearest chair.

"Your bedside manner could do with some work, Malcolm." Da says, in his best Laird of the Manor's voice, causing Malcolm to wince. "We'll wait."

I feel faint, my head swimming, black dots peppering my vision. I wish I could put my head between my knees, but my stomach gets in the way, reminding me I need to keep a lid on my anxiety, if only for the sake of Nick's baby.

We wait as people come and go through the swinging doors for what seems like hours, but when I check my phone, it's not been much more than an hour. I'm close to losing my mind when a middle-aged woman in scrubs pushes through the swinging doors. "Nick Pierce's family?" Her eyes are tired, but she's smiling.

Da leaps to his feet and has his arm around my shoulder again before she has a chance to speak.

"I'm Doctor Love," she starts. "I've had a look at Nick's results. How about we take a seat?"

Take a seat? Does that mean bad news? She must see my terror because she smiles and pats my arm before taking a seat herself.

Da squeezes my hand and I hold my breath, waiting for the doctor to continue.

"Nick was conscious on arrival. The MRI showed a very small hairline crack but no bleeding, which is great news. However, he is concussed, which means he's a little disoriented, although it should resolve itself pretty quickly. He has a couple of cracked ribs, which will be sore but should heal up on their own. We'd like to monitor him overnight to be safe. Try not to worry ..." Dr Love looks at Dad.

"Lulu," he supplies.

"Lulu. He'll be back on his feet in no time. All things considered it could have been much worse."

"Can I see him?" My words are barely a whisper.

"Of course. Once they've moved him to the ward. Although you might like to consider going home. You look exhausted."

And with another pat on my arm, she's off through the swinging doors.

When we get to Nick's room, he's sleeping. They hand over a bag with his belongings and I almost laugh at the sad state of his lovely boots. Just as the nurse is leaving the room she turns back.

"Oh, by the way, we advised his next of kin. So, you don't need to worry about that."

"Next of kin?"

"His mother. Mary Pierce."

My stomach bottoms out at the mention of the woman who caused so much trouble. But at least she's all the way on the other side of the planet.

Once the nurse is gone, I drag a chair to Nick's bedside, take hold of his hand and press it to my lips.

"I love you," I whisper, and resting my face against his knuckles, I settle in to wait.

CHAPTER THIRTY-FIVE

NICK

The room is dim, and without even opening my eyes, I can tell it's a hospital based on the smell alone. I try to speak but what comes out is nothing more than a croak.

"Water?" is all I can manage. There's a foul taste in my mouth, and my throat is parched. Someone slips a chip of ice into my mouth and I sigh in relief.

Suddenly the room is full of movement, doctors and nurses poking and prodding. Maybe waking up was a mistake.

"Nick, you're in the hospital. You bumped your head," a voice says. I open my eyes, but my vision is blurry and it makes the bed spin, so I shut them again.

I have trouble latching onto a thought, but the doctor doesn't seem too concerned, and right now, my head hurts too much to panic.

"Things might be somewhat jumbled for a day or so, but you'll come good. What you need is peace and quiet."

My eyelids are lifted, and bright light flicks back and forth.

"Just relax while I check your pupils. Everything looks good. Get some rest." I don't need to be told twice, so I let myself drift back into sleep.

The next time I wake up, my vision is clearer. Something soft touches my face. I can smell my grandmother's garden, which seems weird. I concentrate on opening my eyes again, but it's not my grandmother beside me. She's young and her clothes are crumpled. Her wild blonde hair is sticking out at all sorts of strange angles, and there are deep purple bruises under her eyes. And she's pregnant.

Impossibly blue eyes lift to mine. It takes a moment, but it all comes back to me. A face I know. A face I love. Lulu is right beside me.

"Nick," she whispers. She's holding my hand, kissing my palm, hot tears spilling down her pale cheeks.

"I love you," I manage to croak, curling my fingers around hers.

"I love you too. Thank God you're okay. Don't ever do anything like that to me again." Between the words falling out of her mouth and her sobbing, she's almost incoherent, but I hear her loud and clear.

And then we're kissing and laughing with joy at the same time.

We're interrupted by another round of poking and prodding by nurses and doctors. Lulu waits patiently out of the way until they all leave.

As though she can sense the throbbing behind my eyes, Lulu soaks a face washer in a bowl of water, wrings it out and places it across my forehead. The relief is immediate and not only physical. To have this woman taking such care of me after feeling like I might never get her back relaxes my mind and heart, as well as every tense and aching muscle in my body.

"What time is it?" I can see it's dark outside, but I have no idea how long I was asleep.

"Just past six."

The comfort is making it hard to stay awake, and Lulu looks as exhausted as I feel. I don't want her to leave, but she needs to rest. For her and the baby.

"Why don't you go home and get some rest?"

"No. I don't want to leave you. I only just got you back. We have so much to say." She clings to my hand, making no move to leave until the nurse comes in and gives her no option.

"Off you go. Visiting hours are over," she says. "What he needs is rest. He'll still be here in the morning and probably ready to go home."

"Yes, but he might need something," Lulu pleads.

"That's what we're here for," the nurse says crisply. And with that she turns off the light and pushes Lulu out the door.

I wake up to a cold, hard hand gripping my fingers. Watery grey light seeps around the closed blinds, and I can hear the rain hitting the window.

"Nicholas? Nicholas, are you awake?" The voice is sharp and adds to the searing pain in my head. I'd recognise it anywhere. More squeezing. I want to go back to sleep. Where it was at least peaceful and nothing hurt. Where's Lulu? And why is my mother here?

The doctor seems as annoyed as I am by the new arrival.

"I'm his mother," Mum says. "I'm here to make sure he's taken proper care of."

"I can assure you, Mrs Pierce, Nick is receiving the best of care. Visiting hours start at ten. You can come back then." And with that he ushers Mum out. I can hear her threatening and complaining all the way to the lift.

I don't understand what my mother is doing here. She's the last person I'd want to see. When the doctor returns, he explains they contacted her as my next of kin, but that doesn't explain how she got here so quickly.

The next time I wake up, I'm more alert but no less uncomfortable, and Lulu is sitting by the bed, holding my hand.

"Good morning. How are you feeling?" She smiles. Is it my imagination or is the slight Scottish burr in her voice stronger?

"Alarmed. My mother was here earlier. I think. Or am I high on pain meds?"

Lulu looks startled, but before she has a chance to say anything, there's a commotion in the hall. "How did she get here this fast?" I have no time to reply before Mum strides in.

"Who on earth are you and what are you doing in my son's room?" my mother barks at Lulu. "He is in a very fragile condition. Kindly leave or I will call security. We don't need a scene."

I feel Lulu's hand begin to pull away, so I grip it tighter.

"She's not going anywhere, Mum. And you're the one causing a scene." I might be groggy, but I haven't forgotten the stunt Mum pulled. Looks like the hellfire I promised is on the near horizon.

Mum stands by the door pointing, signalling Lulu should leave.

"We need to discuss how to salvage this appalling situation, and we don't need your piece of fluff as an audience."

Lulu stands to her full height beside me, holding my hand and looking my mother in the eye. A warrior prepared for battle.

"You will apologise to Lulu, right now."

"I most certainly will not. It's Eleanor who deserves an apology for the way you've been carrying on."

"With all due respect, Mrs Pierce, Nick is the one who deserves an apology for your interfering. But what he needs most of all is peace and quiet to recover from a nasty accident. I think it would be best if you did as he asked and left." Lulu's tone makes it clear she will tolerate no nonsense.

"How dare you? Who do you think you are?" Mum's eyebrow is up, and her face is an unhealthy shade of purple. I've never seen her quite so furious. Her infamous unflappability has well and truly crumbled.

I'm about to jump in and tell Mum exactly who Lulu is, which will no doubt cause her to lose her mind, but Lulu beats me to the punch with a voice of steel to match her spine and ice in her eyes.

"I'm the mother of Nick's child; that's who I think I am. So, you'd best not make *me* get security. I don't think you'd like the outcome."

I attempt to smother a smile.

"You heard the lady, Mum. Time to leave."

"I most certainly will not," Mum chokes out. "We have things to discuss. Not least of which is this ridiculous claim you are the father of this woman's baby. Have you had a paternity test?" Mum looks at Lulu like she's something she found stuck to the bottom of her shoe.

If I wasn't so groggy, I would get up and see Mum to the door myself for that statement alone. Instead, all I can do is give her the Pierce laser stare. "I don't need one. And you should be ashamed of yourself for such an offensive remark."

There's not a trace of humour in Mum's laugh. "I can't believe how naïve you're being, Nicholas. Women trap men with babies that aren't theirs all the time. I insist on a paternity test. If it is your baby, we can make suitable financial arrangements." Mum turns to Lulu. "But don't imagine you will get more than the absolute minimum. There will be no golden ticket for you, missy."

CHAPTER THIRTY-SIX

LULU

I feel like I've been slapped in the face. Nick's expression is a study in fury. It even makes me a little nervous. I can see why he's such a successful lawyer. "There will be no paternity test and no *arrangements*, financial or otherwise. Certainly not with you."

I can't hold in the burst of laughter bubbling up in my chest.

"I neither want nor need a golden ticket, Mrs Pierce. What I want is to be happy. With Nick. And our baby. And it will take more than a few threats from you to stop that from happening."

"Well, we will see about that when Nick comes to his senses. Which he will no doubt do very shortly. Then you'll find yourself very quickly out in the cold." Mary sneers at me as she turns back to Nick. "You're being ridiculous. If you marry Eleanor, you'll be prime minister one day. Think about your future, Nicholas." There's such a frantic edge to her voice I could almost feel sorry for her if she hadn't caused so much heartache.

"I am thinking about it. Clearly. For the first time in a long time. I warned you at the partners' dinner what would happen if you continued to interfere in my life," Nick snaps."

Their voices are so loud a nurse comes in.

"What on earth is going on in here?" Her gaze travels from Nick and me to Mary. "Nick is recovering from a head injury. He needs peace and quiet, not arguing."

"It's okay, nurse; my mother was just leaving." Nick's voice is strong and brooks no argument. It's the Nick I first met in the lift so many weeks ago.

"Are you sure? Do I need to call security?" I can see there's no love lost between the staff and Nick's mother. She's made herself unpopular in a remarkably short space of time.

Mary doesn't even spare the nurse a glance, but I get a boiling look. "You will be very sorry you didn't heed my warning to stay away, young lady."

"Enough of the threats, Mum. Now please leave, and don't come back until you're prepared to give both Lulu and me a full apology for the appalling way you've behaved."

I would love to tell Mary what I think, ugly scene be damned, but Nick has the situation well under control, despite his injuries.

If this is the woman who raised Nick, who was supposed to be his nurturer, no wonder he wasn't interested in a relationship when we met.

The nurse opens her arms to shepherd Mary into the corridor, failing to hide her grin.

"This conversation is not over, Nicholas," Mary warns.

"It is until Lulu gets an apology." I wouldn't want to be in Mary's shoes when Nick feels better.

We're both silent as we listen to Mary's footsteps fade down the corridor.

"You were magnificent." Nick grins at me.

I can feel my cheeks burning. "You're not upset I threw down with your mother?"

"Hell no. She had it coming."

It's an effort to keep my hands gentle as I adjust Nick's pillows. I really want to throw something. "She crossed a line, Nick."

"She did. Several, in fact. Let's hope she got the message. Although I wouldn't count on it. In the meantime, why don't you hop up here with me?" He somehow manages to shuffle over on the bed a little, making room for me, so I climb up and nestle against him, careful not to touch the enormous bruise on his chest, which covers two cracked ribs, courtesy of Mr Gordon's cow.

"That's better. So, what I don't get is how my mother got here so fast."

"The hospital called her as next of kin." Unfortunately.

"And she decided to get straight on her broomstick and fly right over. It still doesn't make any sense. By the way, do you have my phone? I should probably call Claire. She'll be worried."

"Oh, yes." I lean over and grab my bag from the chair. "It smashed as you fell. Or maybe a cow trod on it." I can't help but laugh as I hand over the mangled device. I can laugh about it now that I know Nick is safe. "But I have my old phone. You can pop the sim card in that."

Once the sim has been transferred, Nick goes to call his sister but is distracted by a voicemail.

"Well, that explains it. Evidently, Mum somehow got wind of the fact I'd flown to Scotland and decided to follow me to put a stop to any *ridiculousness*. She was already in Glasgow when the hospital called her. Claire tried to warn me, but the broken phone got in the way. Mystery solved."

"She seems very desperate for you to marry Eleanor." I don't need Mary to like me, but it hurts to see how much pain she's inflicting on her son.

"She is. So, I need to tell you what actually happened at the partners' dinner."

I settle against his chest and listen as he recounts all the dreadful things his mother and Eleanor have done, and about his parents' plan for him to be a politician.

"Do you believe me?" he asks, a little sheepishly, as though he had any control over what those harpies did.

"Yes, I do. But are you sure you don't want to be a politician? I could totally see myself as the First Lady." I give him a wicked grin.

He laughs and then winces, hand going to his chest.

"Oh, your ribs."

"I'm okay. And to answer your question, I'm very sure. I have no intention of standing for a seat now or in the future. So are we good?" I've never seen Nick look quite so unsure.

"Yes. We're good. And I'm sorry for how all this happened. I'm sorry I didn't give you a chance to explain. I'm especially sorry for not telling you about the baby earlier." I don't know how I will let go of the guilt of that decision.

"Lu, I understand. You were scared. But I need you to promise me. No more running away when things get tricky. Talk to me. There's nothing we can't work out."

"I will. I had a long talk with Da about him and my mum, and it helped me to see things differently. I'm not scared now. I'm ready. To trust you. And more importantly, to trust myself."

"So, you're all in?"

"I'm all in. Whatever life brings."

His fingers slide around my jaw and into the hair at the nape of my neck, sending the shiver which was once so unwelcome and is now such a joy over my body. Gently he pulls me forward, and suddenly, we're not in a hospital, we're not anywhere, except in each other's arms. His lips are soft and a little tentative until I melt against him, my lips opening to him. It's the kind of kiss that fades to black at the end of a movie, all warmth and love and beauty. And I know for sure we'll be okay.

Loud throat clearing alerts us to the arrival of Da, who has appeared in the doorway, looking tired and smelling vaguely of sheep.

"Lulu, hen, the nurses said there was a *stramash* earlier. Are ye alright?" He takes in my position in Nick's arms.

"Better than alright, Dad. At last." I can't keep the smile off my face.

"So, you've worked it all out, then?"

We don't even have time to answer before Mary stalks back into the room, apparently having evaded the nurses.

"Here we go again," Nick whispers into my hair. The face he turns to her is not one I would want aimed at me. "Are you here to apologise, Mum?"

Mary takes in the sight of me on the bed before giving Dad the once over. The look she shoots him is pure poison. Until she does a double-take. She's recognised him, despite the smell of sheep dung and hay.

"Duncan MacLeod?" Her hands come up to her chest, and if she was wearing any, she'd be clutching her pearls.

"I am indeed. And who might you be?"

Mary holds out a trembling hand. "Mary Pierce. So wonderful to meet you. I'm a huge fan. I have several of your paintings."

"Well, I expect we'll be seeing more of each other since we share a grandbaby." Da has no idea of the things Mary said to me earlier; otherwise, she'd be getting his Laird of the Manor's voice and a very cold shoulder.

"Grandbaby?" she chokes out, all the colour leaving the cheeks that had been flushed only seconds ago. Her glower swings towards me.

"Yes. You've met my daughter, Lulu, I take it?"

Mary's expression is priceless as she sinks into a nearby chair. I can feel Nick's body shaking with silent laughter beside me.

"That'll teach her," he whispers for my ears only before adding, "Oh, I wouldn't count on seeing too much of my mother, Duncan. She's on her way back to Sydney as soon as she can refuel her broom. Aren't you, Mum?"

CHAPTER THIRTY-SEVEN

NICK

T he doctor sends me home in the early afternoon with a clean bill of health and instructions to take it easy for a week or two.

The plan is for me to recuperate at Duncan's, and frankly, I'm in no hurry to return to Sydney. Partly because I don't want Lulu flying in her condition. But also because we need this time together to get back to where we were before Meddling Mary interfered in our relationship. And before Lulu let her fears get the better of her. It also gives me the circuit breaker I need to decide what I want in life. Other than Lulu. Because, let's face it, everything else is nothing more than background noise now. And what better place to do it than in a spectacular castle in the middle of nowhere?

Lulu fusses as she gets me settled in Duncan's Range Rover for the drive to the farm. She sits in the back with me while Duncan drives and chats about the weather—a common topic of conversation in Scotland—and the goings on at the farm. The heated seats relax me, and it's nice to rest my head on Lulu's shoulder. Being here beside her is enough to make me feel better, despite the aching ribs and head.

We laugh as we recount to Duncan the story of what happened when we pass the spot where a Highland cow almost got the better of me.

We arrive at Duncan's and are met by a beaming Morag and some very happy dogs. In no time at all I'm bundled into a huge bed with a scorching electric blanket, and hot soup.

"You're looking very pale, lad. But I'll have you set to rights in no time," says Morag, who treats me like a long-lost grandson after having met me once for all of two minutes before the accident. But it's so good to be fussed over and feel loved.

The soup is delicious, and I wolf it down. When I'm finished I sink into the pillows. Lulu has been hovering the whole time I ate. I hold my hand out to her.

"Come here, Lu."

She approaches, looking a little nervous and I pull back the covers inviting her in. "I'm afraid I'm not up for any action right now, but could you spare the time for a cuddle?"

Seeing her smile is like looking directly into the sun. She doesn't hesitate. Whipping off her jeans and bulky jumper until she's down to a thermal t-shirt and knickers, she climbs in next to me.

The simple joy of being here with her, alone, is all I need in the world. Feeling her bare legs pressed against mine as I spoon her, smelling her crazy hair, I can finally completely relax. I can't help but nuzzle the tender spot on the nape of her neck. There's no way I'm up to making love to her. I know I won't be able to resist for long, but it's amazing how much comfort this simple contact can bring.

"I love you," I whisper.

"I love you too," she says as we drift off into an exhausted but peaceful sleep, and neither of us stirs until morning.

Now that I'm out of hospital and on a lower dose of the pain meds, it doesn't take long for my brain fog to clear. But there's one thing that's bothering me.

It's crystal clear in my mind that I bought a ring. An engagement ring. There's no sign of it in my belongings, but I have a vague recollection of dropping it on the table in the kitchen. Lulu hasn't mentioned it, so I have no idea where it might be. Whatever happened, I know I want to marry Lulu, and I have every intention of asking Duncan for her hand as soon as possible. It might be old-fashioned, but I get the feeling he would get a kick out of it, and getting in good with the big man seems like a plan. Especially after the vile things my mother said in the hospital which, of course, he eventually heard about.

Christmas Eve dawns cold and clear. This seems like as good a time as any to talk to Duncan, so while Lulu is busy helping Morag with the food preparations for our Christmas Day feast, I hunt him down in the stable. Fortunately, it's a short walk. I'm still not used to the biting cold or the ache in my ribs.

"Och, there ye are, lad. You're looking much stronger already and with colour in your cheeks." Duncan peers at me over the top of glasses covered in paint as he measures out pellets to feed the horses.

"I'd like to talk to you, Duncan, if you have time." I'm a little nervous. I know Duncan likes me, but after everything my mother put Lulu through, I wouldn't blame him for being wary.

He huffs out a laugh. "I was wondering how long it would take you to get around to this." He leans against the wooden divider in the horse stalls, crosses his arms and looks at me with his eyebrows raised. Not intimidating at all.

"I realise, Duncan, that the last couple of months have been somewhat of a train wreck, and what my mother has put Lulu through is unconscionable. But over and above all that, what I know right down to the centre of my being is that I love your daughter, and nothing and no-one will ever change that. So, what I would like to ask you is, do I have your blessing to ask her to marry me?"

He's silent for long minutes, his face inscrutable, and I can feel sweat breaking out on my back despite the frigid drafts creeping in along the stone floor and stirring up the scattered hay.

"Well now, lad, the way your mother behaved was terrible, and no mistake. But you're not responsible for your mother. Lulu could have handled things better, too. Faced up to things instead of running off. So don't go taking all the responsibility for the whole mess." He takes a deep breath, and his eyes lock with mine. "Lulu is the most precious thing in the world to me, and she'd probably roast me for saying this, but I wouldn't be happy to give her over to just anyone."

"I'm with you there, Duncan. Lulu, and our baby, are the most precious things in the world to me too. I promise you, I will never allow my mother or anyone else to disrespect her again. If you see your way clear to giving me your blessing, I will spend the rest of my life standing by her side through whatever life throws at us." I throw every ounce of the love I feel into my words.

"Wise boy. Lulu doesn't need anyone to fight her battles. She doesn't need protecting. What she needs is a partner. I can't think of anyone I'd rather see beside her than you." Despite the paint on his glasses, I could swear I see tears in his eyes. He shakes his head. "Now, if you could hand me one of those feedbags I'll show you how to feed the horses. Might as well make yourself useful around here." I stifle a laugh. Duncan likes to pretend he's a hard man, but that soft underbelly can't be hidden.

Our Christmas celebration is rather light on gifts since, with all the drama, we've not had much opportunity to shop for presents. But what it lacks in wrapping paper and socks, it makes up for in laughter, delicious food and a great deal of whisky and wine. Well, except for Lulu, who sticks to the home made non-alcoholic ginger beer Morag has taken to brewing for her.

By the time we stagger up to bed, we're so full we can barely move.

I had thought about asking Lulu to marry me at lunch, but somehow it didn't feel right. What I have to say to her is between us. Tomorrow is soon enough to tell them.

Since my accident, we haven't had sex. The mind has been willing. Sadly, the body hasn't been up to it. But tonight, that's going to change. It might not be the best sex of our lives, but something is better than nothing, and there's always the opportunity to improve.

We slide under the covers and snuggle together, listening to the wind whipping around the castle, warm and cosy in our big bed.

Without a word, I start to slide my hand over Lulu's breast, flicking and pinching the nipple. They're bigger and even more sensitive than they were before the pregnancy. Just beautiful.

"What are you doing?"

"I thought I might make love to my woman." Her back arches as my hand slides down over her beautiful belly bump and slips between her legs. I had never thought of a pregnant woman as alluring before, but the lushness of her new body is incredible.

"Are you sure? Your ribs. I don't want you to ... oh yes ..." I've found her clit and am busy spreading the moisture building between her folds all over it. That's all the invitation I need.

"You might need to be on top. Can you handle that?"

"I think I can manage that."

She gives me a sassy smile, pushes me gently onto my back and straddles my hips. I reach down and part her with my thumbs before guiding her up the bed towards my head. I remember her smell and her taste, and my cock is rock hard before I've even touched her with my tongue. Lulu hisses, clutching the headboard for support, as I drag my tongue through her swollen flesh and latch onto her clit with a little bit of teeth and a lot of suction. Thank Christ I haven't forgotten how to pleasure her. It's only moments before I can feel she's on the brink.

"I want you inside me," she breathes as she moves down the bed, positions herself and sinks onto my cock. Long, slow and gentle.

"Fuck, Lulu. You feel so good. So tight and hot." We hit a perfect rhythm, and it's as if we've never been apart.

"Nick. I've missed you. Missed this. So much." And before I know it, both of us are coming. Embarrassingly fast.

I can't help but laugh. "Well, that was quick. I'm sorry. I'll do better next time. I promise."

"It was perfect." She smiles down into my face as she holds herself over me on her forearms, careful not to squash the baby or my ribs.

"Are you okay? Is the baby ...?" I roll her to the side and gather her against me, pressing as much of her body to mine as I can.

"Is it clichéd to say better than okay?"

"Yes. But I'm happy to hear it, regardless." We lie in satisfied silence for long minutes, enjoying the feel and smell of each other. I can't wait any longer.

"Lulu, even when I didn't know if I'd ever see you again, there was one thing I knew. And that's how I feel about you. As far as I'm concerned, if I have to give up everything I know to have you, I'll do it in a heartbeat. Because the only important thing in my life is you."

I turn her onto her side so we're face to face.

"So. Lulu MacLeod, mother of my child, owner of my heart, will you marry me? I can't promise life will always be easy, but I can promise you a lifetime of wild, dirty sex if you only take pity on me and agree to be my wife."

Tears start to slide sideways off her face. "Yes, Nicholas Pierce, I will agree to be your wife. Mother of your children. Keeper of your heart." I pull her closer and kiss her with relief and joy. Until she pulls back.

"There is one thing ..." My heart stops as she turns and opens the bedside drawer. "I don't know if you remember this. And honestly, I don't entirely want you to. I was awful and I hurt you." She has a small box in her hand and I recognise it immediately.

"Before you drove away that day, before the accident, you gave me this." She opens the box and passes it to me. "I've been carrying it around ever since. Just in case."

"Things might have been tough the day I gave this to you, Lulu, but there was never any doubt in my mind where this ring should go."

I pluck the ring out of the box and slide it on her finger, sending up silent thanks to the universe because it fits perfectly, and kiss her with all the love she has created inside me.

I can see all the happy years we have in front of us. Maybe in Sydney, maybe in Scotland. But all of them are happy.

I try to dry Lulu's tears with a corner of the sheet but they keep coming, along with a watery laugh, so I know they're happy tears.

"How do you think your mother will react?" she asks, turning her hand back and forth in front of her face so the ring catches the light from the bedside lamp.

"I couldn't care less to be honest. All I want is to be your husband. Nothing else matters. Just you and me."

"You and me. Sounds perfect." She sighs wistfully. "And we are in Scotland, after all. Gretna Green is only a few hours away."

"Gretna Green?"

"You know, small town, famous for elopements ..."

"That sounds like a plan to me. Now, I think it might be time to improve on my earlier performance."

Lulu laughs as I gather her close and do exactly that.

EPILOGUE
ONE

LULU

As it happens, you can't just turn up to Gretna Green and get married anymore. But all you need to do is give them notice. Nick extends his leave of absence from the firm, which freaks Harry out a little bit at first. And although Nick refuses to speak to his mother, we hear from Claire she's threatening to disown him. He's not the least bit concerned.

He sets up a better internet connection at the house, which he persists in calling the castle, and we turn one of the spare rooms into an office for him so he is able to work remotely on a consultancy basis when he wants to. But on most days, he can be found out in the fields with Dad, up to his armpits in sheep and cows, or in the distillery, learning about making whisky. He says he's enjoying reinventing himself and he's not making any rush decisions, but I can see he's working towards a hybrid life of law and farming. And he's having a blast.

Six weeks after Nick left the hospital, we take off down the road to Gretna. We don't tell Dad where we're going. All he knows is we're going away for a few days. This wedding is for us alone. Nick thinks getting married at the Famous Blacksmiths

Shop with strangers as witnesses is perfect, and there is plenty of time for a party later, and I agree.

We arrive at Gretna late in the day, and Nick insists on separate rooms for the night before our wedding. I had no idea he was such a romantic, but the last few weeks have shown me yet again how wrong you can be about someone.

Nick is already there as I approach the Blacksmiths Shop at eleven am on my wedding day. He's wearing a beautiful, dark grey suit. But underneath is a vest in the MacLeod tartan. Above the vest is a face so full of love and joy I can scarcely breathe.

"How are you today, *mo chridhe*?" he asks, palms flattening against my belly as they always do these days, eyes searching mine. Dad is teaching him what he considers all the important words in Gaelic—my love, my heart, my darling. He still butchers the sounds, but I don't care.

"So happy," I sob, two fat tears leaking from my eyes.

The strangers we find to be witnesses are Canadian backpackers, so excited to be part of a real Gretna Green elopement. There's laughing and crying and kissing and hugging—from all of us—and I don't care it's a cliché to say it's the best day of my life. So far. Because I feel like the best is yet to come.

We decide not to tell our families what we've done until tomorrow. Today we want to stay in our own little bubble—just us and our growing baby. Nick has booked a beautiful Airbnb for us and arranged caterers to make us a spectacular lunch. Because we can, we spend the afternoon in bed doing what we love most. Pregnancy hasn't slowed us down at all.

When he first arrived, Nick was a little wary of being too rough, but that didn't last long. Especially after he confirmed with Lydia—much to my embarrassment—that it wouldn't hurt the baby. Although he does whisper 'close your ears, little one' to my belly before he starts with the dirty talk.

Afternoon turns to evening, and we eat leftovers naked in bed before celebrating our marriage all over again.

The next morning, Nick wakes me with a coffee for himself and green tea for me.

"Ready to let the big wide world in, Mrs Pierce?" he asks.

"Do we have to?"

"No. Not if you don't want to. But you can be the one to tell Duncan we got married and didn't tell him for days."

"Alright, alright. But do I at least get a shower first?"

"I think that might be best considering the state of you right now." He grins.

Rolling out of bed, I hit the bathroom and have to acknowledge a shower—and some clothes—are essential. Ten minutes later, I find Nick settled against the headboard, his laptop on his knees.

"Face Time? Do we have to? Can't we call? Or better yet, text?"

He laughs and tugs me down next to him. "You know your father will cry, don't you?"

"Yes. But I'm more worried about your mother." Frankly, telling her scares the tripe out of me. Nick is happy not to bother, but despite everything she tried to keep us apart, that doesn't sit right with me.

"We don't have to call her, you know. She doesn't deserve it." His face clouds over any time her name comes up.

"She's still your mother, Nick."

"She doesn't deserve a daughter-in-law like you." He kisses my forehead before turning back to the laptop.

"Urgh. Let's do Dad first." I roll my eyes, wriggling to get comfortable against the pillows.

"As you wish." He gives me a Westley style smile, knowing how much I love *The Princess Bride*. Nick—who had a shocking gap in his movie knowledge until I stepped in to rectify it—says our love story rivals that of Westley and Buttercup, and I have to agree.

The phone rings a couple of times before Dad picks up. He's in the kitchen with Morag at the Aga behind him.

"Hey, Dad."

"Lulu. How are you, hen? Is everything alright? I wasn't expecting to hear from you until you got back."

"Everything's fine, Duncan," Nick chimes in. "Better than fine, actually. We have some news ..."

"We got married," we sing, and from there it degenerates into happy tears and excitement.

"I couldn't have designed a better man to take care of my little girl, Nick," Dad says, swiping at his eyes with the dishcloth Morag passes him. "I'm so happy for ye both. Now come on home with yourselves so we can have a proper celebration." As we end the call, Morag is already planning the party. I expect the entire village will be invited.

"Okay, now that we're warmed up ..." Nick stretches his fingers over the keyboard as though he's going to play a sonata. "Are you sure you want to do this?"

"Yes. I wish we didn't, but let's get it over with."

Mary picks up the call on the first ring. Since Nick has been in Scotland, they've only spoken a couple of times, and the conversations have been tense. Nick is not in the mood to take any more of her meddling, and she doesn't like it. She's still having trouble coming to terms with my place in Nick's life. Conflicted doesn't even begin to cover it. She resents me for having 'trapped' Nick with a baby. But she has a desperate desire to brag about her 'relationship' with Duncan MacLeod. Quite the conundrum for her. She's also furious Nick has taken extended leave from the firm.

"Nicholas—it's dreadfully late. What's wrong?" Despite the late hour in Sydney, her voice is still sharp.

"Everything is perfect, Mum. But we thought we should let you know we got married yesterday."

"What on earth are you thinking, Nicholas? It's past time you put all this silliness behind you and came home."

"I am home, Mum. Home is wherever Lulu is. What's past time is you accepting that."

There's a choking sound as she tries to work out what to say next. "Claire. Claire. Come in here," she calls, and I hear faint footsteps in the distance.

"Claire's home?" Nick asks, happy for the opportunity to share our news with his sister.

"Yes, for once," Mary mutters as Claire appears in the back of the frame. "Claire—your brother's gone and married that woman. Without even getting a paternity test."

"They're married? Yes." Claire does a happy dance behind Mary's chair. "Congratulations, you guys. I'm so happy for you." Even though his relationship with Mary is strained, Nick talks to Claire every week and she and I have had many Face Time conversations. I love her to bits and can't wait to introduce her to Rosanna one day.

"How on earth am I going to explain this?" Mary moans.

Nick laughs, settling his arm across my shoulder and kissing the top of my head. "I don't care how you explain it, Mum. In fact, I don't know why you feel the need to explain anything to anyone. All anyone needs to know is we're happy and healthy and we'll be back in Sydney sometime after the baby is born."

"After the birth? What about the firm? You've already been away for months. You need to get back to work. Harry will be retiring soon, and you need to be ready to step into his shoes." Mary ignores me completely, not even glancing my way.

"It's highly unlikely I'll go back to the firm full-time Mum. Harry and I are working out a consulting arrangement that allows me to spend time here helping Duncan." At the mention of Dad's name Mary's just-sucked-a-lemon expression morphs into calculating once again, no doubt wondering how she might use her connection with Dad. "I don't want Lulu flying, so we'll be staying here for the foreseeable future." Nick's tone brooks no argument.

Hours later, after calls to Rosanna and Sebastian and Harry and Will, we settle on the sofa in the lounge room.

"You know, that's as much of the outside world as I can take, wife." Nick pulls me in for a gentle kiss.

"Me too. I seem to remember you promising something about a lifetime of wild and dirty sex if I married you. I think it might be time to start paying up." And pay up he does.

EPILOGUE TWO

NICK

I assumed our wedding day would be the happiest day of my life, but I was wrong. Today was. Well, until the next time. Because there *will* be a next time. Three or four next times if I have my way.

My beautiful wife has given me the most wonderful gift of all. A perfect baby girl. I had no idea a heart could double in size in the blink of an eye, but now I know. As I sit on the side of the bed, watching the love of my life coax our baby girl to latch onto her swollen nipple for her first feed, I wonder if it's possible to explode with happiness. And then Lulu looks up at me. Everyone on Skye noticed the earth move on its axis like I did, I'm sure.

Duncan, Morag, Claire and Rosanna are all waiting impatiently downstairs to meet the new arrival. There was a great deal of debate about inviting Mum. Lulu was quite insistent we extend an invitation because she's loving and generous and forgiving. Duncan graciously said he would welcome her if that's what we wanted. But I stood firm that she would not be welcome until she could show Lulu the respect she deserves. And even though Mum is desperate to curry favour with Duncan, she can't seem to let go of her antipathy towards Lulu. So that was that. She's made her bed. To be honest, I'm relieved not to have to deal with her.

But they can all wait. I need more time alone with my girls.

Lulu was determined to have the baby at the castle—I mean house—where her family have lived for generations. I was nervous about not being in a hospital, but everyone knows not to argue with a pregnant woman. And I know not to argue with Lulu. Although it didn't stop me from having the local paramedics on standby and the hospital in Inverness on speed dial. In the end, it wasn't needed. With the help of Lydia, and a doula I flew in from Edinburgh, Lulu coped with labour like a warrior, and after nearly nine hours, our gorgeous girl was born.

"Do you need anything, *mo chridhe*?" I take her free hand.

She looks at me with more love than I could ever deserve. "No. I have absolutely everything I could ever need, right here. Although once she's had her fill, I could really use a shower."

I stroke a finger across the silky ginger fuzz covering our baby's head. "Looks like red hair skips a generation."

Lulu laughs quietly. "Da will be thrilled."

"He will indeed. You know we won't be able to keep them out much longer?"

Lulu sighs. "I know. One more minute? I feel like we need to decide on a name. If we show even the slightest uncertainty, everyone will have an opinion."

She's right. Everyone has been 'helping' with suggestions. Even Mum has been on a naming campaign in the last couple of months, as if anything she had to say would sway us in any way. But she can't help herself.

We have a list of names—which we've been very careful to keep to ourselves—but looking at the beautiful face of our new daughter, none of them seem adequate. I do have one ace up my sleeve, though.

"I know we have a list, but given where she was born, I was thinking. Isla. What do you think?" It's a traditional Scottish name meaning island.

"Oh, I love it. How did we not think of it before? Yes. Isla it is." Lulu beams down at our baby, who is making loud snuffling noises as she sucks, her huge blue eyes closed in apparent ecstasy, her tiny pink hand kneading the flesh of Lulu's breast. It's beyond magical.

"And for a middle name, I was thinking Annegrete. After your mum." Annegrete was Lulu's mother's middle name. It doesn't surprise me one bit when tears start leaking from Lulu's eyes as she leans forward, our baby between us. She kisses me with immeasurable tenderness and a new fierceness, causing my heart to thunder.

"Yes," she whispers against my lips. "Thank you. It's perfect. Isla Annegrete Pierce. It's beautiful. And bonus points, your mother will hate it."

"Of course she will. She can object all she likes, but I have no doubt you will always triumph over her every time, *mo ghaisgeach.*"

"Hmm. That's a new one. What does *mo ghaisgeach* mean?"

Nick laughs. "My warrior. Because that's what you are to me. I'm in awe of how brave you are."

"It wasn't so bad." She glances down at our daughter. "And look what we got. I could do it again. I think. Should we do it again?"

"As many times as you want, *mo chridhe*, as many times as you want."

THE END

SCOTTISH WORDS

M'eudail – my pride
Bairn – baby
Mo chridhe – my heart
Mo ghradh – my love
Heilan' coo/coos – Highland cow/s
Amadan – fool
Mo ghaisgeach – my warrior

ABOUT AUTHOR

Carrie Clarke lives in Sydney, Australia and has been writing stories, in her head and otherwise, since she first picked up a Georgette Heyer as a tween. The Art of Falling in Love is her first full length novel.

Five Fun Facts about Carrie:

1. After writing (and reading), Carrie's favourite thing to do is travel

2. Carrie loves history, bonus points if it's Egyptian

3. In Carrie's world the most important meal of the day is dessert

4. She would love to speak French, but has no talent for languages

5. Carrie firmly believes sleeping in is the only acceptable use for the mornings

Join Carrie's mailing list to receive advance news about upcoming books, exclusive extras and special content.

ACKNOWLEDGMENTS

It really does take a village to raise a book. First and foremost, thank you to my wonderful critique partners, Antonella, Karen, Emma, and Ann, who have encouraged and supported me during many a bout of insecurity.

Thank you to the wonderful members of RWAus, without whom I would undoubtedly never have had the courage to take the next step and actually publish.

To my gorgeous cheer squad Michele, Deb, Lisa, Kay, Linda, Sue and Michelle, thank you. Love you long time.

Much gratitude to Kelly Rigby for her insightful editing, Jo Spiers for her eagle-eyed proofreading, and Ryan Gilchrist for a beautiful cover.

And finally, thank you to my family who never complained when I was too deep in my own head to remember to cook dinner, and who quietly got out of my way and let me do my thing. Moon and stars to you all.

If you enjoyed this book, I'd love to see a review from you on Amazon or Goodreads.

Thank you for reading x

KEEP IN TOUCH

I f you would like to keep you up to date on when the next book in the Falling in Love Series is coming out, receive special bonus content and exclusive offers, including my spicy short story 'What Happens in Singapore', you can join my mailing list via my website at **carrieclarkeauthor.com.au**.

Follow me on:
Facebook.com/CarrieClarkeAuthor
Instagram.com/carrieclarkeauthor
Twitter: @CarrieCAuthor

SNEAK PEEK

BLUEPRINT FOR FALLING IN LOVE

Remember Josh? Nick's sailing friend with the love bite? If you're curious how he got it, read on for a sneak peak of Book 2 in the Falling in Love Series – A Blueprint for Falling in Love, coming in mid-2023...

BLUEPRINT FOR FALLING IN LOVE

CHAPTER 1 - JOSH

Hiking my battered leather laptop bag over my shoulder I check the area around my seat to make sure I haven't missed anything before turning towards the exit. The old lady in front of me is still gathering her belongings, so I entertain myself by gazing down the long corridor of poor souls who travelled cattle class. It's a tangle of cramped bodies struggling out of tiny seats, bags falling from overhead lockers, and people jockeying to get off the plane as fast as possible.

Flights to Australia are interminable. Especially from London. This one was blessed with the added entertainment of not one but two storms. The turbulence was so bad dinner was delayed, and the smell of airsickness wafted through the plane for hours. I don't envy them right now. At least the pointy end provides a little extra space and comfort.

My eye is caught by a swirling curtain of glowing red hair a few rows down in the economy section. Not Ron Weasley red, but a rich, deep, coppery red, framing an elegant profile, tipped up to search the overhead luggage bins. Long slender arms pull out a small backpack. I'm mesmerised by the grace of her movements as she slips it over her back, highlighting small yet spectacular breasts, which bounce under a clingy t-shirt printed with Frida Kahlo's face, as she settles the straps. My body reacts of its own accord. Worn-out old jeans tightening as my pulse picks up. What a shame she wasn't sitting next to me on this long and boring flight. She's not my usual type. I tend to go for curvier women. But there's no getting away from the fact she's piqued my interest.

"Excuse me." The tone belies the sentiment as I hear a throat clear behind me. Someone's in a hurry to get off. "How about you get moving?"

It's the buttoned-up, business-suited guy who was in the seat across the aisle from me. Who wears a business suit on a twenty-hour flight? He gave me the stink eye when I boarded and turned left instead of right. Like he thought I didn't belong there. I get that a lot. I think it's the hair. Or maybe the tattoos. Then again, it could be the biker boots. Sure, I could tone it down for flying, but I get a kick out of irritating the entitled arseholes who fly business. Even though I'm one of them.

I realise the little old lady has gone and I'm free to make my way to the exit.

"Yeah, sure, man. You go ahead." I step aside and let the dickhead pass me, which earns me nothing more than a slight shove and an eye roll. I don't care. If I linger long enough I might be able to meet up with the owner of the hair on the jetway. Maybe we can share a taxi and get to know one another.

No such luck. I'm pushed along by the stream of people eager to get wherever it is they're going. Or at least eager to get out of the cramped and smelly torture chamber we've all been trapped in. I'm in no real rush. I'm happy just to be here, breathing the Sydney air. Even in the airport, where the stench of jet fuel, unwashed travellers and cleaning products is strong, I can smell the familiar scent I can only think of as distinctly Sydney. Eucalyptus mixed with sea air and humidity. It smells like home. I hadn't realised how much I'd missed it.

I wander aimlessly through the booze and perfume filled duty-free shops for a while, happy to stretch my legs, keeping an eye on the walkway. I don't spot the amazing hair again until I get to passport control, where it's organised chaos. It seems the automatic passport scanning system has been fried by a direct hit during a lightning storm last night. So we're back to old-school systems of officers eyeballing you and stamping your passport. Luckily we're the first plane in, so the wait won't be too long. I pity anyone on the ten am from LA.

The delays work in my favour because there she is, in the queue next to me. I can't see her face, hidden as it is by a waterfall of incredible hair while she taps at her phone. Until she tucks her mobile in the back pocket of her faded jeans and looks up. Our eyes connect over the lane dividers keeping us in our neat little lines and I feel like someone's hit me with a taser. Only in a good way.

The face matches the hair for beauty. This woman is drop-dead, kick you in the balls gorgeous. Her eyes are dark blue, almost navy, framed by curved brows and high cheekbones. Freckles dance across a delicate nose, which leads to a full, lush mouth. I can think of many, many things to do with that mouth.

Her face lights up like Sydney Harbour on New Year's Eve when she notices me.

"Hey." I tip my chin at her.

"Hi." She's Australian, and her expression is more friendly than you'd expect from a stranger, even from an Aussie. Her smile is blinding and, for a second or two, I'm spellbound by those navy eyes. "It's great to see you." She leans across as if to hug me but is brought up short by the rope barrier.

That seems like a weird reaction. She doesn't know me. Does she? Okay, I do sleep with a lot of women. Usually only once.

But I think I'd remember her. The hair alone is not something you would easily forget. Although she does seem vaguely familiar, despite the fact I haven't been home for years.

I'm not sure how to respond. "Yeah... ah...you too." It comes out as almost a question.

Elegant brows draw together at my response. She looks slightly confused and opens her mouth as though she's about to speak when the guy behind her gives her a not-so-gentle nudge.

"Ooh. Sorry. Sorry." She smiles at the guy behind her, before turning to me and pointing at the counter. "My turn. Catch you on the other side I guess."

I watch as she chats with the officer. She's beautiful. No doubt. And maybe a little crazy? He chats right back, clearly attempting to flirt, before he stamps her passport and waves her through. She turns again and gives me a wave that's way too cheerful for someone who's just spent twenty hours in economy, before heading down the stairs to the baggage claim.

I get the distinct impression she's as interested as I am. Looks like my welcome home just got a whole lot more interesting.

My line stalls as I wait behind a guy who seems to be arguing the toss with the passport security officer. Airports really do bring out the worst in people. Eventually they come to an agreement, and I move forward.

It's good to be home. I've travelled all over the world and it's not an exaggeration to say Australia has the friendliest border force officers of anywhere I've been. But don't be fooled. They will drop on you from a great height if they get a whiff of something dodgy.

My officer rolls his eyes and cocks his head towards his previous customer who is stomping down the wide stairs, face red and sweaty. I shrug a 'What can you do?' and he smiles. "Welcome home. Sorry for the delays. Technology. Great when it works." He checks my passport and sends me on my way.

The baggage claim is packed with cranky travellers impatient to get through this last torturous hoop of international travel. I scan the crowd. Lucky for me it's not hard to pick out such bright and shiny hair. I edge through the crowd as I spot my bag and lean in to snag it. Most of my belongings are being shipped, so there's only the one case.

This girl is breathtaking and she's aroused my curiosity, not to mention something a little lower. I drift towards her. Bags are starting to come down the chute thick and fast. As I arrive at her side, a guy way too old to be wearing the wanna-be-a-lad track-suit in look-at-me-dayglow he's sporting, drags his bag off the belt, swings it round and hits Red square in the hip. Taken by surprise she lurches left, and I'm there to catch her. Full-frontal on my chest. My hands come up instinctively, supporting her back.

"Hey man, watch what you're doing." I give the guy a glare which has no impact at all on his self-involved arse. I look back at Red. "Are you okay?"

She's leaning against my chest and rubbing her hip, which moves her breasts against me. They're small, firm and perfect. My hands move to her arms where I find the skin smooth and warm, and I have to resist the temptation to circle my fingers. Taking a deep breath I try to calm my body's response, but the reverse happens as a dose of perfume and pheromones heads straight to my boxers. How does a woman get off such a long flight smelling so good? Like cinnamon rolls. Spicy and sweet and buttery. Delicious.

"Yeah. I'm okay. Thanks." She casts a glare at the disappearing back of the dickhead who whacked her with his bag, making no move to step back from my hold. Without pulling out of my arms she turns her head towards the luggage parade, until with a gasp she lunges for a huge red suitcase which is about to lumber out of her reach.

"Let me help you there." I reach for the bag and heft it off the conveyor belt with a grunt. It weighs a ton. "Travelling light, I see."

"Never. Thanks again," she laughs.

"Is this it?"

"What, you don't think that's enough?"

"I wasn't sure if I should wait for the kitchen sink." I look her in the eyes and there's definitely a vibe as she looks right back at me. I don't miss the way her gaze drifts to my lips, continuing on to my chest. Maybe she's not crazy, just flirty. I think about getting her number as she starts wheeling her New-York-apartment-sized bag towards the queue for customs and I fall into step beside her. Close beside her. Our shoulders brush and heat ignites between us.

"Oh no, I had the sink shipped on ahead. Saves on excess baggage fees."

I can't help but laugh. "Good thinking." A good sense of humour is sexy AF.

"I didn't see you on the flight. I guess you were luxuriating in business class?"

I wonder why she would assume that. Especially given the way I'm dressed.

"Guilty. Although turbulence doesn't discriminate. It was a pretty shit flight."

"It wasn't great. Regardless, I still love flying. Even in economy. It means you're going places, which can't be a bad thing." Despite the long flight, and the slight purple shadows under her eyes, she's glowing with some kind of inner joy. It's incredibly appealing. "How have you been? Are you happy to be home?" I've been away a long time, and although I still have the traces of an Australian accent it's been buried under years in America and Britain. How does she know this is home?

"Yeah. Always. You?"

"Yes and no. You know how it is."

Now's my chance. "So, where are you headed? Maybe we could share a taxi?"

"Oh, that would be good, but I think I'm being picked up by the fam."

I check her left hand, which is resting on the handle of her bag. Nope. Bare. Good.

"Right. Well, maybe we could catch up sometime, grab a drink or a meal?"

Her eyes lock on my mouth as she rubs her own pillowy lips together. Yeah, she's interested, for sure.

"That would be great."

I hand her my phone, trailing my fingers across hers as she takes it from me. "Excellent. I'm Josh. Give me your number and I'll give you a call." Maybe if I get her name my brain will twig to whether or not I know her.

She starts typing, a sly smile on her face, handing the phone back just as we get to the head of the queue. I look down and see she's entered her details as *Airport Pickup*. I don't even know her name.

"Hey, wait. What's your name?" I call as she's herded forward to one of the customs desks. She turns, continuing to walk backwards, and with a wicked grin makes the universal sign for call me with her fingers before waving and handing her declaration to the customs guy, who unzips her bag and begins to paw through her stuff. No doubt he wants to get a look at her knickers. Pervert.

The guy at my desk takes one look at my declaration and I get waived straight through. Guess my knickers are not anywhere near as interesting.

The stream of impatient people behind me keep me moving towards the door as I wonder whether to wait for her in the arrivals hall or to give her a call in a day or two. It's entirely possible she's given me a bogus number. Nah. Unlikely. There was a distinct whiff of interest there. Something about her has got under my skin. I really want to see her again. And I don't even know her name.

The doors open and I'm met with chatter and screams of excitement from the waiting crowd. I can hardly believe my eyes when I find my oldest friend, Will, and his parents Harry and Stella, waiting. Their eyes light up and they're waving with delight.

"Hey guys, I didn't expect you to be here to meet me." I can't even remember telling them what flight I was on. Will looks confused as I go in for our customary man hug. His eyes are darting from my face to over my shoulder. Harry and Stella are not even looking at me. They're looking past me. I'm missing something. I turn, and there she is. The redhead from the plane. And Harry is sweeping her off her feet.

Fuck. No wonder she seemed familiar. I know her. It's Greer. Will's little sister.

If you want to know when Blueprint for Falling in Love is available for pre-order, join my mailing list at **carrieclarkeaut hor.com.au**.